THE GREAT
PYRAMID
ROBBERY

D0721292

THE SEVEN FABULOUS WONDERS

is a new series of fabulous fantasy novels based on the Seven Wonders of the Ancient World. Each book is an enticing mix of myth, history, legend and magic...

Book 2 – coming March 2002
The Persian King, Cyrus the Great, plans to capture the prosperous city of Babylon. The hanging gardens hold the key to its defence – but only one person can access their magic...

Book 3 – coming September 2002
Beset by wars and marauding armies, the ancient race of Amazons build a sanctuary for the protection of women. But this holy shrine needs more than simple stone and weaponry to keep it safe...

Book 4 – coming July 2003
Outraged by the popularity of the Temple of Artemis in neighbouring Ephesus, Herostratus builds the Mausoleum to lure supplicants to Halicarnassus. Determined to procure the Amazon's magical defences, Herostratus takes drastic action...

Book 5 – coming April 2004

Alexander the Great is targeted by the Persians in this tale of treachery at the Olympic Games. But daring to offend the King of the Gods on his home ground during such a time proves to be a costly mistake...

Book 6 – coming January 2005

For years a titanic figure guarded the harbour entrance on the island of Rhodes and kept watch over its people. Then a fatal prophecy foretells doom and destruction...

Book 7 – coming October 2005

A terrorist plot to assassinate Emperor Hadrian and take control of the port of Alexandria shakes the very foundations of the Ancient World. But the great lighthouse conceals a secret power that many suspect but few have witnessed...

for Maggie

First published in Great Britain by CollinsVoyager 2001
CollinsVoyager is an imprint of HarperCollins*Publishers* Ltd
77-85 Fulham Palace Road, Hammersmith
London W6 8JB

The HarperCollins website address is:
www.fireandwater.com

1 3 5 7 9 8 6 4 2

Text copyright © Katherine Roberts 2001
Translations from *Ancient Egyptian Book of the Dead* © xxxxx
Illustrations xxxxx

ISBN 0 00 711278 5

The author and illustrator assert the moral right to
be identified as the author and illustrator of the work.

Printed and bound in Great Britain by
Omnia Books Limited, Glasgow

Conditions of Sale
This book is sold subject to the condition that it shall not, by way of
trade or otherwise, be lent re-sold, hired out or otherwise circulated
without the publisher's prior consent in any form, binding or cover
other than that in which it is published and without a similar condition
including this condition being imposed on the subsequent purchaser.

Katherine Roberts

THE SEVEN FABULOUS WONDERS

1

THE GREAT PYRAMID ROBBERY

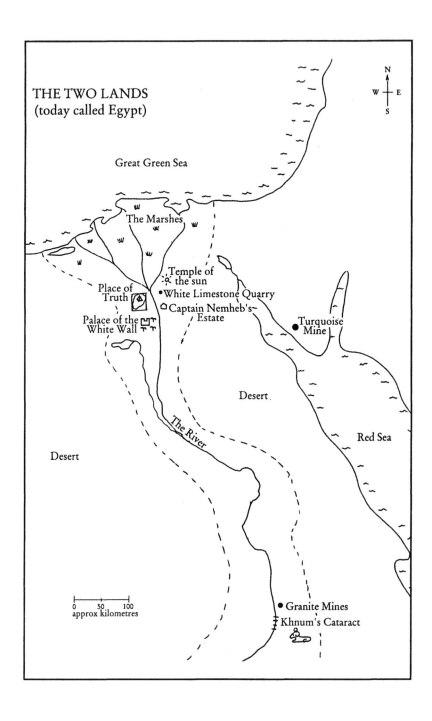

THE TWO LANDS
(today called Egypt)

Great Green Sea

The Marshes

Temple of
the sun
Place of ·White Limestone Quarry
Truth
Captain Nemheb's
Estate
Palace of the
White Wall
Turquoise
Mine

Desert

Desert

The River

Red Sea

0   50   100
approx kilometres

·Granite Mines
Khnum's Cataract

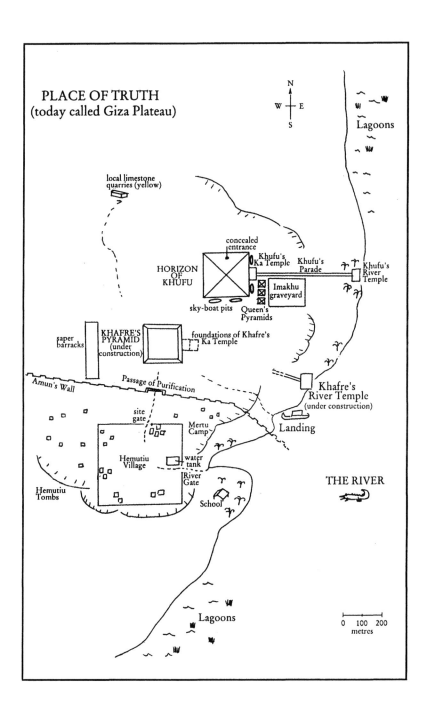

PLACE OF TRUTH
(today called Giza Plateau)

N
W—E
S

Lagoons

local limestone
quarries (yellow)

concealed
entrance

Khufu's
Ka Temple

Khufu's
Parade

Khufu's
River
Temple

HORIZON
OF
KHUFU

Imakhu
graveyard

sky-boat pits

Queen's
Pyramids

KHAFRE'S
PYRAMID
(under
construction)

foundations of Khafre's
Ka Temple

saper
barracks

Amun's Wall

Passage of Purification

Khafre's
River Temple
(under construction)

site
gate

Mertu
Camp

Landing

Hemutiu
Village

water
tank

THE RIVER

River
Gate

Hemutiu
Tombs

School

Lagoons

0   100   200
metres

CURSE OF KHUFU

"I, Khufu, Lord of the Two Lands, made this tomb in a pure place where no one had a tomb, in order to protect the belongings of one who has gone to his ka. As for anyone who might enter the tomb unclean and intending to do evil, the Great One will judge against him."

DARE AT THE PLACE OF TRUTH
Lord Khafre's Reign Year 5
...your ka is with you as a soul... (spell 92)

THE DARE WAS Reonet's idea, but Senu had to do it. And he had to do it better than anyone. The other children thought he was stupid. He'd show them that he and Red could do more than just play tricks on people.

"Stop it, Red," he hissed to his ka, who was performing handstands beside the path. "This is *serious*."

Red reluctantly righted himself and pretended to shake sand out of the ginger ka-tail that frizzed from one side of his head in ghostly imitation of Senu's own. But his ka sobered when they entered the honeycomb of tombs beneath the pyramid site. Reonet had brought a lamp. The other children crowded around its amber glow. Although no one ever saw another person's ka, it was obvious from the others' whispered, one-sided conversations that their otherworldly doubles were close beside them.

They picked their way through the rough tunnels and entered the older chambers beyond, where the smell caught in Senu's throat. One by one, the whispers and giggles fell silent until all Senu could hear was harsh breathing and the shuffle of their bare feet over rock.

At last, Reonet set the lamp in a niche and held up a hand. "Here," she whispered.

They all crowded into the tomb and stared curiously at the dead woman's body, which the priests called a "sahu". It lay on a shelf cut into the rock, unbandaged, its shrunken face almost pretty. It didn't smell much because the desert air had dried its juices, and its organs were in sealed jars beneath the shelf. A goathair wig braided with coloured beads had been placed on its head. Skeletal hands clasped a shrivelled blue lotus to the place where its heart had been.

A boy called Iny sniggered. "It's been here years! It's not going to talk."

"Shh!" Reonet gently touched the sahu's hands, then stepped back and pointed to Iny. "You first!"

The boy turned to the others and grinned. He closed his eyes and chanted a spell Senu thought he'd heard the priests use during one of their pageants. Iny stumbled over the end of the spell, threw his arms to the roof and cried out: "The ka of this dead woman says hello. She says she's starving after all these years and why haven't we brought any food?"

There were a few giggles. Reonet scowled and pushed Iny aside. "Very funny." She pointed to a tall girl. "You!"

The girl performed a similar act, and so it went on. Each time, the message from the dead woman's ka got more inventive and the lamp burned lower. The last few children mumbled their messages in a hurried fashion, casting nervous glances at the flickering flame and the tunnel. Finally, it was Senu's turn. Reonet stared at him as he approached the shelf, a challenge in her eye.

Senu took a deep breath. While the others had been having their turns, he'd taken note of the acts that impressed most and rehearsed his own in his head. Now he raised his arms as Iny had done. But Red muttered in his ear, "Don't be so silly. You're not a performing priest! This lot know nothing. Wait here." And vanished.

Senu let his arms drop to his sides, feeling rather foolish. "Well?" Reonet demanded, hands on hips, her black eyes flashing. "What does she say?"

As Senu licked his lips, wondering whether to wait for Red, more giggles rippled round the tomb. "Senu's too scared!" ... "Let's go back before the lamp runs out." ... "Let's go canoeing instead."

"No," Senu said. "Wait."

Iny faked a yawn. "This is boring! I'm going home." He left with his friends, muttering about stupid dares that made people miss lunch. The others stayed a bit longer, looking expectantly at Senu. But when the lamp spluttered, they made disappointed noises and hurried out, too. Only Reonet and a handful of the girls remained. Senu clenched his fists.

"Red?" he whispered. "This is embarrassing. Come back!"

As he spoke, the oil in the lamp ran out. At the same time, a sudden wind whirled the previously still air of the tomb. Reonet's friends gave little shrieks as a faint blue-green glow appeared above the shelf where the sahu lay. The glow brightened and a ragged hole opened in the darkness. As Senu gaped at it, trying to work out where it had come from, there was a sudden rush of wind and half-glimpsed shadows rushed towards the hole from the other side. Their cries beat at him like wings, making no sense. He staggered backwards and wrapped his arms over his head.

The girls screamed and fled down the tunnel, blundering into Iny and the others. They yelled too, and everyone ran for the exit in a wild, shoving panic. Senu flattened himself against the rock as the light became more intense, the hole larger, the terrifying shadows closer.

"No!" Red was almost transparent with fear. "Get them away from me, Senu! Please!"

"Stop it, Senu!" Reonet shouted through the blinding light and wind. "You're scaring the kas. Moon, come back here! It's only one of Senu's tricks."

Senu could not move. The blue light blinded him. The shadows were still shouting in the way grown-ups shouted at foreigners who didn't speak the language of the Two Lands. He saw bodies of humans with the heads of birds and animals, or were they bodies of beasts with human heads? For a horrible moment, he couldn't find Red and thought the monsters had eaten him. Then Reonet fought her way across the tomb and grabbed his wrist. She dragged him into the tunnel where the wind was quieter. Red came too. Behind them, the ghostly shapes sucked back into the light, which grew smaller and fainter until it was a tiny blue star shining above the sahu. The darkness rushed back.

Senu could still see spots behind his eyes. He clung to Reonet's hand as they stumbled after the others.

"That sahu was your mother's, wasn't it?" he said in sudden understanding. "You should have warned us."

Reonet said a word they weren't allowed to use at school and wrenched her hand free. "You and your stupid tricks, Senu! Why did you have to go and scare everyone like that? You've ruined it all. We won't get another chance now."

At first he didn't realize what she meant. Then he heard the men's voices outside. Sandalled feet marched into the tunnel, blocking the daylight.

"We know you're in there," called a stern voice. "Come on out, all of you! These tombs aren't a playground."

Senu glanced back the way they'd come, wondering if he could hide and find another way out later. But the thought of going back there in the dark on his own brought a cold sweat. Meekly, he followed Reonet out into the sunlight and joined the huddle of subdued, blinking children surrounded by a detachment of sapers from the site. Reonet tried to explain she'd only been making an offering to her dead mother's ka, but was told to be quiet.

Two of the men ventured in to check the tomb. They came out shaking their heads. "Nothing in there except sahus," said one. "Silly things scared themselves, I expect." Getting little sense out of the frightened children, the saper leader settled for lecturing them on the dangers of playing in the caves. With emphatic thrusts of his spear at the crumbling sandstone, he told them they'd been very lucky and he'd let them off this time. But he'd have to make a report, so if any of them were thinking of coming down here again without adult supervision, they could expect trouble when they were caught.

Senu started to tremble. Every time he shut his eyes, the blue light blazed in his head, muddled with the monsters and the wailing. "What did you do in there, Red?" he whispered. "What happened?" Then he had a terrifying thought. "Those were the kas of the dead, weren't they? They actually came! What were they trying to say?"

His ka, almost invisible now, sighed like the wind. A delightful coolness spread where the colours and the images burned, fading them out. "Nothing," Red whispered. "They said nothing. Forget it ever happened. Forget..."

Chapter 1

GLYPHS
O Eye of Horus, save me... (spell 92)

SENU SAT CROSS-LEGGED in the shade of an awning on the river bank with the other children from the hemutiu village, a limestone slate balanced across his sunburnt knees, a reed pen clutched in one sweaty hand. It was far too hot for serious work. The stink of open sewers and raw fish blew down from the plateau, mosquitoes swarmed, and dust from the building site got into everything. Yet old Batahotep had decided that the last day of school before the long Akhet holiday was the perfect time to give his class their most important test of the year.

"Don't try so hard," Red whispered invisibly from the air. "You won't pass, anyway."

Senu kept working. True, he'd failed the apprenticeship exam every year since he'd been old enough to sit it. But the nightmares had stopped now.

All his friends had already done apprenticeships during the holidays, and this particular test was to decide who would be allowed to help the craftsmen decorate Lord Khafre's river temple. Senu's father was Chief Artist at the Place of Truth. If Senu didn't pass this year he'd shame Tefen before the entire site. Worse still, his failure would be quoted as yet another reason he should cut his ka-tail.

"Go away, Red," he muttered under his breath. "Can't you see I'm trying to concentrate?"

"Your father's ka said you've got to fail," Red insisted.

"*What?*"

This was so unexpected, Senu committed the greatest sin in their teacher's eyes. He looked up from his slate.

Batahotep had erected the awning so his pupils couldn't see the activity beyond Amun's Wall. Less distractions that way. In front of Senu, neat rows of heads bent over their work. The younger pupils who didn't have to worry about the outcome of the test still wore their hair in ka-tails like Senu's, that hung over their ears. But everyone else of Senu's age now wore their hair in the all-over adult style that indicated they'd given up their kas and were ready to start work.

Luckily, no one seemed to have noticed his exclamation. Batahotep lounged on his stool in the coolest spot where palm leaves shaded the awning, watching a huge granite slab being unloaded from its barge by a gang of thirty sweating, bare-chested mertu labourers. As the men strained at the ropes, their teacher picked at a loose thread in his wig and yawned. Red remained invisible.

Senu stole a look at Reonet. Her regrowing hair was just long enough to be confined in a turquoise clip. She crouched over her slate, chewing her lower lip as she completed Batahotep's glyphs. They'd be perfect, he knew. He considered asking his ka to sneak across for a look, then shook his head. He'd promised himself he wouldn't cheat this year.

"That's not funny, Red! This isn't easy for me, you know."

He bent back over his work, spat on his slate and carefully wiped off a line. He chewed the end of his reed, dipped it into the soot and began again.

"That bit's not right," said Red unhelpfully.

Senu scowled. "I *know*."

"You need a steadier hand. Here, let me-"

There was a shimmer at the corner of Senu's eye as his ka's semi-transparent body became visible against the reeds. As usual, it was like looking at his own reflection, only the right way around. Gangly limbs that had grown too fast for the rest of him, knobbly knees, frizzy red ka-tail... even his squint from being kept behind too many times after school copying old Batahotep's glyphs in the fierce afternoon sun.

A shiver went through him as Red's otherworldly fingers rested upon his hand. There was the familiar crackle of intense *longing* that still, after all these years, made him want to throw his arms around his ka and cry. The next thing he knew, a jagged line had appeared across his slate, ruining the only three glyphs he'd completed so far.

He threw his pen at his ka's chest in frustration. "Oh, why don't you go jump in the river?"

Because kas were not solid, the pen went right through Red and landed in Iny's lap. The boy, who sat next to Senu not out of choice but because Batahotep had told him to, yelped as he dropped his slate. Then he seemed to remember he was supposed to act grown-up now he'd cut his ka-tail. The snooty look he gave Senu as he retrieved his work and dusted it off would have been worthy of a priest.

Batahotep's head snapped up. He heaved himself to his feet and adjusted his wig with a sigh. "Senu son of Tefen, our class joker! I might have known. Come here. Bring your slate."

Senu clutched the precious slate against his chest. A whole morning's sweaty, finger-cramping work! He wondered if he could pretend not to have heard. The site was noisy with preparations for the huge influx of labourers who would come up from the fields over the next few days. Some of them were here already, building temporary huts outside the village walls.

"*Now*, Senu. Is there something wrong with your ears? Shall I send for the doctor?"

The last thing he needed was a dose of the site doctor's hippopotamus-blood-and-cat-hair paste. He clambered quickly to his feet. Reonet peered at him through her fringe and pretended to continue with her work. The rest of the class fidgeted in anticipation. Whispers passed around the awning. "Bet he'll get a beating!"... "Yeah, five lashes." ... "No, ten!" ... "Not on the last day, silly. Even old Batahotep wouldn't do that."

Iny added loudly, "No point him doing the test, anyway. Everyone knows babies who bring their kas to school aren't allowed in the temple. It's bad luck."

"Why don't you grow up?" Senu hissed back, which only earned him splutters of mocking laughter.

Their teacher clapped his fleshy hands. "Settle down, all of you! Or the whole class will be staying after school. And I'll be taking the awning down, so you can sit out here and get sunstroke. I mean it." He glowered at them from under thick black brows.

The class quietened at once. No one wanted to miss the first afternoon of the holidays.

Senu approached Batahotep's stool, trying to look as if he didn't care. Beatings were nothing compared to the shame he'd feel tonight, when he had to admit to his father he'd failed yet again. Maybe if he apologized he'd be allowed to stay after school and finish the test?

"Sir, I-"

"Quiet. A boy your age should have more respect for his materials. You're a hemutiu craftsman, not an uneducated mertu! One day your work might adorn the walls of Lord Khafre's ka-temple, and it's my job to make sure you don't disgrace his name. This punishment is for your own good."

Senu's heart sank. But Batahotep did not reach for his rod, simply held out one pudgy hand. Reluctantly, Senu passed his slate into it. Batahotep considered his work in silence. He raised a surprised eyebrow. "Not bad," he said. But even as Senu's heart stirred in hope, the teacher took a crumpled cloth from his waistband, spat on the slate and rubbed out every last line of his hard won glyphs.

"No...!" He'd taken half a step forward, fists clenched, before Red's hand touched his shoulder. Very lightly, flooding his body with a confusion of love and sympathy.

"Don't," his ka whispered. "Or he'll beat you as well."

The class had gone still. Even Reonet had stopped working, her wide kohl-lined eyes fixed on Senu's face. He quickly looked away and set his jaw. Without a word, he took the slate back from Batahotep.

"Now, go sit out the back and start again," Batahotep said. "I won't be recommending you to help in the temple this year because you obviously lack the required concentration. But if you can show me twelve glyphs of a similar standard by sunset, I'll consider putting your name forward next year. You can use the holiday to say goodbye to your ka. I've no idea what your father means by letting you keep him so long." He looked meaningfully at the air behind Senu.

Under different circumstances this might have been

funny, because Red had already rippled from under the awning and was doing handstands on an abandoned slab of cracked limestone, pulling faces at their teacher. Behind the ka, high above Amun's Wall, the golden apex of Khufu's pyramid dazzled against the sky.

Senu blinked hard and looked away. The one time in his life he'd actually tried to do something right, and his own ka had betrayed him.

At the end of the sixth lighthour, when the shadows under the palm trees had shrunk to feathery fingers, Batahotep collected the slates and dismissed the class. Twenty-eight boys and girls streamed from under the awning. Whooping and laughing, they ran up the path to the village, while behind them Batahotep's servants dismantled the awning and took it away.

Reonet hesitated. Since her father was usually drunk on fermented gruel by the time she got home from school and she had no mother to look after her, she'd often come to Senu's house for lunch. Then they'd spend the afternoon messing around with Iny and the others down at the lagoon. But Batahotep frowned at her, so she waved and promised to bring Senu a radish. The teacher warned Senu not to move until he'd finished his task, gathered up his slates and puffed up the path after his pupils.

Senu got back to work. He couldn't remember how the Eye of Horus went. As he rubbed the glyph out for the fifth time, he wondered if Batahotep could be right. Maybe his hopelessness *did* have something to do with still having his ka? After all, Reonet had cut her tail and released Moon years ago. She claimed she could concentrate better without her ka hanging around all day and had found herself a kitten to play with instead. Perhaps he should get a cat, too? He'd still be able to talk to Red in his dreams, the way adults spoke to their kas. Then he glanced at Red's transparent arm hanging limply over the edge of the slab and his heart twisted. No.

Reonet dropped off the promised radish on her way to help the village women with the washing. It was gone all too soon, a brief, sweet crunch that barely moistened his throat. Ignoring the rumbles from his newly-woken stomach, Senu licked the end of his reed and set to work with fresh determination. Sunlight shimmered across the river. Papyrus and palm leaves waved in the breeze. The gang-songs and endless chiselling from the site grew sluggish as the afternoon heat increased. The lines on his slate blurred. For his father's sake, he tried his best. But he'd never had Reonet's passion for writing. Somewhere between the eighth and ninth glyphs, he dozed off.

He woke with a jolt to find a big, ebony-skinned man looking down at him. The white tattoos on the man's cheeks marked him as one of the warriors known as "medjay", who came from beyond Khnum's Cataract and hired their services to the highest bidder. There were always a few of them on site helping the regular saper guards investigate thefts and other crimes, and as a result everyone was slightly afraid of them. Behind the medjay's dark head, Khufu's pyramid cut into the setting sun, its polished walls aflame. All noise from the site had ceased. Reonet and the women had gone. It was cold in the shadow behind the stone.

Heart thudding, Senu scrambled to his feet. His slate fell off his knees and landed at his feet with a thud.

"Senu son of Tefen?" asked the medjay in his thick accent, tattooed face impassive.

"Er, yes..." He looked round for Red, but his ka was invisible again.

"Come with me."

"Why? I haven't done anything wrong! I'm supposed to finish my test..." His heart sank as he bent to pick up his slate. He'd never manage twelve glyphs now.

The medjay's dark hand closed on his arm. "Leave it."

"But-"

"This way."

Before Senu could think, the medjay had steered him on to the path that led round the south of the escarpment. "Where are we going?" he said, starting to feel scared. Red was beside him, strangely quiet. Then he saw the dark openings in the cliff ahead and sweat bathed his neck. He hadn't been down here since the day of the dare six years ago.

He dug in his heels, but the medjay had already stopped. As Senu nervously eyed the entrance to the tombs, his captor unwound a strip of linen from his waist, folded it in half and stepped behind him. "Sorry about this, boy," he growled. "Master's orders."

Before Senu realized what he was up to, the bandage dropped across his eyes.

He clawed it off in panic, ducked under the medjay's arm and raced back along the path, his breath coming in gasps. The medjay cursed in his native tongue and pounded after him. Senu ran faster, looking over his shoulder. A mistake.

"Watch out!" Red materialized in the middle of the path and tried to catch him with his ghostly arms. Unable to stop in time, Senu plunged straight through the ka – a horrible feeling, like wading neck deep through the river – and blundered into a short, stocky figure that seemed to have appeared out of nowhere. The medjay caught up and grabbed his arm again.

As Senu kicked his captor's shins, yelling for the sapers, for his teacher, for Reonet, for anyone, the newcomer said in a gentle voice, "This obviously isn't going to work. Let me."

"Don't let it touch you!" Red cried. "It's a monster without a ka-shadow. Oh, it's horrible..."

The medjay held Senu firmly as the stocky figure stepped closer. He struggled in despair. Then he saw Red's "monster" and almost laughed. It was only a wrinkled old dwarf with the bone sickness that stopped people's legs from growing. The dwarf's right hand was missing three fingers and his eyes were like silver clouds. Senu stopped struggling to stare at them.

"Careful," said the medjay. "Remember he still has his ka."

Smiling, the dwarf stood on tiptoe and pressed a knobbly finger to Senu's forehead. Senu's ears roared. The desert sparkled with blue stars. He was still trying to work out what had happened, when everything went dark.

Chapter 2

PERFECT CRIME
I am the Child! (spell 42)

IT WAS THE OLD nightmare. Darkness... rock against his left cheek... musty, underground smell... a dull ache in his head... something over his eyes...

Buried alive!

Terror sent him sliding briefly back into unconsciousness. Then Red's arms went around him, easing the fear.

"Don't panic," his ka breathed into his ear. "You're not a sahu yet. It's the black human's cloth over your eyes – remember? There's a lot of men in here. The monster with no ka-shadow is here too. Shh, something's going on. Pretend to be unconscious."

This made sense. Many of the best tricks relied on pretending to be asleep. Somehow, Senu managed to lie still until the fear resolved itself into voices. He realized the odour of the tomb was overlaid by men's sweat, the whiff of barley gruel that formed the labourers' main diet, and another, more homely smell. He couldn't think straight enough to identify it. One of his arms had gone numb, squashed beneath him. But he wasn't bound. He could remove the blindfold any time he wanted and the kas of the dead weren't shouting at him. These were the voices of the living. The panic faded. He made himself relax and listen.

"I know you're not starving yet," a clipped, educated voice was saying. "But the flood's low again this year, and the royal grain stores are far from full after the last harvest. Our late Lord Khufu – may his ka roam wherever it pleases – cleaned them out building his pyramid, and they haven't had time to recover. You've all seen the extra huts going up in the mertu camp. It's no secret Lord Khafre's summoned twice as many men as usual to work on his tomb this year. What the authorities haven't told you yet is that they'll be stopping the grain ration to non-working family members. Lord Khafre's anxious there should be enough to feed the work force until the completion of his own pyramid. There's a rumour going round that the non-working members of the hemutiu families will be sent off site entirely next year so Lord Khafre can use the space to sleep yet more men. If the harvests don't improve, it'll be half rations before you know it. Then you'll be hungry and have to do your own washing and cooking, but still be expected to work from Re's rising to his setting. And we all know what'll happen if you dare go on strike. Remember what

Lord Khufu – may his ka roam wherever it pleases – did when the priests spoke against him?"

Uneasy mutters and grumbles greeted this speech. Senu frowned, trying to make sense of it. Sent away? This was his home! All his friends were in the village, and-

"Concentrate!" hissed Red. "I think we're in trouble."

The grumbling died down. Another voice spoke up. From the thick Kush accent, it sounded like the medjay who had brought him here. "Strikes are bad for everyone. It's a good plan. The sapers won't investigate the theft, since the victim will hardly be complaining to the authorities. Once you've got the stuff out, you reseal the entrance tunnel and no one's the wiser. No punishments, no interrogations, and your families needn't worry about starving. It's the perfect crime!"

Senu frowned again. His father said copper tools were always going missing from the site, and offerings had even been stolen from Lord Khufu's ka-temple. But he'd never heard of a thief needing a tunnel before.

It made less sense the longer he listened. Other, rougher voices joined in and the volume rose. Several arguments seemed to be going on at once. People seemed concerned about how to get the treasure off site. Where to hide it while they arranged transportation. Who to approach when they wanted to exchange it for food. How to melt it down so the bigger pieces wouldn't be recognized. Whether they dared keep any in the camp.

How much they should take. How many bribes they should budget for. And so on, and so on.

Senu stopped listening. Very slowly, he worked his hands nearer the blindfold.

Then someone asked why Lord Khafre didn't simply limit the size of his work force to allow for more harvests, since he surely didn't expect to die so soon? The tomb quietened as the educated voice explained.

"It's all to do with face." The voice sounded amused. "I don't have to tell you how determined Lord Khafre is to outdo his father in everything. He was devastated when the priests told him a larger pyramid wasn't possible because it would fall down, and only agreed to the present plan after his Chief of Works assured him we'd build his pyramid on higher ground so it would *look* bigger than Khufu's. Employing more men than he needs is his way of showing everyone how powerful he is. He doesn't care if you all go hungry and the sewers block up and everyone gets stomach ache just as long as he's seen to be the greatest Lord ever to rule the Two Lands."

This sparked off yet more grumbling. A few people shouted out individual complaints. The educated voice silenced them.

Finally, someone said, "What about Lord Khufu's ka?"

There was an intense silence. Senu's neck prickled.

"Keep still!" Red hissed. "They're all looking at you. Oh, this is bad."

Another man shouted, "That's why the boy's here, innit?"

"Ain't he awake yet?"

"You sure you didn't damage him, Dwarf?"

Their rough laughter cut off as Senu sat up, nails tearing at the knot behind his head. His stomach was jumping and his legs felt like water. But he'd had enough of being blind.

Firm hands caught his wrists. The next two words turned his world upside-down. "No, Senu," said a quiet voice. "It's there for your own good."

His struggles ceased. Confusion washed through him. *"Father?"* he whispered. That smell, the homely smell... of the pigments that permanently stained Tefen's fingers and clogged his nails.

"Great! Now he's recognized you!" someone muttered. And the clipped voice added, "We agreed you wouldn't speak, Tefen."

The men took this as permission to grumble again.

"How long's he bin awake? That's what I want to know."

"He's a sly one. You'll have to watch 'im on the gang, Sobek!"

"No names, you fool!" a rough voice bellowed. "I told you no names until we're sure of the boy! How'd you like to drag a stone all by yourself tomorrow?"

"That's enough, Sobek," said the clipped voice. "We're all in this together, remember."

With an effort, Senu swallowed his confusion.

"What's going on, Father?" he whispered. "What are you all doing in the tombs?"

"Don't worry, son. I won't let them hurt you again. This has gone far enough."

His father helped him to his feet and gently turned him to face the muttering assembly. His long, clever fingers rested on Senu's shoulder. "Listen to me, all of you! I didn't like this when it was first suggested, but it's done now. Senu's my son. He won't betray us. Let me take the blindfold off. There's no point terrifying the boy like this. We want him to work willingly with us, don't we?"

"And if he refuses?" someone called.

"Then you'll just have to trust him! It wasn't my idea to bring him here like this. I could just as easily have had a quiet word with him at home one night."

"Oh yeah? And had your wife spread the gossip round the entire village in the morning? We all know how loose hemutiu women are with their tongues!"

Tefen's fingers tightened as the men laughed. Had he been able to see, Senu would have thumped the man who'd insulted his mother.

"Father?" he whispered. "What's this crime you're all talking about? What was all that about Lord Khufu's ka? Why do I have to be blindfolded? I don't understand-"

"Shh," Tefen said. "Captain Nemheb will explain now."

The reassuring weight of his father's hand lifted. He was left standing in darkness, surrounded by sweaty strangers and the underground smell of the tomb. Red hovered, a prickly presence at his elbow. Then hands tugged at the blindfold, catching his ka-tail as they pulled, and suddenly he could see.

He blinked. Lamps cast shadows on to rough rock and gleaming copper flesh. It looked like one of the newer tombs with a low, lumpy roof and debris still on the floor. Behind the men, niches could be glimpsed in the walls with empty shelves for future sahus. Half finished tunnels twisted into darkness. Senu shivered, wondering which one led to Reonet's mother's tomb.

"Concentrate!" Red hissed. "This is no time for day dreaming!"

About thirty men crouched in the small space, mostly mertu labourers fresh from the fields. Their shaven skulls brushed the roof. Cheap amulets of blue and green faience chinked around their necks as they fidgeted. Their fingernails were black and broken. Their eyes glittered hungrily as they watched Senu. The medjay sat on his heels at the very back in the shadows. The dwarf was next to him, his cloudy eyes staring through Senu in a manner that made his skin crawl.

Then a small man with a thin face pushed through the crush and Senu stiffened. At once, he knew this was the man who had ordered him blindfolded. He carried a scribe's staff which he used to thrust the mertu out of his way. A golden collar gleamed around his neck, indicating he was much more important than Batahotep. He looked Senu up and down in a lazy manner.

Scared and angry, Senu glared back.

Amusement registered in the kohl-lined eyes. "You've grown since I saw you last," he said in his clipped voice. "I'm sorry for the manner you were brought here, but I'm sure you're old enough to understand we have to be extremely careful in this matter. Pehsukher was instructed to be as gentle as possible. He doesn't know his own power sometimes." He glanced at the dwarf, who stared back without blinking. The scribe smiled slightly. "I'm Captain Nemheb. You might wonder what I'm doing here?"

Senu nodded, not trusting himself to speak. A *Captain*. That was only one rank below the Chief of Works.

Nemheb went on smoothly, "The truth is, it'll help no one if there are rations, discontent and strikes on this project. Lord Khafre's pyramid won't get built as grandly as he wants. Then he'll start to apply pressure and everyone will suffer for it. My job will be harder and I'll be forced to call in extra manpower to keep order." He glanced at the medjay. "That'll make life difficult for all of us. Yet there are riches enough to feed the entire population of the Two Lands for more years than you can count, buried just a short walk from where we stand. The priests will tell you they're put there for Lord Khufu's ka in the afterlife, but I've had lengthy discussions with my own ka on this matter and can assure you it's all a lot of temple mumbo-jumbo." His smile did not touch his eyes.

Uneasy whispers rippled round the tomb. Nemheb silenced them with his raised staff and looked meaningfully at Senu. "I know some of you don't trust me because I've done temple service myself. Why don't we let the boy ask his ka what need he has of gold?"

The tomb quietened. All those eyes, fixed on him, made Senu's skin crawl.

"Red," he managed in a dry voice, embarrassed to be seen talking to his ka before grown men. "Uh, do you need gold?"

Red rippled in amusement. "It's quite pretty to look at."

"What I meant was-"

"I know what you meant. You know I can't touch anything in your world except you. Gold would be about as much use to me as the food the priests leave in Lord Khufu's ka-temple! All the kas laugh at them, you know. Especially when they sneak back at midnight and eat the offerings themselves."

Senu hadn't known they did that. He fought a sudden urge to giggle.

Nemheb frowned. "If you're not going to take this seriously, we'd best return you to the village right now and find someone who will. You realize what'll happen to your father and mother and your sister's family if the merest whisper of this reaches Lord Khafre's Royal Ear, don't you?"

Senu turned cold. "I wasn't laughing at you, sir! It was just Red... uh, that's my ka..." He faltered under

Nemheb's hard stare. "I mean, Red says gold is quite pretty to look at, sir." He hated the way his tongue tied itself into knots when he was nervous. But he got the words out.

Chuckles erupted around the tomb. Nemheb scowled and struck his staff on the floor.

"See?" he said. "Even a ka-tailed boy knows the truth! Lord Khufu's gone to his horizon. His soul is safe and his ka is happy, gold or no gold. But we're not going to take all Lord Khufu's treasure, not by any means. Just small pieces that can be easily carried, transported, and hidden under the hearth until they're needed. Enough to feed all your families until Lord Khafre's tomb is finished and he's no longer concerned with earthly matters. I'll select some nice pieces of jewellery to keep my servants quiet and a few hefty bribes to further my career. The priests needn't know about it. Everybody's happy. As our Kush friend said, it's the perfect crime."

"Re's breath!" Red exclaimed, rippling around the tomb in agitated circles. His half-visible form blurred the mertu's faces and cast a strange watery shadow as he passed before the lamps. "They're going to rob the *Horizon of Khufu*!"

Senu had worked this out a fraction before his ka. After he'd turned cold, then hot, then shivery, then weak all over, excitement took root deep in his belly. He didn't agree with Nemheb and the medjay. Being at the receiving end of various punishments over the years, he could think of quite a lot of things that might go wrong.

But robbing a pyramid beat playing tricks on old Batahotep. Suddenly, his interrupted test didn't matter. *This* would show Reonet and the others he didn't have to banish his ka to be useful!

Nemheb was watching him closely. So was the medjay. So, in his creepy way, was the dwarf, Pehsukher. In the corner, Tefen chewed a paint-stained nail. Senu's excitement subsided slightly.

"Uh, why exactly *do* you need me, sir?" he asked.

Red hovered behind the Captain like a flame flickering in the dusty tomb. Nemheb breathed out, perhaps sensing the ka's curiosity. "We need a child," he said. "Someone who can distract Lord Khufu's ka while we're busy in the burial chamber. None of us can do it because we have to dream to communicate with our own kas, and I'm sure you'll agree that's a bit of a hindrance when you're trying to carry out a robbery?" Again, the smile did not touch his eyes.

There were one or two chuckles, but not many. Senu didn't feel much like laughing any more. "You want Red to talk to Lord Khufu's ka?" he whispered. He could feel Red's fear, shivering through him.

"Please don't make me do that," his ka whispered. "Please Senu, don't. You know what happened last time. It's dangerous."

None of them could hear Red, of course. But something of his reaction must have shown in Senu's face. Nemheb glanced at Tefen, who looked uncomfortable. Pehsukher leant forward, his strange eyes luminous blue in the shadows.

"If you're afraid to do it, we'll find someone else," Nemheb said, turning away.

Red was still shivering, raising goosebumps on Senu's arms and making his ka-tail crackle with sparks. Some of the mertu gave him amused looks. Others watched him sympathetically, as if he were about half his age.

He clenched his jaw. "Don't be such a baby!" he muttered, pushing Red off – easier said than done, like trying to spear a fish in the river, never quite where it seemed to be. "This is all your fault, remember? If you hadn't jogged me this morning, we wouldn't even be here. All that nonsense about having to fail Batahotep's test! You should have found out why before you blindly did what Father's ka told you! What's so hard about talking to a dead person's ka, anyway? If you could do it when we were eight, you can do it now."

Red shivered one last time and faded from sight.

Senu frowned. He experienced a moment of unease as he recalled the nightmares he'd suffered after the dare. But he'd only been a baby then, fled the tomb before he even had a chance to hear what the kas were saying. Stupid.

He straightened his shoulders and took a deep breath. "Will I have to go into the burial chamber?"

"No. It'll be safer for everyone if you can lure Lord Khufu's ka outside. We'll take what we want and seal everything back up just the way it was. When Lord Khufu's ka returns, he'll never notice the difference."

Senu's relief was tinged with disappointment that he wouldn't get to see the fabled treasure. "I'm not afraid!" he said. "What do I get for helping you?"

Nemheb looked taken aback. "Your family will get a larger share, naturally. It's up to your father how much of it he lets you have, but I'm sure some reward will be in order." He glanced at Tefen, who nodded, fighting a smile.

Senu thought of Reonet. How much did it cost to go to scribe school? "I'll do it," he said firmly. He looked round for Red, but his ka was still hiding behind the boundary between worlds.

Nemheb nodded as if he'd never believed he would refuse. "Good. I'm attaching you to the Scorpion Gang for the duration of Akhet, which means you'll be working under Gang-Chief Sobek over there. His men call him 'the Crocodile', so watch out for his teeth."

Senu glanced uncertainly at the big man, remembering how he'd threatened to make one of his gang haul a stone on his own. Then he caught Sobek's wink and managed a small grin back.

"Sobek will keep you informed of when we need you," Nemheb went on. "We'll probably require you to distract Lord Khufu's ka while we make certain, um, preparations. The men you see here are all sworn to secrecy. Not a word to anyone else. I'll have my eye on you. Understand?"

Senu glanced at the medjay, who had not moved a single ebony muscle the entire meeting. He nodded. There was some boring talk about quotas, after which

Nemheb dismissed the men. The lamps flickered eerily as the mertu made their way out, bent double to avoid scraping their unprotected scalps on the tunnel roof. The dwarf left with Nemheb, the medjay a silent shadow at their heels.

When everyone had gone, Tefen rested a hand on Senu's head. He sighed and said, "This won't be easy for you, son. The other boys'll tease you about working on a gang. They'll be encouraged to think it's your punishment for failing the test today, but you can't tell them any different, however hard it gets. You realize that, don't you?"

Senu nodded again. "But it'll be all right to tell Reonet, won't it? She can keep a secret, and-"

His father frowned. "You can't tell *anyone*, Senu. I thought Captain Nemheb made that clear." He stared along the tunnel a moment, then tweaked Senu's ka-tail. "Come along, we'd best get back before your mother thinks we've been eaten by a crocodile – I told her I was taking you night fishing so she wouldn't wonder where we were. How's your head? Did that weird dwarf of Nemheb's hurt you? I said you wouldn't go off with a stranger, and that business with the blindfold was stupid, only Captain Nemheb's a difficult man to argue with..."

Senu hardly heard. As his father steered him through the tunnels and out under a sky blazing with stars, his thoughts were racing ahead to Reonet's face when he showed her the gold he'd earned.

Chapter 3

SCORPION GANG
Do not be hostile to me in the presence of the Keeper of the Balance, for you are my ka... (spell 30B)

IT TOOK A few days to sort everyone out. Mertu were arriving from the fields at all hours of the day and night, desperate to build themselves somewhere comfortable to sleep before work started in earnest. The rocky area between the village and Amun's Wall filled with shaven-headed men and rough-looking boys erecting mudbrick shelters and hide tents. Shouts of greeting filled the air. Coarse songs. Angry yells. Fist fights. One night there was a murder, and the sapers dragged off one of the mertu to be judged behind the White Wall. In the morning, the murderer's partly built hut was claimed by a family fresh from the fields, who set about finishing it.

Other Akhets, Senu had kept well out of the way, canoeing in the freshly filled lagoons until Re sank into the desert and he had to head home. But since this year he was among the apprentices, he had to stay in the village. He paced the little house with Red rippling at his shoulder, until his mother shouted at him to get out before he drove her crazy. "The sooner you start work, the better!" she said. Then she dropped her head in her hands and gave a little moan. "Oh Senu, why couldn't you have tried harder in the test? I daren't even think of you working up there with those savages. Re's breath! I *hate* this time of year."

Several times when Iny and the others teased him about his "punishment", Senu came close to blurting out the truth. But the other apprentices were worrying about their own assignments, so their taunts were half hearted. Even when he plucked up the courage to tell Reonet he was going to join the Scorpion Gang, he didn't think she realized how unusual it was for a hemutiu to work on a gang. "I'm to work under your father's personal supervision in the river temple!" she told him in return. "Batahotep thinks I'll just be mixing paints and trimming brushes. He says there's no point me learning spells and things because I'm a girl, but I'm sure your father will teach me if I ask him. Then I'll be able to go to scribe school, no matter what old Batahotep says! Isn't that wonderful?"

"Wonderful," Senu muttered, thinking: *That should have been me.*

Reonet looked at him closely and said, "I found your slate. Your glyphs weren't at all bad, you know. You could have finished if you'd only stuck with it a bit longer." She sighed. "Why do you always give up so easily, Senu?"

He stiffened. "What was the point? Batahotep had already failed me."

"He might have changed his mind."

"He wouldn't have, all right? You don't understand!" He turned his back on her hurt look and fled home before she could ask any more awkward questions.

That night the official notification came, instructing all hemutiu apprentices to report for work at the Passage of Purification at first lighthour the next day. Senu didn't sleep a wink. Red had vanished in a sulk when he heard the summons, leaving him with nothing better to do than watch the shadows dance around his sleeping mat until the carefully rationed oil in the lamp ran out just before dawn. His ka still wasn't back when the sky paled.

After a special breakfast of date and barley gruel, of which he couldn't force down more than a few mouthfuls, his mother plaited his ka-tail and tied her precious copper ankh amulet in the end. When he protested, she gripped his hand hard and stared into his eyes. There were tears in hers. "Wear it for me, Senu." she said softly. "Please?"

Not wanting to hurt his mother's feelings, he left the ankh where it was, though he was sure mertu boys didn't wear such valuable amulets on site.

There were at least fifty people waiting to get through the shadowy passage under Amun's Wall. Senu joined the back of the queue, nervously winding his ka-tail round his finger. The ankh glittered in the early sunlight. The circle with the cross beneath was supposed to be a powerful spell for "life". Senu only hoped it would work.

Everyone moved forward a step as the duty scribe marked another man off his list. Important craftsmen like Tefen had gone through early to avoid the crush. Those left waiting with Senu were the younger apprentices or spare labour not yet assigned to any specific task. He twisted his head, hoping to see Reonet so he could apologize for running off last night, but there was no sign of her.

Another step, and another man disappeared into the gloom under the Wall. Senu broke into a sweat.

"Red?" he whispered.

But his ka was still in a sulk and didn't answer.

Now he was at the mouth of the Passage. Framed perfectly by the far opening, Khufu's Horizon shimmered pink, white and gold in the heat haze. For a breath, Senu was lost, dizzy. The plateau shifted under his feet. He caught himself against the wall and closed his eyes.

"Name?" snapped a voice. "Wash your ears out, boy! You're holding things up here."

Senu blinked. "Er, sorry sir..."

"Wait a moment!" The scribe squinted at him over his papyrus and his tone softened. "You're Tefen's son, aren't you? Recognize that red tail of yours anywhere."

Senu stared at his toes. "Yes sir."

"What you doing up here still? Why aren't you with your father in the river temple? He reported in half an hour ago."

"I – er -"

"He's being punished, sir," piped a voice from behind. "Got to work in a dirty mertu gang till he learns to write properly, hasn't he? You're late, ka-baby! You'll be in big trouble."

Senu turned with a scowl and saw Iny grinning at him. The boy gave him a sly shove between the shoulder blades. "Go on then, dirty ganger. Get through there where you belong!"

The scribe's forehead creased. "This true? You're on a gang?"

Senu aimed a backward kick at the Iny's shin, but missed when the boy danced out of range. "Yes sir."

"Then you're in the wrong place. You should have been here much earlier. Do you know which gang you've been assigned to?"

"Scorpions, sir."

The scribe made a note. "All right, since it's your first day and you didn't know any better, I'll mark you down on time. So much confusion anyway today, I doubt anyone'll notice. Tefen probably didn't realize but for future reference, mertu start an hour earlier than hemutiu. The Gang Chiefs have permission to give one lash for each hour their men are late. Scorpions are hauling today, so you'll probably catch them on the road to the quarry. Hurry along now."

Iny jeered as Senu hurried through the passage. His stomach, already jumpy with nerves, knotted itself into a painful ball. An hour late! Why hadn't Captain Nemheb warned him? Did he *want* him to get whipped on his first day?

The noise hit him as soon as he emerged from the Wall. Mertu laughed and called to one another in rough voices as they collected their tools and dispersed through the site. This was the closest Senu had ever been to the first layers of the new pyramid that would one day house Lord Khafre's sahu, but there was no time to have a proper look. Reluctantly, he turned his back on the pyramids and raced along the quarry road following the jumble of bare footprints in the dust. "You could help me here, Red," he grumbled under his breath as he ran. "Isn't it about time you stopped sulking? No one's likely to want us to talk to Lord Khufu's ka today, are they? It'll take ages to sort this lot out. At least tell me if I'm going the right way-"

He was so busy following footprints, twisting his head to look for Sobek and hoping to see Red, that he forgot to look where he was going. He ran into a wall of hard copper muscle and landed on his backside in the middle of the road, all the breath knocked out of him. "Oof!" he gasped.

The mertu he'd blundered into turned and looked down at him. He bared dazzling white teeth.

Senu scrabbled backwards and picked himself up. "Er, I'm sorry, I was just-"

A callused hand closed about Senu's ka-tail. "I've found your water-boy, Sobek!" his captor called. "What'll I do with him?"

About fifteen men in stained loincloths with coils of rope slung over their shoulders looked round. Senu thought he recognized some of them from the secret meeting in the tomb. Three boys who looked about his own age stared curiously. None had ka-tails. Two of them carried wooden yokes with jars roped to each end. "Hold 'im tight, Father!" called the one without a yoke, his rough accent clashing with his remarkably handsome face. "Late, ain't he? He's got to be whipped."

The boy's black eyes fixed on Senu, bright with a hatred he didn't understand.

He wondered vaguely if a whip would hurt more than Batahotep's rod and started to prepare himself for the pain. But Sobek pushed through the others and rested a large hand on the handsome boy's shoulder. "That's enough, Gef," he said.

Senu stood as straight as he could with the mertu holding his ka-tail. "Senu son of Tefen reporting for work, sir!" he managed.

Sobek regarded him steadily, taking in the ankh and Senu's flush when he saw him looking at it. He nodded slowly. "I see you've met my deputy. Let him go, Adjedd. Get him a yoke and explain his duties. We'll have to get movin' if we're going to shift our quota of stones today."

There was hostile muttering from the three mertu boys.

"But he was late, sir!" Gef protested.

"It's his first day," Sobek said firmly. "Allowances must be made. Adjedd?"

Senu could feel Gef's hostile eyes on his back as he followed the deputy over to a collection of ropes and tools laid neatly under an awning at the side of the road. Two sapers were handing out the tools to the men as they passed, while a scribe made careful notes on a sheet of papyrus. The chisels and adzes were shiny, the ropes neatly coiled and unfrayed. After a few words with the scribe, Adjedd selected a yoke and balanced it across Senu's shoulders. As the deputy tied a jar to each end and measured the ropes until they were of equal length, Gef stared straight at Senu and ran one finger slowly across his neck.

Senu looked away, heart banging.

"Least you're not a runt," Adjedd said, knotting ropes. "Got good bones under that gangly frame of yours. Some boys we've had can hardly lift the jars off the ground when they're empty, let alone full. There!" He gave one of the jars a tug, making Senu stagger. He laughed. "You'll get used to it, lad! Just what you need to build up some muscle on that soft hemutiu body. Soon be havin' you entering the End of Akhet Wrestling with the rest of the lads. But don't get above yourself," he warned as Senu turned on his heel and experimentally swung the jars. "Chief Sobek's a fair man and he might have let you off a whippin' today, but he won't stand for any nonsense. You be on time tomorrow, right? And sun-up means *here* when Re peeps over that horizon, not just staggering out of your fancy hemutiu house rubbing your sleepy eyes."

Senu surreptitiously rubbed his knee, where a jar had caught him on the back swing. He nodded. "Yes sir."

Adjedd gave him another slap on the shoulder. "Glad to see you've got some respect. You carry on like this, and we'll get along just fine. Now then, you follow Patep and Teti down to the river an' fill those jars. By the time you're back up, Sobek'll have a stone on the rollers. Then we'll see how nimble you are. But don't hang around down there chattin' and holding up the work, now! Or you'll feel the Chief's teeth, hemutiu or not."

Senu hurried after the other two, who were already on their way down the steep path to the river, swinging their yokes with practised skill. He bit his lip as one of his own jars tangled round his leg and almost sent him flying. He hadn't really thought about the physical work involved, or the possibility the mertu boys might be hostile. He'd thought the hardest thing would be keeping his mouth shut.

Looked like he'd been worrying about all the wrong things.

The quarry road wasn't far from the site if you were a hemutiu youngster playing tricks on the labourers. But it was as long as the journey to Khnum's Cataract and back when you were carrying two full jars hanging from a yoke across aching, sunburnt shoulders. Each time Senu reached the huge limestone block the Scorpions were hauling from the quarry to the site, he had to unhook his jars and add them to the line of full ones waiting at the side of the road. Under Sobek's watchful eye, one of the boys poured water on the wooden rollers beneath the stone, while the other two ran round behind and carried the last roller to the front, thus ensuring their sledge moved as smoothly as possible when the men leant into the ropes. Scorpions weren't the only gang assigned to haulage. The road was a sweaty, fly-infested, dusty river of blocks being dragged from the quarry to the site, to the accompaniment of the men's gang-songs and the cracks of the Chiefs' whips.

Senu kept his mouth shut and did as he was told, trying to stay out of trouble. It was cool by the river, and he could thrust his head under the water once he got down there, bringing momentary relief. It wasn't until he'd staggered up the hill for the ninth time that he realized the boys on the other gangs were taking turns under the yoke so the ones who had just fetched and carried water could take a breather pouring or moving rollers.

"The little snakes are doing it on purpose!" he muttered, seeing Gef, Patep and Teti glance knowingly at him and chuckle among themselves.

"About time you came to your senses," a familiar voice whispered in his ear. "Maybe we can go home now?"

Senu's heart lifted. For the first time that morning, he forgot how much he ached. "Red!" he said, whirling. The jars swung dangerously. Water slopped out. Gef, who was on his way across to collect them, scowled.

"I thought you'd gone for good," Senu whispered, quieter. The last thing he needed was for the mertu boys to hear him talking to his ka.

"'Course not," his ka said. "You haven't cut your tail yet, have you?"

"Don't just stand there!" Gef snapped. "The rollers are dryin' out!"

"Bully! Bully!" Red rippled around the boy, pulling faces and sticking his tongue out. "Yah! Dirty mertu bully!"

Gef couldn't see or hear the ka, of course. But Senu could. Before he could control it, a giggle escaped.

Gef's black eyes narrowed. "What you laughin' at, Red-Tail? Get on over there, or I'll make you burn as hot as you've let our sledge get." He glanced over his shoulder to check Sobek wasn't watching and gave one of Senu's ropes a sly tug.

Already off balance because of the full jars swinging and sloshing their contents, Senu staggered. Gef's foot was suddenly in the way. He tripped over it, tried to right himself, got one of the ropes fouled around an ankle and sprawled full-length with the yoke on top of him. Water spilled into the dust. One of the jars bounced off Senu's spine. The other rolled across the road under the Scorpions' feet and was crushed by an advancing roller.

"Clumsy hemutiu oaf!" Gef shouted, his expression triumphant. "You've broken a *jar*!"

Senu lay face down, ears burning. The coolness of the water trickling over his aching back and legs was rather pleasurable. Nearby, Red was urging him to get up. It seemed much easier to lie still. But despite the yelling men tugging backwards on the ropes, the Scorpion's stone was still rolling towards him. It was too big to stop in a hurry and the road here sloped downhill.

He fought off the yoke and shook his head. The gang working behind the Scorpions yelled in alarm and leant back on their ropes too, desperately trying to slow their stone before it crashed into the back of the one in front. There was a lot of shouting and cursing. Clouds of dust obscured everything. The Scorpions' stone had almost stopped when the one behind hit it. Rollers skewed sideways. Men scattered, yelling warnings, as the enormous block tilted like night falling over Senu's head.

I'm going to die, he thought and closed his eyes in terror.

Something cool closed about his wrist and the ground went soft. At the same time, a resounding thud shook the road behind him. When he'd wiped the dust out of his eyes, the stone wasn't as close as he'd thought. He must have rolled clear, after all.

Red released his wrist and backed away. "Don't make me do that again," he said in a small, shaky voice.

Senu blinked. Was his ka *blue?*"

Sobek shrugged off his harness and hurried across,

coughing and wafting dust aside in an effort to see if Senu was hurt. Gef, who was closer, just stared, his smirk replaced by a frown.

"Gef!" Sobek snapped. "Go ask the Overseer for another jar to replace the broken one."

Grumbling, Gef went. Sobek retrieved the yoke and silently handed the surviving jar to one of the other Scorpion boys. Senu scrambled to his feet and brushed himself off. His shin was bleeding.

Sobek looked him up and down, frowning. "What happened?"

Senu eyed the Scorpions. They leant against the fallen stone, easing their muscles and scratching bites. The gang behind exchanged amused comments concerning boys in general. Senu flushed. Patep and Teti glared at him, daring him to tell.

"I tripped, sir," he muttered.

Sobek's eyes narrowed. "I been watching you. You seemed to have the hang of it."

Senu stared at his toes. "I was tired."

"I see." The Gang-Chief glanced at Patep and Teti, then turned to his men. "All right, we'll make this the last stone before lunch. Adjedd, you're in charge. I'm taking Senu to have his cut seen to. You two boys, get down the river and fill another pair of jars each before you break off."

Catching the others' scowls, Senu tried to protest that his leg wasn't that bad, but there was no arguing with Sobek. Gef was on his way back with the replacement jar. Patep and Teti paused to exchange a few muttered words with their friend before they headed for the river. As they did so, all three glanced Senu's way. He winced.

Sobek took him to the edge of the plateau where the midday sun reflecting from all the stone made his eyes hurt. The smaller pyramids where Lord Khufu's family were buried, the dead Lord's ka-temple, and his Parade with its frieze of painted animals were lost in a shimmering cloud of dust. But Khufu's Horizon rose out of this, dazzling and untouchable above the noise and heat. For the second time that day, Senu felt dizzy.

Mistaking his faintness for pain from his wound, Sobek steered him towards a patch of shade under an awning where some hemutiu women were doling out plain barley gruel and radishes for the labourers' midday meal.

"Sore, huh?" he said. "You'll feel better when you've had something to eat. We've caught up our quota, so you should be able to take it a bit easier this afternoon. Don't worry, the other boys'll come around once they get the idea you're here for the stretch. Don't let 'em bully you. There's no funny business on my gang, and they know it. Gef might be Adjedd's first-born, but he knows I won't spare him the lash if he steps out of line."

Senu glanced round. The only people close enough to overhear were busy crunching radishes or slurping gruel straight from their bowls in disgusting mertu fashion. "Er, sir?" he whispered. "How long before... you know?"

Sobek gave him a sharp glance. "You'll be told when. Shh now, we can't talk here." Pulling him across the tent, he said in a hearty tone, "Here we are! These ladies serve the best grub this side of Khufu's Horizon! A special lunch and a clean bandage for my water-boy here," he called. "It's his first day on the job, and the poor lad's feelin' it a bit."

The women took one look at Senu's ka-tail and immediately turned motherly. Before he could protest, one of them had smeared some foul-smelling paste on his shoulders where the yoke had rubbed the skin raw, and another had bandaged his shin as tightly as a sahu's leg.

"There you go, lovey," she said, giving his ka-tail a tweak. "Tell your mother that ankh of hers is working just fine."

Senu fought his way out of the lunch tent, cheeks burning. Red's giggles tickled his ears like invisible feathers. He didn't notice the Scorpion boys sneak in behind the next gang. Or the way Gef's black gaze followed his ankh, narrow and thoughtful.

Chapter 4

SECRETS
Hail to you, you who descend in power, chief of all secret matters! (spell 14)

UNLIKE THE CRAFTSMEN'S apprentices, boys assigned to the gangs worked afternoons along with the men. Senu was so tired and it was so late when he staggered home, he didn't see any of his friends all week. He filled the time trying to think of a way to pay Gef back for tripping him under the stone.

The mertu boy hadn't tried anything else since that first morning. But Senu felt those black eyes on his back as he struggled up and down the path from the quarry road to the river. Once, when he turned to glare at the boy, he caught a puzzled expression on Gef's face. He assumed Sobek must have threatened him with the whip and breathed a sigh of relief.

The opportunity for revenge came at the end of the week, when he and Gef were sent down to the river to fetch water while Patep and Teti stayed to move rollers. Senu hung back as Gef hurried ahead, neither boy wanting to get close enough to talk. It was Gef's habit to fill his jars straight away and leave them on the bank while he splashed water over his face and washed the dust out of his hair. Senu waited until the boy's back was turned then quietly dropped handfuls of broken stone he'd collected from the site into Gef's jars. Some of the boys from other gangs saw, but grinned and said nothing. Senu ducked back into the reeds to watch.

When Gef retrieved his yoke, he staggered with a look of surprise. But, seeing the others watching, he struggled determinedly up the path. He didn't realize there was rubble in the jars until he reached the Scorpion's sledge and tipped the sludgy, gritty mess over the rollers. The men stopped singing in surprise as the sledge juddered. Sobek looked down and cursed. "What's got into you today?" Adjedd yelled at his son. "You've bin on this gang long enough to know not to bring sandy water!"

Gef's face darkened. He walked close to Senu and viciously threw one of the stones at his foot. "You wait, Red-Tail!" he hissed. "You just wait!"

Senu danced clear, trying not to laugh. Even Red, who usually sulked the whole time they were on the wrong side of Amun's Wall, broke his self-imposed silence and giggled from the dusty air.

It was only after the duty scribe had checked him off site and he was nearing the river, where he came every night to wash off the worst of the blood and dust before heading home, that Senu remembered Gef's threat. The hemutiu's favourite bathing spot was usually deserted at this hour but tonight faint giggles and splashing carried on the air. Where better to ambush him?

He ducked into the reeds, heart banging, crawled towards the noise and peered out. The relief was so great, he laughed. It was only a group of hemutiu girls, knee deep in the still waters of the lagoon, stretching their wet hair and measuring its length against their arms. One of them had made a garland of wilting lotus flowers, luminous blue in the dusk, with which she crowned the girl who had the longest hair.

Reonet.

Red rippled mischievously into the middle of their game and passed a transparent hand through the petals, pretending to pluck them and throw them in the air. Senu smiled as he extracted himself from the reeds.

The girls whirled at the sound of cracking stems. "It's a dirty mertu spying on us!" one of them screamed, clutching her dress to her in fright.

"It's only Senu, you idiot." Reonet splashed out of the lagoon and put her hands on her hips. "Finally!" she said. "I thought we were going to have to wait down here all night."

The other girls splashed out of the water, too, and wrung out their skirts. Whispering and giggling, they headed up the path to the village. "Got to lose that ka of yours soon, Senu!" one called as they went. "She won't wait forever, you know."

Senu blushed furiously.

Reonet's normally spotless dress was streaked with coloured pigments and she had a blue smudge on one cheek. She looked him up and down in silence. Her gaze settled on the now rather tattered bandage around his leg. She laughed tensely. "Practising for when you're dead, Senu son of Tefen? Won't be long, the way you're going."

"I've just come down for a bath," Senu said, flushing again. "You don't have to wait."

"Fine. I'll go then."

They glared at each other.

"I'm... uh... sorry about what I said in the village," Senu said. "I was worried about going on the gang."

She looked confused. But she tightened her lips again. "Am I supposed to feel sorry for you? It's your own silly fault."

His flush deepened.

Then Reonet said, "How is it on...?" And at the same time, Senu said, "What's it like in...?"

They stopped and stared at each other. Then they both laughed properly, and everything was all right again.

"You first," Senu said, settling his back against a shadowy palm trunk.

Reonet sat beside him and told him about her mornings in the river temple, mixing paints and watching Tefen work. "It's brilliant, Senu!" As she spoke, her eyes shone and her fingers described arcs in the air. "I've just mixed so far, but I'm learning so much! I know how to make all the colours we're never allowed to use in school. And your father explains everything to me as he does it. He says I'm getting on so well, he might let me do some filling-in tomorrow. And maybe, if I work hard and keep learning as fast as I am, he'll even teach me how to make the red squares on the walls so I can draw my own outlines! The other artists don't like it much with me being a girl and all, and the priest who came today to see how we were getting on was really snooty. But Tefen's in charge, so they got to let me learn. And I plan to learn a lot more than how to draw pictures! There are spells all over the place, Senu. You should see them. I'm not afraid of them like the others are. I'm going to learn everything I can, and one day I'll show old Batahotep and Father. I'll show them all!"

Her voice had risen with excitement. The reeds behind them rustled and a duck flapped out, making them both jump. Reonet giggled, then glanced round as if she'd said too much. "But what happened to you? You look like you've been in a fight."

In return, Senu told her about the Scorpion gang, Sobek, Adjedd, and Gef and the others, though not how he'd nearly died under a stone on the first day. She'd only have told him off for being so hopeless. Reonet made sympathetic noises and examined his blisters and bruises with morbid curiosity. It was such a relief to have a friendly ear, they talked and talked until the stars came out and dazzled the water.

Then Reonet said, "How long do you have to stay with the gang? I can't see how it's supposed to teach you how to write. You're more likely to lose fingers like your sister's poor husband and never be able to hold a pen again."

Senu's stomach gave an uncomfortable lurch as he thought of his older sister, whose family never had enough to eat. One of the obelisks destined for the imakhu graveyard had slipped whilst Tamuwy's husband had been carving its owner's name into its base, leaving the young sculptor with a crushed hand and unable to work. Tamuwy was always round their house, begging spare food for her two small daughters.

Senu stared across the lagoon and shrugged. "I dunno. Till Father thinks I've had enough, I suppose."

Reonet frowned. "Looks like you've had enough already. I can't think why he won't let you in the river temple. You're not that hopeless."

Senu forced a grin. "Why are you so anxious to have me there? I thought you liked being Tefen's star apprentice."

Her lips tightened. She sprang to her feet, planted her fists on her hips and stared down at him in disgust. "I wish you'd grow up!" she said.

His cheeks went hot. "What's that supposed to mean?"

"You know what it means! You're such a fool, Senu. Look at you. Is it really worth crippling yourself just to spite your father and old Batahotep? Do you want to spend the rest of your life with leathery skin and bent bones? Even if you manage to keep all your fingers, the dust up there makes people go blind, you know."

Senu's stomach gave another lurch. "That's not true!" he said. "Anyway, there's interesting stuff happens up on site, too. Sobek says we're on the pyramid all next week. I'll get to see how the lifting machines work tomorrow, and I'm bound to learn something about measurements and things. Anyway, I'm not going to be on the gang *that* long. Only until-" He bit the words off. But she was staring at him. Her frown deepened. Red groaned and put a hand across his eyes.

"Until what?"

"Nothing."

"Yes there is. You were going to say something important. Your eyes went all bright and silly, like they do when you're looking at your ka."

"My eyes do *not* go all bright and sill-"

"Don't change the subject. Until what?"

Reonet was more of a crocodile than Sobek. Once she had hold of something, she rolled it round and round until it stopped struggling. "Until... until I realize I'd rather be a scribe than a labourer, I suppose," Senu muttered.

Reonet gave him a long, hard look, then shook her head and reclipped her hair. "I've got to go. I've got to feed Miu, and there's something else I want to try tonight. You'd best hurry if you're going to have a bath. They'll be shutting the village gates soon, and then you'll be in double trouble, Senu son of Tefen!"

She marched back up the dark path like a boy, swinging her arms, completely fearless. Senu watched until she was safely round the bend then pinched his nose and jumped into the lagoon. The water was refreshing, but he didn't stay in long. His bruises were stiffening and visions of Gef with a gang of mertu boys intent upon revenge kept springing out of the dark. Even the sight of Red doing backstroke through the reflected stars failed to cheer him up.

He splashed out, shivering in the night air, dried himself with his loincloth and started back to the village. It was darker on the path than he'd thought. A new row of mertu tents cast black shadows in the moonlight. He thought he heard a stealthy footfall and stared over his shoulder, heart banging. Why, oh why, had he stayed so long talking to Reonet?

"Who's there, Red?" he whispered.

"I don't know," his ka breathed in his ear, increasing his nerves. "Hurry, Senu!"

Senu forced his aching legs into a run.

By the time he reached the River Gate, he was gasping with imagined terrors. The saper on duty laughed at him as he let him through. "Scare yourself, boy? You shouldn't stay out so late. They say Lord Khufu's ka goes down that lagoon at night to sail his star-boat. Better watch out, or he'll steal your ka away."

Shuddering, Senu raced through the moonlit alleys until he was out of sight of the gate. He leant against a wall to get his breath back. Red collapsed beside him, imitating his distress, although there was no need. Kas didn't have trouble with breathing. They didn't need air to stay alive.

"That's not true, is it Red?" Senu puffed. "About Lord Khufu's star-boat?"

Red made a strangled sound and vanished. Senu's heart started up afresh as an ebony-skinned man slipped out of the shadows. He'd been almost as invisible as Red in the dark. It was too late to run. Senu pressed back against the wall, skin prickling, as the medjay strode towards him.

But the medjay didn't stop. "Tomorrow," he whispered out of the side of his mouth as he strode past. "Sobek will tell you when."

Chapter 5

AMULET GAME

I have come to you bearing the amulet which is in my hand, my protection for the daily course. (spell 182)

"GET IT OVER with, Red," Senu said as brightly as he could, as he hurried through the Passage of Purification the next morning. "Then we won't have to come up here any more."

No answer.

He sighed. After the incident with the stones in Gef's jars, Red had stopped sulking to the extent that if Gef came near Senu, the ka would appear between them with raised fists as if he could fight the mertu boy. He'd hoped this meant his ka was resigned to his task. Evidently not.

His steps slowed as he approached the Scorpions' meeting place. He was in good time. The sun had yet to rise and the cold of the desert night still lingered on the plateau. Khufu's pyramid loomed dark against the sky, raising goosebumps on Senu's arms. Not everyone was here yet. The men sat on the base of the ramps or leant against the blocks waiting to be raised, laughing and exchanging coarse jokes. The Scorpion boys could be seen playfully pushing each other as they made their way across the site. Gef and Patep were throwing something between them that the shorter boy, Teti, jumped and tried to catch. Senu couldn't see what it was.

Sobek spotted him and came over, a grin cracking his wide jaw. Still trying to see what Gef and his friends were playing with, Senu stumbled over a coil of rope and nearly fell.

"Steady there, lad!" Sobek caught his elbow. "I wanted a word with you before the others got here..."

This is it.

"...so don't be afraid to ask if there's something you don't understand," Sobek finished. He frowned. "Senu? You listening?"

"Y-yes, sir." He licked his lips. "I mean... would you mind repeating that, please? I couldn't quite hear. The noise..." He waved a vague hand at the gangs converging on the ramps. Although they'd worked a ten-day week hauling stones from the quarry and now had to lift them up the seven finished layers of the new pyramid, the men didn't seem tired. In fact, they seemed to be looking forward to the change of task.

Sobek grinned again. "Yeah, it can be a bit rowdy up here till you get used to it. All I said was the liftin' machines are dangerous. Your task today is to help lift water for the rollers up top and bring us poor hoisters regular refreshment to oil our throats! Stay clear of the machines unless you're called across for somethin' specific." He gave him a meaningful look.

Senu swallowed and nodded. "Yes sir."

So it wouldn't be until later? Maybe Gef and his mates would have dropped a stone on his head by then. Save him the bother of trying to talk Red into distracting Lord Khufu's ka.

As usual first thing, all the boys were sent to the river for water. Gef and the others raced off, uncommonly keen to return to the site with their full jars. This was both a relief and a nuisance. It gave Senu another opportunity to try to tempt Red into an appearance. But by the time he got back to the ramps with his water, the gangs were busy setting up their machines and there was no one to help him lift the jars up the layers above the ramps.

Senu found a place near one corner where there was no scaffolding, untied the ropes from the yoke and retied them round his wrist. He caught the edge of the first step and swung himself up, heaved the full jars after him one by one, and jumped back down to collect the yoke. No one took much notice of him. There seemed to be some kind of competition to see which gang could set up the quickest. Around all four sides, the stones were levered on to sledges ready to haul up the ramps to the first level of machines. On the flat square platform of the seventh layer, other gangs waited with sledges and rollers ready to drag the raised stones into position. They were building the eighth layer from the centre outwards.

About ten blocks were already fitted neatly together in the middle. A handful of hemutiu craftsmen lounged against them, tools at their feet, while the harassed-looking Overseer and his accompanying scribe rushed back and forth checking that everything was set up correctly.

Legs dangling over the edge, Senu paused to catch his breath. Even seven layers up, barely a foundation, the partly-built pyramid provided a fine view of the site. Water filled the valley where heavily laden barges and boats sailed through the heads of drowned palm trees. To his left, Khufu's Horizon gleamed in the early sunlight. The colourful Parade with its carved animals and birds was like the tail of some fantastic beast resting on the hill with its square end – Khufu's river temple – dipped in the edge of the flood. A little way upstream was Lord Khafre's river temple, as yet isolated and unfinished. His father was down there somewhere, with Reonet mixing his paints. To his right, Amun's Wall stretched from the river's edge to the desert, sun-glints on top showing where sapers patrolled. Senu wrenched his gaze away. Better not to think of those sharp spears and what the sapers would do to people caught robbing a pyramid.

He picked up his jars and made his way to the centre, which seemed the safest place to be until the new blocks arrived. One of the hemutiu recognized him and asked after his father. Senu mumbled a reply. Gef and the other Scorpion boys were in a huddle with some boys from other gangs. For once, they ignored Senu.

He glanced round to make sure no one was listening. "Red?" he hissed. "Come on out, you coward! If you don't, we'll have to stay on this stupid gang all Akhet!"

Still no answer.

Senu wrapped his arms around his knees with a sigh and rested his chin on them. He kept one eye on Gef and the mertu boys, the other on the southern side of the pyramid where the Scorpions had set up their "machine". There were shouts below. Whips cracked. Ropes creaked. And, like every morning, gang-songs filled the air as the mertu threw themselves into their work. Patep extracted himself from the huddle of boys, ran to the edge, peered over, then ran back. There was more excited whispering. Senu tensed – curious, but too wary of Gef's tricks to go to the edge and see what was happening.

"If he thinks I'm going to take a look so his friends can shove me from behind, he can think again," he muttered.

The creaks and strange cracking noises grew louder. Then, as if by magic, an amber block floated slowly up over the edge. The Overseer gave a shout and the nearest gang raced to the spot. With smooth practice, the stone was drawn inwards on to their sledge. Boys poured water and under the Gang-Chief's watchful eye the stone rolled smoothly towards the waiting craftsmen.

"Scorpions for ever!" Gef shouted.

The other boys groaned as Gef, Patep and Teti scooped several amulets each from the pile in the middle of the group and hung them around their necks.

Gef swaggered across to Senu, his new amulets rattling and flashing in the sun. "See, Red-Tail? We're still the best, in spite of 'aving you as a handicap! S'pose we should thank you. The others wouldn't bet so much normally."

The other two laughed obediently.

Gef stared down at Senu, a challenge in his black eyes. Senu clenched his fists and thought of the robbery. He daren't get into a fight, not today.

When it became obvious he wasn't going to rise to the bait, Gef seized his ka-tail and peered closely at the ankh. "Mmm, fancy hemutiu craftwork. Copper, too. Might be worth a bit. Your ankh against my three-legged hippopotamus here, that Scorpions get the most stones up by midday break. Shouldn't make much difference to you, havin' a broken charm. You've always got your ka to rescue you from a tight spot, haven't you?" He gave Senu a very strange look, then flicked his ka-tail so the ankh caught Senu in the eye. Chuckling, he led Patep and Teti back to the others.

Senu glared after them, furious but a bit worried, too. Gef couldn't do much up here with all these people around. Nevertheless, he decided to keep well away from the edge. Just in case.

Midday break came and went. The boys were sent back to the river for more water. More bets were made and won – mostly by Gef, whose collection of amulets grew by the hour, though thankfully he seemed to have forgotten his self-made wager with Senu. More stones were lifted over the edge and fitted efficiently into place. The mertu sang, the hemutiu chiselled and scraped, the dust rose in clouds that obscured Khufu's Horizon. As Re sank towards the western dunes, Senu began to relax. The medjay's message might have been wrong. Nemheb might have changed his mind. What person with any sense would choose to rob a pyramid in broad daylight, anyway?

Curiosity and boredom finally lured him across to watch the machines at work. The ramps took care of the first two levels. From there, each gang took on a stone. The strongest men levered the stone up at each end, while the rest of the gang inserted wooden planks underneath, slowly building a platform until the stone was high enough to be levered on to the next level. Then the gang on that step repeated the process. The machines were staggered so if a gang dropped part of their equipment, it wouldn't hit the men below. At first Senu couldn't imagine how many men it would take to lift stones as high as Lord Khufu's pyramid. But when he'd watched one block lifted all the way from the ramp into its final position at the centre of the eighth layer, something clicked in his head.

"It's clever, Red," he whispered. "Less stones each time, so you only need the same number of gangs, no matter how high it gets."

"Quite the mathematician, aren't you, lad?" Sobek said softly behind him, making him jump. "Shh now, the scribe's listenin'."

The big Gang-Chief dusted off his palms and drew Senu round the north side of the central layer. The scribe, his papyrus rolled under one arm, peered short-sightedly after them.

"Nosy officials," Sobek muttered. "Give 'em somethin' else to think about in a moment. Now then, you sit over here where it's nice an' quiet and... you know."

Senu's mouth dried. "Now?"

"What you're here for, ain't it? There's goin' to be a little rumpus on the south side. People'll come over and look. You take no notice. Don't worry, it's all bin fixed. Nobody'll get hurt unless they're in the wrong place."

"Uh, but Red-"

"Shh!"

The scribe was glancing their way again, talking to the site Overseer now. He pointed at Senu. The Overseer stood on tip-toe to see over the eighth layer. Sobek swore and pushed Senu down. "Keep your head low. Leave this to me."

Sobek slid over the edge to rejoin his gang. The hemutiu were still busy chiselling, trying to finish their quota before sunset. All the north side stones seemed to have been raised, so Senu had a good view of Khufu's pyramid through dust tinted orange by sunset. The scribe and the Overseer were still looking his way. He leant back against the warm stone and hissed, "Red! Come *on*. We've got to do this. *Now.*"

His ka didn't become visible, but he whispered very faintly from the air, "We don't have to."

"Yes we *do.*"

Senu's voice squeaked and one of the hemutiu working nearby gave him a strange look.

He tried again. "Come on, Red. If we do this, it'll all be over and we'll be rich. Wouldn't you rather spend the rest of Akhet canoeing and fishing than getting hot and dirty up here?"

"I don't get hot and dirty."

"That's not the point! You're supposed to be my ka. Please, Red? You do this for me today, and even if it's not over, I'll do whatever you want tomorrow. Be off sick, whatever. Promise."

Silence. The Overseer and his scribe had been called across by one of the hemutiu to answer a technical question, but any moment now they would remember him.

"Red!"

"I can't. You heard what the kas said-" He broke off and there was an intense stillness by Senu's ear.

Senu frowned, trying to remember exactly what the kas of the dead had said in the hemutiu tombs. It was no good. The only thing that stuck in his mind was the silly babyish way they'd panicked and fled into the arms of the sapers.

He set his jaw. "We survived, didn't we? It can't have

been that bad. Get over to that pyramid, Red. Stop being so stupid."

The stillness persisted. Senu started to worry. "Red? You still there?" Nothing. He sighed. "All right, if you don't want to-"

"We don't have to!" his ka said, rippling into view with a strange expression. "I've been over to check, and he can't see them."

Senu frowned again. "What do you mean?"

"Lord Khufu's ka. He's..." Again, that strange look. "...otherwise occupied. So you don't have to worry."

"But-"

They were interrupted by a great, echoing crash from the south side of the pyramid. Screams, shouts and the rattle of wood and stone followed. A vast cloud of dust puffed against the setting sun. Heads snapped round and people whirled. Hemutiu dropped their tools and rushed across. Boys jostled one another to see. The Overseer cursed under his breath and puffed over with his scribe in tow, fighting his way through the crush at the edge. "Stand back!" he yelled. "Men down! Give them room!" Gang-Chiefs with loud voices passed the order on, bellowing it over the edge with cupped hands and modifying it slightly on the way. "MEN DOWN! ALL HANDS TO THE PYRAMID! EMERGENCY! MEN TRAPPED!" Mertu streamed towards the accident from all corners of the site, abandoning their tasks and calling through the dust. "What's happened?" ... "I can't see a thing!" ... "How many are dead?" ... "Look out!

Another stone's falling!" There was the sound of another avalanche. Panic swept through the crowd like fire before the wind. Sapers left their posts and raced across to restore order.

"No, you idiots!" shouted the Overseer. "It's not that bad. No one's dead, no one's trapped-"

By this time, of course, it was too late. Just about every person on site, including the water-boys and the women on refreshment duty, were swarming over the southern ramps in a confused riot of excited, sweaty flesh.

Senu had jumped to his feet with the rest. Then he realized. That stone had fallen from the Scorpions' machine. He sat down again with a grin and squinted at Khufu's pyramid, a little disappointed not to see the robbery in progress. But of course they'd be round the far side, hidden from the site.

"How long do you think it'll take, Red?" he whispered. He peered at the panicky people below and had a horrible thought. "Are their kas here too? What if Lord Khufu's ka comes to see what's happening?"

Red, in a better mood now he'd escaped talking to the dead, gave him a scornful look. "Don't be stupid. Kas of dead people don't care what happens to the living."

"But I thought-"

"How *sweet*!" said a familiar voice. "Red-Tail's talking to his ka!"

Senu scrambled to his feet. Gef and the other mertu boys, bored with the "accident", had come looking for more interesting entertainment. Senu darted a glance across the pyramid. Everyone else was still watching the activity below. The boys closed, trapping him against the eighth layer. Gef was in front, his neckful of amulets flashing the setting sun into Senu's eyes. He pushed Senu back against the stone. "Wondered where you'd go to. Come for my ankh, haven't I? Scorpions won this morning, in case you didn't know."

Senu's skin prickled. "You can't have it," he said. "It's my mother's."

One of the older boys from another gang picked up an abandoned adze and tested the edge. He eyed Senu speculatively. "Shall I cut 'im, Gef?" he said. "Learn 'im what 'appens to people who don't pay their debts?"

But Gef shouldered the big boy back. His handsome face pushed close to Senu's. He said in a low voice, "I don't think that'll be necessary. Red-Tail an' me understand each other, don't we? Wouldn't want me to tell on you and that precious ka of yours, would you?" He waggled his fingers. "So hand it over."

Patep and Teti giggled nervously. Senu's eyes flicked from Gef to the boy with the adze and back again. "Tell what?" he whispered, his legs weak with fear that Gef might have overheard him and Red arguing about Lord Khufu's ka. "I haven't done anything wrong."

"It's all right, they don't know anything." Red puffed himself up and made a frightening face at Gef. The only trouble was, none of the boys could see him.

Gef smiled. "Oh come on, Red-Tail! I'm not blind,

you know. It's either the ankh or your ka. Your choice."

Were they threatening Red?

"You can't touch my ka," Senu said, relieved the conversation had taken a turn away from the robbery. "I'm not that stupid."

"We can touch *you*, though, can't we?" said the boy with the adze. "'Urts just the same."

Gef gave him a hard look. "Keep out of this, Hori. We'll do it my way." He smiled at Senu, fingered the amulets around his neck and whispered, "Maybe I got a temple scarab right here. Ask your sweet little ka about *that*."

Though he tried not to look, Senu's eyes flickered to Gef's amulets. There were stories, of things the priests did...

"He's only a dirty mertu," Red said. "He's lying." But his ka's tone was strange.

"Well?" Gef said, staring hard into Senu's eyes. "What did he say, then?"

Senu licked his lips. From the corner of his eye, he could see order returning to the site, gangs going back to their stations. Soon the Overseer or his scribe would notice what was happening.

He straightened his shoulders and stared Gef in the eye. "He said you're lying!"

Big mistake. The boy with the adze, Hori, swung the sharp tool with a yell. Red immediately rippled between Senu and the descending edge, but the adze flashed right through the ka. A line of fire scored Senu's cheek. There was an awful grating noise, as if he'd crunched a bone between his teeth. Gef seized Hori's arm with a yell. Hori swung the adze at him. Patep and Teti tried to defend their friend. The pyramid dissolved in a wild flurry of fists and feet as the other boys flung themselves into the fight. Someone's elbow got Senu in the eye, a starburst of blue. Hands tugged his ka-tail, dragging him towards the edge. He kicked frantically. Everything was a blur. Dust... blood... spinning, whirling sky... Then there was an "Oof!" and the hands let go. Someone shouted "*Heka!*" and the boys scattered.

Senu lay still, curled into a ball. He couldn't understand how Red had managed to hit someone, or why people were shouting about heka. Then he remembered that doctors sometimes used heka-powers when their patients needed a spell to help the healing process. Had someone called the site physician? He hoped so. His ka-tail felt as if it had been pulled out by the roots. His cheek burned. Blood was splattered everywhere.

Sobek's roar came from a long way off. "What in Re's name is goin' on here? Thought I told you to look after the lad, Gef! Did you do this? If you did, you're off my gang this instant, son of the deputy or not!" He helped Senu into a sitting position and peered at his cheek. Red hovered, trying to staunch the wound with his ghostly hands. Senu moaned and hid his face against Sobek's chest. Even his ka's feathery touch was too much.

"We had a bet," Gef said, his black eyes fixed on

KATHERINE ROBERTS

Senu, a deep frown between them. "Wasn't me that started the fight. Others got excited."

Sobek frowned at Senu. "This true, lad?" he asked softly. "Did you have a bet on with Gef?"

He nodded. It seemed the easiest thing to do. The Overseer arrived, out of breath, and demanded to know what had happened. One of the boys pointed to the adze Hori had dropped, still covered in Senu's blood. The Overseer took one look and sent for the sapers. As Senu drifted in and out of a beautiful blue light, two grave-faced sapers arrived and questioned the boys. They tied Hori's elbows behind his back and hauled him away. The adze was wrapped in linen and taken away, too, presumably as evidence. Red hovered anxiously. Senu was too dizzy to think.

Sobek sighed. "Someone should have warned you about bets with Gef." He scowled at the subdued knot of boys. "You boys go help the others clear up the mess down there. I'm takin' this poor lad home." He lifted Senu as easily as an empty water jar and carried him to the edge of the pyramid.

Something stirred in Senu's memory. "Sir? Was it... did it go off all right?"

Sobek gave him a startled look and grinned in relief. "Life in you yet! Yes, it all went to plan. They made a good start and there was no ka-trouble. Well done. You just do the same thing over the next few weeks, and everything'll be nicely on schedule. Without the fighting, though," he added with another grin. "Captain

Nemheb'll never forgive me if you get invalided off site."

Same thing? Next few weeks? "But I thought – didn't they get the treasure?"

"Shh!" Sobek's head twisted nervously. "Lad's delirious," he explained to the nearest mertu. "Lost a lot of blood."

"But-" Senu insisted. Over Sobek's shoulder, he could see Red's worried face. One of his ka's cheeks glistened with mock blood. He closed his eyes, feeling sick.

Sobek sat him on the edge and passed a rope under his armpits, securing it with a deft knot. "Didn't think we'd do the whole thing today, did you?" he whispered. "That was just so we could smuggle tools and stuff into the pit. Got to make a new tunnel in, take a bit of time. You concentrate on gettin' well. We need you back here soon as possible."

He swung Senu over the edge and raised his voice. "Look out below! Injured man comin' down!"

Only then, swinging in the sunset above the wreckage of the fallen machines, did Senu realize how sly Gef had been. His mother's precious ankh had gone.

Chapter 6

WARNING
...I have come and I have removed the evil... (spell 4)

SOBEK CARRIED HIM through the Passage of Purification, past the fish-drying racks and the bread pots where women stared and whispered, all the way into the hemutiu village. The huge, dusty mertu soon gathered a tail of giggling, ka-tailed children who stuck out their tongues behind his back, but he took no notice and carried Senu to his house.

Senu's mother snatched him from Sobek's arms and hugged him hard as the Gang-Chief tried to explain about the accident on the pyramid. He apologized over and over for letting Senu get hurt. She gave him an icy glare and told him to get out. It would have been embarrassing, had Senu not felt so dizzy and sick.

The village physician was sent for. His cheek had to be stitched and the doctor shook green powder over the wound. It stung like crazy. Senu bit his lip and squeezed his mother's best mat into sweaty fistfuls, determined not to cry. From the shadows of the main room, his mother and Tamuwy watched the operation anxiously. Tefen was still down at the river temple and didn't know about the accident yet, although a messenger had been sent. Tamuwy's two small daughters clung to their mother's legs and stared at Senu, unusually silent. Red peered over the doctor's shoulder, wincing every time the needle punctured Senu's skin. Senu shut his eyes so he wouldn't have to see the neat row of ghostly stitches appear on his ka's cheek.

After the fierce heat and noise of the site, the house was cool and quiet. It smelt of fish oil, fresh bread, barley, and his mother's perfume that she made herself from wild lotus. Home. He sighed, feeling better already.

Then the doctor said, "Open your mouth," and one of Tamuwy's little girls gave a gasp of fright.

"Ugh!" Red said. "It's still alive."

Senu opened his eyes. The doctor was leaning over him, dangling a long black wriggly thing above Senu's lips. Before he knew what was happening, the doctor's other hand clamped his chin and his bitter-tasting fingers forced their way into the corners of his mouth. The black thing slipped between Senu's teeth and down his throat.

He grabbed the thick wrists and tried to rouse himself far enough to spit, but the doctor had dosed reluctant patients before. He chuckled, holding Senu's mouth shut and pinching his nose until his throat convulsed of its own accord. The black thing slipped down. He felt it wriggle all the way to his stomach and he curled up, gagging.

"The eel will eat the poison from the wound and bring it safely out of the boy's body," the doctor explained. "I've a spell here somewhere..." He rummaged through his medicine box, unrolling papyrus scrolls and rolling them up again. He swore softly and glanced at Senu's mother. "I seem to have left it at home. I can get it for you if you want. But between you and me the boy's better off resting. Heka's fine for priests and the unseen sicknesses, but where injuries like this are concerned, modern thinking holds that powders and eels do a much better job."

His mother shook her head, too upset to decide. But Tamuwy gripped her hand and whispered, "Look, he's right! You can see the eel working."

They all regarded with interest Senu's attempts to throw up.

The doctor smiled and pushed him back on the mat. "No dirty work until the wound closes, but he should be up and about in a day or two. Good strong boy you got there. His ka will help him pull through, don't worry."

Two jars changed hands in payment for the doctor's services. Senu was far too busy trying to choke up the eel to notice what his mother put in them.

"Leave it," Red said, pulling at Senu's wrist to stop him putting his fingers down his throat. "You heard what the doctor said. It'll make you better."

"Leave me alone," Senu moaned. "It's all right for you. You don't know what it's like to get sick. Go back to your Land of Dreams or wherever you go, and leave me in peace."

Red looked hurt. "It was a different story this afternoon, I seem to remember."

"Don't, Red. I'm not up to arguing."

When the doctor had gone, Tamuwy removed one of her own amulets and tied it about Senu's ankle. His mother placed the little bandy-legged house god, Bes, near his head. She rested a hand on the statue and muttered a quick prayer. "That's it," she said in a tight little voice. "You're not going back on that gang, whatever your father says."

"But I've got to-" Senu protested.

Tamuwy shook her head. "You get some sleep, little brother. You're not thinking straight. When the eel comes out of you, you'll know we speak sense."

Tamuwy's smallest daughter tried to touch Senu's stitches but got the sight of the eel, asked, "Can you feel it wriggling around inside you, Uncle Senu?" She stared at the air beside her and giggled. Soon both girls were rolling on the floor, clutching their stomachs and shrieking with laughter at something their kas must have said. The women pulled them up, shushed them sternly and dragged them out of the house.

Senu was about to put his fingers back down his throat when he heard his name mentioned. He lay still, the eel forgotten.

"Tefen's been acting real strange lately," he heard his mother say to Tamuwy. "I know he was angry about Senu's school work, but this is going too far..."

"...hoped it'd make him grow up? He's the oldest child in the village to still keep his ka. People are starting to think there's something wrong with him..."

"...such a big baby sometimes. Won't go to sleep unless I leave the lamp burning..."

"...don't think he's got – you know..?"

There was a pause before his mother said, "I used to wonder when he was younger. The tricks that ka of his used to get up to! But he's never shown any of the other signs..."

"...boys his age can be secretive..."

"...no, he can't have. If he had, he'd have used the ankh to protect himself instead of losing it like that..."

"Maybe we'll get to the bottom of this after the eel comes out..."

As Tamuwy spoke, there was another wriggle in his belly. Senu turned over with a groan. Red curled sympathetically around him. Love and warmth flowed from his ka.

"Sleep," Red whispered. "Forget."

He woke briefly when Tefen came home. After a heated argument Senu knew he wasn't supposed to overhear, his father came over to the mat, rested a paint-stained hand on Senu's feverish forehead and whispered, "Don't worry, son. I'll have a word with Captain Nemheb. This has gone far enough."

Senu opened his eyes long enough to check the lamp was still burning and closed them again with a smile. That night he and Red slept curled together as they hadn't done since he was eight and used to have nightmares about the hemutiu tombs.

One good thing came of his injury. His mother was so relieved he hadn't been crushed by a falling stone in the "accident", she didn't make a fuss about the lost ankh. Best of all was the "no dirt" holiday the physician had decreed. Once Senu had persuaded his family he wasn't going to faint the moment he stepped out in the sun, he was allowed to go canoeing with the other hemutiu children in the afternoons.

By this time, of course, Reonet had heard all the gossip from the other apprentices in the river temple and some of the truth from Tefen. All the same, his appearance seemed to shock her. When they met down at the lagoon on the first afternoon, she took a long, silent look at his cheek and pressed her lips together. "Who did it?"

"It was an accident."

"Senu! I'm your friend, not your mother! Tell me the truth, or I'll ask Moon to get it out of Red."

"Red won't tell."

"I wouldn't be so sure of that. I've been learning a spell for summoning kas, you know."

A shiver went down Senu's spine.

…ad already taken their canoes and …to the reeds, laughing and calling for …atch herself in case Senu tried any dirty …s. This side of the lagoon was sheltered from … . Huge, feathery papyrus heads missed by the harve… .ers nodded in the heat. Senu's head felt as if it were stuffed with half-baked bread. He hadn't felt quite himself since the eel came out, though it must have worked. His cheek didn't hurt any more.

Reonet peered closely at him. "Don't look like that, silly! What have they done to you up there? You used to enjoy a good joke. C'mon, let's get my canoe. I've got a surprise for you."

Senu didn't think he could take many more surprises. But arguing was too much like hard work, so he followed Reonet's turquoise clip through the reeds. He smiled when he saw her canoe. Like the others, it was a simple bundle of reeds roped at both ends with a wooden platform in the middle. But Reonet had decorated the wood with animals and birds, painted in glowing yellows, reds and blues. Miu crouched in a basket in the centre of this bright platform, hissing at rustles in the reeds. When the cat saw her mistress, she put her paws against the side of the basket and miaowed in delight.

"You'll be in trouble if an official sees that paint," Senu said.

Reonet put her fingers through the holes in the basket so Miu could lick them. "No I won't. Tefen let me have it. It's leftovers. Can't be used the next day because it cracks. Miu, my pretty one! Were you frightened? You know I'd never leave you!" She turned to Senu. "I'm training her to fetch back birds. You can help, so long as you promise not to mess about."

The cat was a lot bigger than when Senu had last seen her. Her coat had lost its fluffiness and gained stripes of rich gold and brown. In the reeds, she'd be harder to see than Red in one of his sulks. "Aren't you worried you'll lose her down here?" he said, smarting at the way she'd suggested he couldn't act responsibly.

Reonet gave him a withering look. "She'll stay on a leash until she learns. Besides, she loves me – don't you Miu?" She opened the basket and gathered the cat to her, smoothing the golden coat and murmuring into its tufted ear.

Senu watched, uncomfortable, remembering what Reonet had once told him about the cat replacing Moon.

"You try cuddling *me* like that, and I'll bite you," Red warned as he perched cross-legged and weightless on the front of the canoe.

Senu grinned and picked up one of the throwing sticks. He whirled it around his head, making Reonet duck. "Well?" he said. "What are we waiting for? Let's go find some birds!"

Hunting wasn't good near the Place of Truth. Too much noise and dust, too many people, too many smells. Any bird with half a brain had migrated to the marshes at the beginning of Akhet, and even those who hadn't much brain flapped off when they saw the hemutiu canoes coming with their giggling, splashing, stick-wielding occupants. Each day, Senu and Reonet ventured further from the others in search of somewhere quieter where Miu wouldn't be distracted from her training. As they explored the hidden lagoons on the west bank of the river, scraping their way along irrigation ditches suddenly to find themselves in some secret, deep pool that reflected the sky, Reonet stopped nagging him for the real story behind his cheek and Senu began to enjoy himself.

The fresh air and laughter worked even better than the doctor's eel. Soon he felt stronger than he had since Batahotep rubbed out his glyphs. His days on site faded to an uncomfortable memory. He'd just about convinced himself the robbery would succeed without him and Red, and that his father would give him a share of the gold anyway, once he'd managed to find Nemheb and explain, when the doctor pronounced him well enough to go back to work.

Reonet decided they should celebrate his return to the land of the living by making a special effort to catch something. On their final afternoon of freedom, they ventured further upstream than they ever had before. In a lagoon ringed by tall papyrus they flushed a couple of small fowl, which Senu promptly missed with the stick. Miu got excited and tried to chase them anyway, only to end up tangling her leash around the reeds. The stick did not come back as it was supposed to and Senu had to go swimming after it. Giggling helplessly, Reonet lay full length on her decorated platform to untangle Miu's rope.

Senu had his hand on the stick when Red came rippling across the surface of the water and clutched his ka-tail. "Someone's watching us," he whispered. "Over there."

Senu trod water and twisted his head. He couldn't see anyone. But the reeds were dense here. All at once, he realized how far they'd come from the site and how quiet it was. He couldn't even see Khufu's pyramid on the horizon. He grabbed the throwing stick and splashed back to the canoe, heart thudding.

"Who is it, Red?"

"The monster." His ka faded, then vanished completely. "The monster with no ka-shadow."

Senu's skin prickled. He pulled himself on to the platform behind Reonet and stared so hard at the reeds, the shadows and sunlight blurred. He thought he saw another canoe, low in the water. A short, thickset figure crouched on its platform, watching them.

"Reonet!" he hissed. "Hurry up!"

She stopped giggling and looked round. "What's wrong?"

"There's someone in the reeds over there."

She relaxed when she saw the short figure. "It's just one of the others, spying on us. Iny, I expect. He's jealous, you know." She giggled.

"No, I think it's a dwarf..."

There was no time to explain. With a cracking and snapping of reeds, the other canoe came straight for them, its occupant crouched awkwardly over the paddle. With his tiny legs crossed beneath him and the muscles in his shoulders straining, he looked exactly like the house-god, Bes. But those silver-clouded eyes were unmistakable. It was Pehsukher.

Reonet grabbed Miu, half strangling the cat. "Quick, Senu! Get the rope untangled!"

He stared in dismay at the loops tangled in the reeds.

"Hurry up – oh stop it Miu, you're scratching me."

"Tell Moon's human to leave the cat," Red suggested.

Senu threw a desperate glance at the approaching canoe. It was coming faster now, more sure of the direction. The dwarf's cloudy eyes stared creepily, even as they had stared at Senu during the meeting in the tombs.

Reonet dropped the hissing cat and picked up her paddle instead. She held it across her body like a weapon, legs spread for balance, chin raised. "You touch us, and I'll report you to the sapers!" she said.

At the sound of her voice, the dwarf's head tilted and he back-paddled. Not soon enough. His canoe, with his weight driving it along, swung into theirs. Water slopped over the side. Miu's basket fell overboard with a splash and the cat abandoned the platform for the mudbank. Reeds snapped as her leash jerked free. Unfortunately, Reonet had untied the end to help the untangling process. The rope whisked off the canoe and disappeared after the cat's striped tail.

"MIU!" she cried, whirling in dismay.

"Sorry," Pehsukher said in his gentle voice. "I get the distances confused sometimes."

Reonet rounded on him, still gripping the paddle. "It's all your fault, you weirdo! Get away from us! If you dare touch us-" She broke off and frowned at his eyes. She swung the paddle across them and back again, then lowered it warily. "You're blind, aren't you? Who are you? Don't you know there are crocodiles down here? And hippopotamuses? And-"

The dwarf's wrinkles creased into a smile. "And two hemutiu youngsters and a half trained cat in a canoe, all alone a very long way from the village. I can look after myself. Can you?"

Reonet raised the paddle again. "Don't you dare come near us! Go back to – to – wherever you belong!"

"First I want a word with the boy."

"Senu?" Reonet frowned. "Why?"

Pehsukher sighed. "Soon I'll be rejoining my ka and facing my judgement. I've done some things in my time that make my heart heavy, but I won't stand by and see a young lad's life ruined like mine was." Something stirred in the clouds of his eyes, quickly gone. "Watch out for the Captain, boy. He is the serpent that speaks with two tongues. Tell your father."

Senu had been staring at Pehsukher's maimed hand with its single knobbly finger. He touched his forehead and shuddered in memory. He gave Reonet an anxious look, but she was too busy scowling at the dwarf to notice.

"As for you, child." The creepy eyes stared right through Reonet. "Take care what questions you ask. You mightn't like the answers." He raised his head, listened to the cries of geese a moment, then pushed off and paddled slowly back into the reeds.

"Hey, where are you going?" Reonet called, struggling to keep her balance on the rocking platform. "What do you mean? Wait!"

Pehsukher did not stop.

Reonet's lips compressed. "Who does he think he is? Nearly sinking us and scaring off poor Miu! And who's he calling a child, anyway? I cut my ka-tail three years ago!" With a determined expression, she dug in her paddle and set off after the other canoe.

Senu gripped the sides. "Don't follow him," he whispered.

She kept paddling.

"Reonet, don't."

"I don't like people who scare me. I *don't* like people who chase my cat. I *don't* like stupid dwarfs who don't speak sense! What did he mean by all that nonsense about two tongues? And how come he knows you, *anyway*?"

She was making vicious stabs at the water with each accented word, not good paddling technique. Despite his handicap, the old dwarf's canoe drew ahead and slipped out of sight.

Reonet said a word that would have earned her a stripe of Batahotep's rod had she said it in school. Then a muffled growl came from the mudbank and she instantly forgot the chase. "Miu! Come to Reonet, come on!"

The cat leapt on board trailing her soggy leash, a bedraggled mass of feathers clamped in her mouth. She deposited the duck at Reonet's feet and miaowed again, lashing her tail in pride.

"Good girl! See, Senu! Isn't she clever? We've got meat for supper tonight."

"She's chewed it half to bits," Senu muttered. "No one'll want to eat that." But Reonet was too busy praising her cat to care.

They were nearly home before they mentioned the encounter with the dwarf again. The sun was sinking behind Khufu's Horizon and the last barges of the day were hurrying for the landings beyond Amun's Wall. Miu was asleep, curled happily on the front of the canoe with Red. A royal barge passed them on the current, carrying a huge statue of Lord Khafre destined for the river temple. It lay on its side and its black granite eyes stared straight at Senu as if it could guess every thought in his head. He shivered.

"Creepy, huh?" Reonet said.

For a moment Senu thought she meant the statue. "Wh – what?"

"Wash your ears out! That old dwarf back at the lagoon, with all his weird talk." She giggled. "Bad as the priests!"

Senu wrapped his arms around his knees and shivered again. They'd stayed out too long. He was cold, yet the adze scar on his cheek burned. "You were scared too," he pointed out.

"Only at first. He was old and blind. I could've drowned him with one swipe of my paddle. Soft in the head, I reckon."

Senu licked his lips. "Yes, I expect that was it." *No ka-shadow.* He'd thought Red simply meant the dwarf's ka was away, as adult kas often were, particularly when their humans were as old as Pehsukher. Now he wasn't so sure.

"You ever seen him before?"

"Er... no."

She frowned at his hesitation.

"I might've seen him around the site. You know how it is... difficult to remember with so many people. Some of the old ones hang around to watch."

"Even you'd remember a weird old dwarf! Anyway, he can't watch. He's blind. And he doesn't speak like a mertu."

"Er... maybe he likes to listen? Or smell? Lots to smell up there!" He smiled, trying to make a joke of it.

Reonet steered the canoe into the reeds and rested her paddle across her knees. She frowned at him. "I know when you're lying, Senu. That dwarf knew you, and your father's been acting real strange since you got hurt. I'm your friend, aren't I? We used to tell each other everything. Come on, Senu! You can trust me. My lips are sealed like a statue's. Promise. On Moon's life."

There was no more binding promise than that.

Senu closed his eyes. What did it matter now, anyway? He wouldn't be on site much longer. And Reonet *was* his friend.

Red tugged his ka-tail. "Don't tell her! We'll be in trouble. Please Senu, don't."

"We're going to rob Lord Khufu's Horizon," he whispered.

No one rushed through the papyrus to drag him away for questioning. Lord Khufu's ka didn't come out of his pyramid and attack Red. Miu carried on purring. Senu relaxed slightly.

Reonet didn't react at first. Then she said, "What?"

"We're going to rob Khufu's pyramid. Captain Nemheb – that's the Captain the dwarf was talking about – needs me and Red to lure Lord Khufu's ka out so he won't notice the men digging the tunnel..." It was such a relief to share his problems, he rushed on without noticing Reonet's incredulous expression. "But Red's too scared to talk to Khufu's ka, so we just pretended, and I hope we won't have to do it again because if we pretend and Lord Khufu's ka comes back while the men are inside, they'll be caught and Sobek'll be in trouble. I like Sobek, he's been kind to me. So it's probably best if they get someone else to do it-"

"Hey, steady on, slow down." Reonet gripped his hand. Miu woke up, stretched, and blinked sleepily at them before going back to sleep. "Are you saying a

Captain is going to rob Lord Khufu's pyramid? That's a bit unlikely, isn't it?"

Senu scowled. "Well, he is! He probably won't go inside himself, though. There are lots of other people involved, and everybody will get a share of the gold. I thought it would be all right at first, but that was before I'd worked in the gang. You think the mertu are bad enough in their huts, but they're tired then. Up on site it's... it's like a really horrid nightmare I can't wake up from!"

Reonet's lips twitched. She controlled it at first, then burst out laughing.

"Oh, Senu!" she spluttered. "That was a good one! I nearly believed you there! You and Red and an imakhu Captain robbing a pyramid together? That's the best yet!" She giggled again and picked up her paddle "C'mon, it's getting late. We'd best get back."

"But it's *true*," Senu said.

"Yeah, like that time you scared us all in the tombs, pretending the kas of the dead were coming after us? And that time you told us old Batahotep was a Palace agent sent to spy on us? And that time you said Red went into the ka-temple and saw the priests walk through a wall?"

"All right, so I made that up." Senu flushed. "But the tombs-"

"You made them *all* up, Senu. I know you too well."

"What about the dwarf, then?" he said, annoyed now.

"Yes, convenient, wasn't he? I bet you thought it was funny, getting him to scare me like that. Sooner you're back to work, the better, Senu son of Tefen! Better keep quiet about robbing pyramids when you're in the river temple, though," she added, glancing back at him. "The priests don't have a sense of humour like I do. They might believe you and drag you off behind the White Wall to be judged by Lord Khafre and impaled on a spike for all to see. It takes days for people to die that way, or so I've heard. I hope they impale the person who did your cheek."

"He got taken away by the sapers-" He bit his lip as Reonet laughed again.

"See! I *knew* it wasn't an accident! Got it out of you in the end, didn't I?"

She dug in her paddle again, a loud plop. Senu clenched his fists and stared at her hair clip, wanting to shake her and shout that it was true, true, TRUE! But that would only make her believe him less. She was still giggling softly to herself about the robbery. He shook his head.

"Don't believe me, then," he muttered. "I was going to give you some of my share of the treasure so you could go to scribe school. But since it's only *joke* gold, it won't be any good to you, will it? At least I won't have to worry about your priests, though. I'm going back on site tomorrow."

Reonet stopped giggling and looked round. "But I thought-"

"It's complicated. Captain Nemheb's been away, and you know how everything needs to be sealed in triplicate before anyone does anything. Father says I'd better go back on the gang. Just for a few days until he can sort things out properly with the authorities. Besides-" He set his jaw. "There's something I have to do. One of the Scorpion boys stole something that belongs to my mother. I'm going to get it back."

She sobered and glanced uncertainly at his cheek. "Senu... don't you think you've been in enough trouble?"

"It's not me who'll be in trouble this time."

Chapter 7

HEKA
I am the beloved of my father, one who greatly loves his father... (spell 99)

SENU LAY AWAKE all night trying to think of a way to get the ankh back off Gef. Red didn't help by coming up with silly suggestions such as telling Senu to steal a spear from the saper barracks and ambush the mertu boys in the Passage of Purification. When Senu ran out of ideas and started worrying instead about the dwarf's warning and how he was going to convince Reonet he was telling the truth about the robbery, his ka vanished completely. The lamp beside his mat flickered. Demons lurked in the shadows. Senu fixed his eyes on the window and watched the sky pale in a mixture of relief and trepidation.

His mother was very quiet as she plaited his ka-tail after breakfast. She squeezed the end and muttered a prayer to Bes before letting him go. Tefen told Senu not to worry, he'd sort it out, and left the house before Senu had a chance to tell him what the dwarf had said, his lips set in a grim line. Senu reported for work at the usual time and found himself sitting in the dust at the Scorpions' meeting place still without the faintest idea what he was going to say to Gef.

Sobek spotted him and broke into a grin. "How're you feeling, lad? Glad to have you back. We're quarryin' today, so we don't need so much water. You can fetch tools and run errands. Get you back into the swing of things gently, eh?"

Was that good or not? Senu mumbled something about feeling much better, thanks.

The deputy, Adjedd, gave Senu an awkward pat on the head. "Won't happen again," he promised. "I've had a word with my son."

Senu's heart sank. That would make Gef hate him more than ever.

He half hoped the mertu boy would come swaggering to work wearing the ankh openly around his neck, so he could confront him in front of Sobek and the other men. But Gef was too clever for that. When he saw Senu, his black eyes widened slightly. He whispered something to Patep and Teti, who were staring at Senu as if he had sprouted an extra head. Then the three boys went to collect their tools as if it were a perfectly normal morning.

Which it is for them, Senu reminded himself. I'm the one who doesn't belong here. "At least we won't have to worry about talking to Lord Khufu's ka if we're in the quarry," he whispered to Red.

By lunch break, the Scorpions had cut five rough slabs of limestone from the desert side of the plateau, which hemutiu stone dressers squared to match the Overseer's strict measurements. The quarry was sheltered from the wind. Thick amber dust hung in the hot air, making the men cough and Senu's cheek sting. No one mentioned the accident, or Senu's imminent transferral. Maybe they hadn't heard yet.

He made sure he ate his lunch of gruel and a sweet onion in full view of the other men. As he crunched the onion, he watched Gef from the corners of his eyes. The boy watched him in return. A couple of times, Gef looked as if he would leave his friends and come across. Finally, he pointed to a jumble of rocks at the worked-out edge of the quarry and made a signal with his head.

Senu quickly looked away and chewed his lip. The last thing he wanted to do was play to Gef's rules. But once they were working again, there wouldn't be another opportunity to confront the boy until this evening.

Red flickered into view. "You're an idiot if you go over there alone," he whispered.

Senu mopped up the dregs of his gruel with the last of the onion. "He's not getting away with it," he whispered back. "That ankh was Mother's special amulet. She's really upset about it. C'mon, there are plenty of people around. If there's trouble, you can easily contact one of their kas and raise the alarm."

"You know I can't! The men's kas have to wait till they're asleep to contact them. By then it'll be too late, because you'll be dead."

"Sobek's asleep. I heard him snoring just now."

Red rippled over to the big man. Sobek's shaven head rested against the Scorpions' fifth slab, eyes closed and mouth open. Red shook his head and rippled back. "He's not properly asleep."

"Then he'll hear with his own ears if there's any trouble, won't he?" Senu said. He felt stronger for the food. The thought that he wouldn't have to stay on site forever helped too. Only a few more days, at most. With any luck, his father might even have sorted it out by tonight, since Captain Nemheb was expected back today.

Trying to look more confident than he felt, he sauntered towards the rocks Gef had indicated. They were bigger than he'd thought, reaching well over his head. Gef cast a glance at the dozing Sobek, tucked his thumbs into his loincloth and followed.

In a narrow cleft out of sight of the gangs, the two boys stopped and faced each other. Senu's heart started to race. He was acutely aware of the quarry wall at his back, too high and smooth to climb. All the things he'd planned to say deserted him. He stared at Gef like an idiot.

Gef regarded him steadily. "Didn't think you'd be back," he said.

"That's obvious. Dirty mertu thief! Took my ankh, didn't you? Thought I was too hurt to notice, but I'm not stupid."

The black eyes narrowed. Gef took a step towards him, his handsome features dark and dangerous. He seized Senu's ka-tail. "Listen, you hemutiu idiot! I didn't take your precious ankh, all right? I spoke as witness to the fight, got myself a stripe for my trouble!"

The mertu boy was strong. Heart thudding, Senu made himself meet his gaze. "You touch me again, and I'll call Sobek," he whispered.

"Go ahead. Then you won't hear what I have to say."

They glared at each other. Senu's eyes were watering. He bit his lip, determined not to let Gef know how much he was hurting him.

The boy relaxed his hold slightly and lowered his voice. "Something's goin' on," he said. "I got contacts up here, Red-Tail. You tell me what you're after, an' I might be able to help – if you help me."

Senu's stomach fluttered. "Nothing's going on! Let me go."

Gef shook his head, eyes still narrow. "Oh, yes it is! First my little brother gets taken off the gang at the last moment when he'd bin lookin' forward to working on site all year, and if that's not bad enough our whole family's rations get cut because of it. Then you turn up, all fresh from your fancy school, and take his place. It's obvious you're as useless as a water jar with a crack in it, but do you get punished for your clumsiness? No! Not even when I tripped you that day and made you drop the jar. Any other boy would've bin whipped on the spot. But you just get a pat on the head from old Sobek!

Finally you get sick, an' we all breathe a sigh of relief. But when I ask if my brother can come on site to replace you, Sobek whips *me* for lettin' you get hurt. Is that fair?"

Senu had opened his mouth to protest. But Gef's admission that he'd tripped him that day stopped the words in his throat. He closed his mouth and pushed irritably at Red, who was trying to prize Gef's fingers off his ka-tail – as pointless as a baby trying to open a crocodile's jaws.

"You hit Hori, didn't you?" he said, a few things falling into place. "I thought it was Red, but-"

Gef grimaced. "But you're so hopeless, you can't even use the powers you're born with! Least you admit it." He let go of Senu's hair, though he still blocked the way out of the cleft. "You got heka, Red-Tail. I seen you go blue. Why didn't you use it to stop yourself gettin' hurt?"

So *that* was what his mother and sister had been talking about.

Senu rubbed his scalp and eyed him warily. "But I haven't... I don't..."

It would explain a few things, though. Red was fading in and out of view, shaking his head. Senu felt dizzy again.

Gef cursed under his breath and thrust something into his hand. "Here!" he said. "It was a lot of trouble getting it back. Hope you "preciate it!"

Senu stared in confusion at the little copper ankh. The

cord was frayed at the ends where it had snapped during the struggle on the pyramid. He frowned at Gef, unable to think, then tightened his fingers around the amulet and set his jaw. "So it *was* you who took it! Think you can mend things by giving it back, do you?"

Gef scowled. "When are you goin' to grow up, Red-Tail?"

It was too much. Everything that had happened since the beginning of Akhet – the tension of keeping the robbery secret, his injury, the theft, the eel treatment, the dwarf's warning, Reonet not believing him – exploded in a swift lunge to the boy's eye. Gef staggered backwards in surprise, recovered quickly and returned the blow.

"No!" Red shouted, rippling between them. "No, oh no, not again-"

As Senu held his eye, seeing stars, the ankh grew cold in his hand and a blue wind knocked him backwards. Both he and Gef sat down, breathless, squinting at each other through a column of suddenly swirling sand.

"Sorry," Red mumbled. "Stronger than I thought."

At first Senu couldn't think what had happened. But to his surprise, Gef began to laugh. "So you *can* do it, Red-Tail! Afraid of people findin' you out, is that it? You're a spy, aren't you? The priests send you up here to make sure we don't carve any evil spells into the stones, huh? Don't forget to tell 'em how I got your ankh back, Red-Tail. My little brother could still do with that job." Still grinning, he got to his feet and dusted himself off.

"Could've saved yourself some trouble if you'd used your powers before, though. Hori, too."

Feet were pounding towards them, alerted by the column of sand.

"What happened to Hori?" Senu asked, curious.

Gef snorted. "Fifty lashes from the saper captain. Serves 'im right. Everyone knows you don't touch hemutiu tools."

Senu winced, trying to imagine Batahotep's rod lashing him fifty times.

Gef chuckled. "You're soft, Red-Tail! He'll survive. He just won't do it again in a hurry."

Suddenly the men were there. Hands pulled Gef away, helped Senu up. Adjedd scowled fiercely at his son. Sobek frowned. Red hovered, anxious. Gef's eye was already colouring. He had blood on his elbow and sand stuck all over him. From Red's appearance, Senu guessed he must look just as bad.

The Overseer arrived, out of breath, demanding to know why the afternoon's work hadn't started on schedule. The men muttered something about a fight. Senu eyed them uncertainly. Had they seen that blue light?

Sobek shook his head and sighed. "What am I going to do with you, Senu? All right, who started it?"

"No one, sir," Gef said. "It just happened."

Adjedd frowned at him.

"Give 'em ten lashes each," the Chief of one of the other gangs advised. "Works wonders with my boys."

"Na, link their ankles with a short rope till they learn to work together," another called. "That way, they soon get tired of beatin' each other up. You'll see."

"Silence!" snapped the Overseer. "If neither boy will admit to starting it, I'll call the sapers to sort this out. I don't want a repeat of what happened on the pyramid. Not in my quarry."

Senu's back prickled. But Sobek shook his head. "I don't think that'll be necessary, sir. Looks to me like this was a return match. You boys quite finished now?"

Gef winked at Senu and nodded. Trying hard not to giggle, Senu nodded too. The men sighed.

The Overseer stared suspiciously at them both, then clapped his hands. "All right, back to work! Excitement's over. You've time to make up if you don't want me to mark the lot of you down for reduced rations tonight."

All that afternoon, Senu turned over in his head what little he knew of heka. Needless to say, Batahotep's lessons hadn't covered such things. His pupils were beaten if they asked such questions. Senu knew only that heka had something to do with spells. That was why doctors used it. And priests. Would his father know about him having heka powers? Reonet, maybe? No, she'd only think he was joking and laugh at him again.

He shook his head. Gef must have got it wrong. How would a mertu know about such things, anyway?

After the fight, Sobek allowed the two boys to rinse

the grit out of their eyes and wounds. But he forbade a visit to the river to get properly cleaned up until work stopped at sunset. Senu was pretty certain the Gang-Chief hadn't seen anything unusual, otherwise he'd surely have dragged him aside and said something before now. Or – and a niggly suspicion took the edge off his triumph at getting the ankh back – maybe he'd known all along? He watched the big mertu from the corners of his eyes, trying to decide. But when Sobek eventually called him across, it was only to send him to the site for a replacement mallet. By the time he got back, Gef had been sent on a different errand. And so it went on. It wasn't until the sun began to sink behind the dunes that Senu realized the big Gang-Chief had been deliberately keeping him and Gef apart. He consoled himself that his mother would be pleased about the amulet, at least.

"Wouldn't it be funny if I really did have heka, Red?" he whispered to his ka as they hurried home through the Passage of Purification. "We'd be able to play some brilliant tricks. Maybe we could-"

He broke off. Red was hissing between his ghostly teeth, the way he did when something especially bad had happened.

Senu's neck prickled. The streets were quiet, the women having called their families inside for supper. The little mud-brick houses seemed to close around him, their shadows suddenly threatening. Above the village wall the evening clouds were aflame. At the corner of their street his mother waited like a statue of the dead, staring out for him.

"What's wrong?" Senu whispered, his stomach hollow. "Red? *What is it?*"

His ka hissed, flickering in and out of the shadows.

Senu broke into a run. His mother ran towards him, her black hair loose, her cheeks stained with tears. Tamuwy appeared behind, her daughters clinging to her legs and sobbing. From their neighbours' houses, eyes watched them through the windows.

"What is it, Mother?" Senu whispered. "What's wrong?"

His mother fell to her knees and gathered him close, squeezing so hard he could barely breathe. "Senu, oh Senu – it's your father-" Half the village was watching and he was way past being hugged in public, but he didn't push her off. The panic in her voice scared him.

"What's wrong with Father?" he whispered, his own legs going weak.

"They've taken him, Senu," she sniffed, trying to be calm but failing. Her voice rose hysterically. "The sapers dragged him from the temple and put him on a barge with chains around his ankles! My Tefen, Chief Artist at the Place of Truth! Conscripted like a common mertu!"

Fear and confusion rippled through Senu. He stared at Red, who was still flickering like a dying flame in the sunset.

"B-but why? When?" He couldn't get his head around what she was telling him. "Taken him where?"

His mother burst into tears. Tamuwy was left to tell

him the details in a quiet, worried voice. "He's been conscripted to mine the granite at Khnum's Cataract," she said. "The barge left this afternoon. I'm sorry, Senu-"

"No..." Senu staggered out of his mother's grasp, senses reeling. Khnum's Cataract. Where savages with burnt-black skins attacked from the mountains and men died from strange southern fevers and overwork. "No!" he screamed, imagining Tefen's clever fingers blistered by mining work and crushed beneath huge blocks of black stone. "Not Father! No!"

He ripped the ankh from his ka-tail and threw it in his mother's direction. Then he was running, blinded by tears, through the darkening streets towards the River Gate.

"Senu!" Tamuwy called, her voice faint. "He's gone, Senu, there's nothing we can do. Come back! Your mother needs you now, we all need you..."

He shut his ears to her words and ran faster, fists clenched. The scar on his cheek throbbed as the blood rose to his face. One thought burned in his head, fiercer than the flood-star. "Betrayed!" he gasped to Red as he ran. "Someone's betrayed us!"

The River Gate was shut for the night and guarded by a saper. He was supposed to protect the hemutiu from the unruly mertu camped outside the village wall. For the first time, Senu wondered if this was the whole truth. Guards and locked gates kept people in as well as out.

He turned up a shadowed alley, waited until the guard was looking the other way, and scrambled over the wall.

Red rippled through the bricks and met him on the other side.

"What are you *doing*?" he whispered. "The mertu are all drunk at this time of night. They'll beat you up if they see you."

Senu was too busy jumping at every shadow and rustle to answer. Up on site, a survey was in progress. Tiny pricks of light glimmered around the base of the new pyramid. He ran through the mertu camp, neck prickling. No one challenged him. The path to the river was deserted, silver in the moonlight. Senu cut across the school site to reach the lagoon, keeping to the shadows under the palms. Still no outcry. He plunged into the cover of the reeds with a rush of relief.

"This is really stupid," Red moaned, rippling through the black stalks beside him.

Senu concentrated on keeping his footing. The flood was raging. The bank where he'd sat with Reonet that first night was under water. Papyrus seeds got into his eyes and mouth as he fought his way through the reeds. He kept stumbling into irrigation ditches, hidden under the flood. He was making far too much noise, he knew. But the faster he went, the more chance he had of catching up with the conscripts' barge.

Reonet's canoe was where she always kept it, carefully secured to a palm trunk. He freed the rope and scrambled aboard. Geese flapped from their nests in alarm. Somewhere in the dark, a hippopotamus roared. Senu still felt faint from the heat in the quarry and the confrontation with Gef. The stars whirled overhead as he paddled along a ditch towards the main river, cursing Hapi and any other god he could remember when the canoe got stuck on unseen mudbanks.

Red flickered in agitated circles around the canoe. "Where are you going? This is dangerous. You'll get sunk by that hippopotamus! You'll get eaten by crocodiles! Please, Senu, let's go back now?"

"I've got heka, haven't I?" Senu hissed, paddling furiously.

His ka went quiet.

The reeds thinned and suddenly the open river glittered before him, a vast expanse of silver and black water swirling under the moon. There was a barge near the far bank, a black smudge against the dunes. "*Father!*" he shouted. "I'm coming!" His legs trembled. The canoe lodged itself on a mat of twigs and he swung the paddle at the blockage in fury. The reeds exploded with black wings and wild screeches. Then he was free, out in the current, chilled by the night breeze.

Without thinking, he struck straight across the river, his mother's warnings about the strength of the current at this time of year forgotten. Canoes this small had to keep close to the bank during Akhet or risk being overturned in the flood.

Red tried to stop him, hanging on his arm like a fierce but weak kitten. Senu swung the paddle at his ka. "Stop it, Red! They've got Father over there!"

"Don't be stupid! There are no humans on that barge. It's moored for the night."

Too late, Senu realized his ka spoke the truth. He back-paddled, but the current had already seized the canoe and whirled it downriver. He started to panic as Amun's Wall rushed closer. The sapers had permission to kill intruders after dark.

Then the worst happened. Speeding out of the dark, straight for him, came a monster with huge spiked arms trailing a clotted mass of reeds and mud. A cloud went across the moon. His ka vanished.

"Come back!" Senu screamed, his words swallowed by the black water. "Red!"

Pieces were falling off Reonet's canoe. Senu desperately tried to hold the reeds together, but that meant he had to stop paddling. The many-armed monster whirled past – a great, twisted branch which must have been in the river since Khnum's Cataract, at least. Senu clutched the sides and stared at it, frozen with fear. Most of the branch had passed when the heavy stump swung towards him and struck the little canoe broadside. The reeds parted like sticks. One moment Senu was kneeling on the platform holding on to the sides. The next, he was in the water.

"RED!" he screamed, trying to swim towards the bank. A spike hit him on the back of the head and he went under, fought his way up spluttering and coughing.

Heka, he thought vaguely. *Must use my heka.*

But he didn't have the first idea how, and was sucked down again.

Chapter 8

SERPENT'S TONGUE
Get back! Crawl away! Get away from me, you snake! (spell 39)

WHEN SENU HAD struggled out of the dark and could breathe again, he became aware of something heavy and cool across his eyes. A sweet, unfamiliar scent caressed him. He was lying in feathers softer than anything he'd lain in before. A strange tinkling sound played at the edges of his hearing, bringing memories of the music he'd heard drifting from rich imakhu barges as they sailed past the Place of Truth on their way to make offerings at the Temple of the Sun.

He sighed. If this was what it was like to be dead, why had he been fighting so hard to stay alive?

Red ruined it all by hissing into his ear, "You're not dead, stupid. Though you made a good attempt at it that time."

Even as his ka spoke, all Senu's bruises began to

throb. He turned over with a groan. Feathers puffed into his nostrils, making him sneeze. The thing across his eyes fell to the floor with a wet *splat.*

There was a creak beside him and a soft hand felt his forehead. "How are you feeling?" asked a female voice. "I wanted to send for the doctor when they brought you in, but the Master wouldn't hear of it. Said it wasn't worth bothering him in the middle of the night for such a small thing. You slept so long, you had me worried."

Senu opened his eyes and thought for a moment that he was back on the river. All around his bed, birds and fish of every variety flew or swam through lush reeds. Squares of sunlight brightened the colours until he had to squint. Walls, he realized. Just paintings on walls. The ceiling was much higher than in his mother's house, smooth and white. Painted swallows swooped across it.

He raised himself on one elbow to have a better look. Was this a temple? No, the pictures were all wrong. His father was always complaining he had to paint endless gods and goddesses in strict squares when he'd much rather do freehand work...

His father!

It all came back in a rush. He pushed the woman's hands away and swung his legs over the side of the bed, noticing in confusion that it had a proper raised wooden support for his head of the sort only the richest imakhu could afford. More feathers puffed out of their linen bag in clouds of grey and blue. He sneezed again.

"Take it easy," said the woman, trying to pick up the fallen cloth, push him back on the bed and pour him a drink at the same time. "You nearly drowned, you know. Lucky for you the Master was on site taking star measurements last night, or you might have been swept all the way to the Marshes by now. Whatever were you doing so far out in the current in a canoe?"

"Where's my father?" Senu demanded.

"Your father?" She frowned. She was pretty, he noticed vaguely. Her shoulder-length wig had been threaded with coloured beads and she wore a dress of fine linen. Barefoot, though. A servant. "Oh, were you night fishing? Irresponsible of him to take a boy your age out at this time of the year. The flood was at its height last night. He should've known better."

Senu's blood rose. "I'm not a baby!"

"You're a big lad, true, but-" Her fingers brushed his ka-tail.

Senu jerked away and looked at the row of high windows. The sun must have been up for hours. "I've an important job on site," he told her. "I'm late. I've got to get back."

He had no intention of going back to the gang, but she didn't have to know that. It was starting to make sense now. This fine house must belong to some important scribe. He must have been taking readings from the stars above the river and seen Senu in trouble. Lucky for him.

"Luck had nothing to do with it." Red said, rippling

back from where he had been examining the paintings on the walls. "I fetched help."

Senu frowned. "You called a stranger's ka?"

Red fiddled with his ghostly ka-tail, tangled with weed to mimic the current state of Senu's own. "Well, not exactly..." He avoided Senu's gaze. "I didn't have much choice. You were drowning! Shh, here he comes now."

Sandalled feet approached the door with a quick, confident tread. The woman stopped trying to make Senu lie down and backed into a corner, still clutching the goblet and jug. She lowered her eyes as a thin man clad in a calf-length kilt of fine linen stepped into the room. Senu's heart missed a beat, though he supposed he should have guessed. Who else would be allowed to build such a big house so close to the Place of Truth?

Captain Nemheb's kohl-lined eyes studied him with amusement. "So you're still with us? Good."

The clipped words brought back all the terror of their first meeting in the hemutiu tomb and Nemheb seemed to know this. He smiled again and clicked his fingers at the woman. "Bring the boy a drink. He still looks a bit faint to me."

Senu sat up properly and clenched his fists. "I'm fine," he said.

Nemheb raised one eyebrow.

"-sir!" Senu added.

Another twisted smile. "I'm glad to hear it. But I think you'd better have a drink, anyway. It's a special brew my servants make, clears the head. We need to have a little chat and I don't want you collapsing on me before we're done."

The woman tiptoed over with the goblet. With a nervous glance at her master, she held it out to Senu. Senu eyed the contents suspiciously.

"Drink up," Nemheb insisted.

Red hovered anxiously as Senu took the goblet and sniffed the contents. It smelt all right, like warm honey. He tried a sip. Sweet. He took a large gulp and sighed as the smooth liquid slid down his sore throat.

Nemheb motioned the woman out and dragged a reed stool across to the bed. He perched on it and stared into Senu's eyes. "So. What were you doing on the river last night?"

Senu bit his lip. Remembering Pehsukher's warning, he wondered if it was wise to tell Nemheb anything. But the drink had made him warm inside. Dust danced in the shafts of sunlight. The pictures were so colourful, the room so peaceful and cool. Through the high windows, birds sang and the unseen fountain tinkled. It was such a relief to be comfortable. And Captain Nemheb had saved his life. All the dwarf had done was knock him out by the tombs and scare him in the lagoon.

"It's my father..." He choked, tried again. "Captain Nemheb, he's been arrested and taken to Khnum's Cataract!"

The scribe's expression did not change. He sighed. "I know. I heard last night. I'm sorry, I couldn't do anything to stop it."

Senu stared at him. "You knew? But– but *why?* I don't understand."

One of Nemheb's hands rested on his. It was clammy and made Senu's skin crawl, but he so needed sympathy he didn't pull away.

"Senu," Nemheb said in his educated voice. "You have to understand. We can't jeopardise the robbery just for one man. The sapers heard a rumour that Tefen was involved in a plot against the Double Crown. He's safer where he is, believe me. Safer for us, too. Don't worry, as soon as this is over I'll work for his release."

It was no comfort to discover he'd been right about the betrayal. He couldn't imagine what the sapers had heard, nor who could have told them. Gef? But he hadn't guessed about the robbery, just thought Senu was a spy.

"Moon's human knew," whispered Red.

Senu closed his eyes. What if Reonet had said something to one of the others, still thinking it was a joke, and a saper had heard? He turned cold inside.

"If I make a fuss now, the Chief of Works will start to get suspicious," Nemheb said, mistaking his reaction for worry over his father. He stroked the back of Senu's hand. "What I want you to do is carry on as if nothing has happened. I'll take you back with me and explain why you're late today. People will understand you were upset about your father. Don't worry, I'll make sure your family's rations aren't docked. Your mother and sister are relying on you now, Senu." He narrowed his eyes. "You do realize that, don't you?"

Senu shook himself. Nemheb's story seemed to make sense. Yet he didn't quite trust him after that time with the blindfold.

"It's very kind of you to bring me to your house, sir," he said firmly. "But Father said he was going to take me off the gang, and I'd rather not go back up on site until he's home, if that's all right with you. Mother will be worried about him. The last thing she needs is to be worrying about me as well."

Nemheb's whole manner changed. He drew himself straight on the stool. Darkness walked behind his eyes as he said, "If you don't go back to work, I won't be able to help you. Your mother and your sister's family will be turned out of their houses and have to beg for scraps with the rabble outside the White Wall. Tamuwy's husband won't be fit to work for a long time, and there's no room for unemployed layabouts at the Place of Truth."

Senu's stomach did a peculiar little dance. "But that's not fair! They haven't done anything wrong!"

"No. But your father has – at least as far as the authorities are concerned. Until he's back from Khnum's Cataract, your whole family will be under suspicion, you included."

"Then you'll have to find someone else to talk to Lord Khufu's ka!" Senu said, relieved about that, at least. "If the sapers are watching me, Red won't be able to do it."

"It changes nothing. Sobek will set everything up, just like he did before. You did a fine job last time, despite that unfortunate tussle with the mertu boys afterwards. Don't worry, I'll make certain they won't bother you like that again."

Senu shivered. "But I don't understand. You said you could get another child to help you if I didn't do it. Why don't you use one of the mertu boys? Some of the water-boys on other gangs still have their ka-tails, I've seen them."

Nemheb took the goblet from Senu's hand and placed it on the tiled floor beside the stool with a little click. He leant forward, gripped Senu's wrist and stared into his eyes. Senu wanted to pull free and run, but the stool and its occupant blocked the way. Red, who had faded to a mere shadow at the mention of Lord Khufu's ka, stared at him over Nemheb's wig.

The Captain spoke in a soft undertone, so close to Senu's ear he could feel the heat of his breath. It reeked of dates.

"You don't realize how special you are, do you?"

Senu leant backwards until his shoulders met the wall. "I'm not special..." But he let his voice trail off, remembering what had happened when he hit Gef.

"You still have your ka when everyone else of your age said goodbye to theirs years ago. Haven't you ever wondered why?"

Senu looked at Red, who was shaking his head violently.

"Why?" Senu whispered, little chills going up and down his spine. But he thought he knew.

"Think about it. Why do you think so many scribes are employed the length of the Two Lands writing letters to the dead for those who can't write themselves? Wouldn't it be easier and simpler if people simply got their children's kas to ask their ancestors' advice directly?"

"I suppose..."

"Exactly how many of your friends' kas have ever spoken to the dead?"

"Um, well, we..." He thought of the dare, the way no one else had really tried. He'd always told himself it was because they'd been too afraid of looking stupid when the kas didn't answer.

The Captain was smiling again, as if he guessed Senu's thoughts. "None of them managed it, did they Senu? Only you."

"No, no, no, no," Red said, rippling around the walls faster and faster, as if he were trapped by them like a human.

"We're the only ones who can really do it," Senu whispered, the panic in the tombs starting to make sense. "Me and Red are the only ones in the whole world who can talk to the dead!"

Nemheb chuckled. "Not the only ones, no. You're not that unique. But it's a rare gift these days. Tefen was never that important to us. We only brought him on board because of you."

He paused to let this sink in.

When Senu didn't say anything, he added, "So maybe

now you realize why we can't use another boy? It's to your advantage, really. Your job and your family's rations are guaranteed, at least until the robbery. And afterwards neither you nor your family will have to worry about work or food again." Another twisted smile.

Senu's legs felt so weak he didn't think he'd be able to run, even if Nemheb let him go. Red stopped rippling around the room and pushed against him like a strong wind.

"Letters are best," the ka breathed in his ear. "The kas of the dead don't like being bothered by the living, see? They prefer letters, really they do. Maybe you can write one to Lord Khufu's ka?"

He hardly heard. Nemheb was still watching him with those shadowed, kohl-lined eyes.

He took a deep breath. "It's to do with my heka, isn't it?"

The eyes did not flicker. "Talking to the dead is a heka skill, yes."

"You knew I had it! All along."

"Let's say I suspected. The sapers who caught you in the tombs made a full report. They didn't understand about the heka, of course, but they're trained to report the facts and let those of us with superior education and intelligence interpret them. One of you had to have it. I just wasn't sure who until the others had cut their tails. I thought it was Iny for a while."

"But why didn't you *tell* me?"

Another chuckle. "All Captains have to do Temple service before we can take up our positions. Mostly it's boring, but I learnt a few things about heka. How it needs to be awakened. How some people don't realize they have it until they grow up and it's too late. How those who show the power early enough are snatched away by the temples before they can cut their ka-tails. I've done you a favour, Senu. If I hadn't kept my mouth shut about what happened in the tombs that day, you and your friends would have been tested by the priests and you'd be behind temple walls now. Besides, I seem to remember you were willing enough to help us for your share of the gold. As a gesture of goodwill, I'll double your family's share to make up for this unfortunate business with your father – how about that?"

He released Senu's wrist and retrieved the goblet. "Now then, drink up, and we'll see about getting you back to the site. I'm sure I can trust you not to draw attention to yourself, heka-wise?"

Senu transferred his gaze from Nemheb to Red. The thought that his ka could have kept such a thing from him hurt more than Nemheb's deceit.

"I couldn't tell you, Senu! I couldn't!" the ka said. "I love you! You had such horrid nightmares. Captain Nemheb's ka said if I let you forget what happened, they would go away!" A pause. "They did go away, didn't they?"

Nemheb's smile hinted that he could guess what the ka was saying. "It was for the best, believe me. You don't need to go to a temple to learn about heka. My dwarf can teach you – you remember him, don't you? He's getting old, but he had the power once. After the robbery, you can come and live with us here on my estate. Would you like that?"

Senu's head was spinning. The hemutiu tombs, the nightmares, the heka powers even his parents hadn't guessed he had... Captain Nemheb had been watching him. All his life.

He shuddered.

"You sent me up on site to awaken my heka, didn't you?" he whispered. "You knew the mertu boys would give me a hard time, and you sent me up there deliberately. You tricked Father! You tricked us all!"

Nemheb raised a perfectly shaped eyebrow and brushed Senu's cheek with his finger. "Tricked is a strong word. I merely arranged things to make it easier for you and Red to talk to Lord Khufu's ka. I admit things got a bit rougher than I intended, but that's the mertu for you! Can't trust them to do anything right." He smiled again. "I hope you don't blame me for some peasant boy's small brain. If I'd told you my plan, it wouldn't have worked. Heka's funny like that, and it seems you've more than anyone suspected locked away in that bright ka-tail of yours. I can help you and your family, Senu. But you must help me in return."

"All right." He made himself meet Nemheb's stare. "I'll go back! But you've got to promise to get my father free! And I need to know when the robbery will take place." At Nemheb's narrowing of eye, he said quickly, "It'd help me and Red if we knew, sir. Then we can say the right things to Lord Khufu's ka. Don't worry, I won't tell anyone else. I'm not *that* stupid."

The scribe laughed. "I know you're not. But it's best if you don't know the details. You might get nervous, and it'd only transmit to Lord Khufu's ka through Red. The last thing I want is to lose you now. Any other questions?"

Senu had hundreds, but not ones he wanted to ask Nemheb. He shook his head. He couldn't look at Red.

"Good!" Nemheb said. "Then that's settled. I'm glad we had this chance to chat, man to man."

Man to man. In spite of everything, Senu couldn't help a flicker of pride. A Captain, an *imakhu*, talking to him on equal terms!

Nemheb stood in a single fluid movement and clapped his hands. The door opened and the same woman as before came in. Her eyes took in the empty goblet and she smiled at Senu. He assumed he must look better, despite what he felt like on the inside.

"Clean the boy up and bring him a fresh loincloth and something to eat," Nemheb ordered in his clipped voice. "We'll be leaving for the Place of Truth at the fourth lighthour. And I don't want any gossip about how the boy came to be here last night. Understand?"

The woman lowered her eyes and nodded.

When the Captain had gone and she'd started mothering him again, Senu tried questioning her about the dwarf. But it was hopeless. At the very mention of Pehsukher's name, she paled and glanced at the door. All he could get out of her was, "The Master saved his life. He was being tortured by the sapers and the Master stopped it."

"Was that how he lost his sight?" Senu said, his skin crawling with a mixture of horror and curiosity. "Why did they chop off his fingers?"

She shook her head. "It was a long time ago. I was just a baby, and you shouldn't be worrying your head about things like that at your age. Be thankful the Master's been so good to you and don't make trouble for yourself asking questions about things that don't concern you. You're a very lucky boy having such a clever, quick thinking ka. Forget old Pehsukher. He lost his ka completely, more fool him."

She rubbed his scalp vigorously with a thick linen towel, making Senu's eyes smart and further questions impossible. Yet he'd discovered something. The dwarf *had* lost his ka.

"How did it happen, Red?" he mumbled through the towel, chilled. "Was that part of the torture, too? I didn't think anyone could kill a ka..."

But Red, who had vanished in another of his sulks when Senu had agreed to go back on site, made no answer.

Chapter 9

DISAPPEARANCES
Open to me; then I will tell what I have seen. (spell 86)

SENU HAD HOPED Pehsukher might accompany them on the journey downstream to the Place of Truth. But the barge was manned by four impassive medjay who, following their master's example, treated Senu as if he were no more than a spare paddle. As the flooded fields slid past in a blur of reflected blue and gold, he decided to confront Gef, find out exactly how much the boy knew about heka.

But when Nemheb escorted him to the quarry where the Scorpion gang were on their last day cutting stone for the new pyramid, there was no sign of the mertu boy.

"Bin transferred to another gang," Sobek informed him shortly when he asked. The big man's glance at Nemheb, who had stayed to talk to the Overseer, warned against further questions.

Patep and Teti seemed to blame Senu for their friend's

transferral and refused to talk to him. He spent the afternoon carrying thin gruel to wet the men's throats and trying to find out from the other boys which gang Gef was working on now. None of them knew, or said they didn't, which amounted to the same thing. In desperation, he even asked Red to contact one of the younger boy's kas. But Red was still sulking about Senu's decision to come back on site and pretended not to hear.

Home was worse. He found his mother and sister sitting in silence in the unlit house, holding each other's hands. When Senu came in, they rushed across and hugged him so hard he thought his bones would break. He didn't receive the telling off he'd expected, but was fed a special supper of fresh fish that must have represented a whole week's rations. His mother and sister then left him to eat while they retreated to the flat roof to discuss Tefen's arrest. When Senu crept part way up the stairs to listen, however, their whispers changed to a new recipe for bread. His mother was pretending to work on a basket she'd been weaving when Tefen was taken. She was fooling nobody, but gave Senu a brave smile. He shouted up that he was going to see Reonet and fled into the alley before they decided they couldn't let him out of their sight.

Reonet's house was dark and empty. Even Miu wasn't there. He called Reonet's name, his voice echoing in the quiet streets, until the woman who lived next door stuck her head out of a window and yelled at him to keep the noise down. "No one's in," she told Senu, looking disapprovingly at his ka-tail. "Go home, boy, and let the rest of us get some sleep."

"Where are the people who live here?" Senu demanded.

The woman shook her head. "It's none of my business, and none of yours either. That girl was always too wild for her own good. Didn't surprise me in the slightest when that priest turned up."

"What priest?" Senu said, thoroughly alarmed now. "What happened?"

But the woman withdrew her head, muttering about troublesome youngsters who were allowed to keep their ka-tails far too long these days. Senu kicked the wall. Not knowing what else to do, he went home.

It was the second darkhour before Red came out of his sulk. He rippled into view and planted himself in front of the night lamp as Senu was filling it with oil. Senu's hands turned icy cold as he realized they were inside his ka. He snatched them back, the hairs on his arms standing up. "Don't *do* that!"

Red didn't move. "You do things I don't like."

"You know I had no choice." He glanced up the stair to the roof where his mother and sister were still talking. He lowered his voice. "You heard Captain Nemheb. It's the only way to help Father. It's not like you haven't spoken to the dead before. I forgive you for making me forget, but you got to help me now."

His ka looked sideways at him. "It's all right. We can just keep pretending."

"No!" He clenched his fists. "No, Red, we have to do it properly this time, or Sobek and the other men'll get hurt."

"They won't."

"They will! Nemheb wouldn't be going to all this trouble to get us to help him otherwise. If Lord Khufu's ka attacks them, it'll be our fault."

"He can't attack them," his ka whispered, sparkling faintly.

Senu frowned. "What do you mean?"

"He just can't. Shall I try to contact your father's ka now?" he offered in a brighter tone. "He might be dreaming."

Instantly, Senu forgot Lord Khufu's ka. He sat up and hugged his knees in excitement and trepidation. "Can you really, Red? All that way?"

"Ka journeys aren't the same as human journeys," Red informed him. "Shall I go, then?"

There was no question. Senu gave his permission. Red was away all night. He didn't get a wink of sleep, nor another chance to ask his ka about heka or what exactly the kas of the dead had said when they'd been eight, or whether he could ask Moon where Reonet was. Nor did he get to talk to Tefen – though by the time he realized Red wasn't going to succeed, the sky was paling and it was time to leave for the site.

Somehow, he struggled through to sunset. The Scorpion gang were back on the pyramid for another week, lifting stones – Captain Nemheb's influence, no doubt, since it wasn't their turn. There was still no sign of Gef. But there were no more "accidents" like the one that had destroyed the lifting machine and no trouble in the robbers' tunnel, although Senu found Red's story that Lord Khufu's ka was "otherwise occupied" harder and harder to believe as the days crawled by.

Every night he went round to Reonet's house, but she was never there. When he checked the lagoon, only geese answered his call. It was the end of the week before he caught her father in, and then he got the door slammed in his face. "Don't want my daughter hanging around with the sons of criminals!" a slurred voice shouted through the window. "If you come back here again, I'll call the sapers."

Senu thumped on the door. "Where is she?" he yelled back. "You'd better tell me, or I'll tell Captain Nemheb you've been fermenting gruel again!"

He didn't think Reonet's father would take any notice. But there was a crashing and cursing inside, and a flushed, unshaven face appeared at the window. "Gone down her mother's place, hasn't she? Pourin' her little heart out to that sahu, no doubt. Stupid stupid girl... I keep tellin' her it does no good. Her mother's dead, she ain't never coming back..." He slid down the inside of the wall and began to sob.

"He knows nothing," Red said. "Fermented gruel stops his own ka reaching him, let alone anyone else's."

"Leave him alone, Red." Senu was more embarrassed

than afraid now. "Down her mother's place... I should have guessed. C'mon!"

At bedtime, he checked the lamp was full of oil, curled on his mat and closed his eyes as usual. He waited until his mother was asleep, hid the lamp under a fold of his loincloth and slipped out of the house. It was a beautiful Akhet night. The sky glowed deep purple and the stars dazzled above the site, as if the world wasn't about to end when Sobek's men broke into Khufu's Horizon and plundered his treasure right under the nose of his ka. Trembling slightly, he scrambled over the village wall and took the path to the hemutiu tombs.

He did wonder what he'd do if Nemheb had called another secret meeting. But the tombs were quiet and still, their entrances like black eyes watching the moonlit desert. A single bored saper dozed on his spear in the shadow of the escarpment, just like the guard six years ago. Refusing to think of what had happened that day, Senu crept past him.

Inside the first tunnel, he stopped and uncovered the flame. Light licked the walls, showing every lump and crack. Being on site where the hemutiu laboured to make every stone smooth and clean edged, he'd forgotten how rough and ready these tombs were. The musty smell brought memories of when he'd been blindfolded.

He took deep breaths until the fear dulled. "You'll have to lead the way, Red. I don't remember."

His ka rippled ahead of the lamp, throwing a ghostly blue shadow on the wall. Senu frowned at it. He didn't remember *that* happening before. As they crossed the cavern where Nemheb had held his secret meeting, Senu tripped over a discarded lamp. He hesitated, remembering the feel of his father's fingers on his shoulder and his soft voice. Then he thought he heard a scrape in the dark and hurried after Red. Deeper in, the tunnels became twistier and so low he had to stoop. Surely they hadn't been this small six years ago?

Red stopped before a narrow entrance from which a sweet smell drifted. "Up there," he whispered.

Unaccountably, Senu broke into a sweat. He set his jaw and ducked into the tunnel, one hand cupped carefully around the flame. He hadn't taken many steps when a quiet chanting came out of the darkness ahead.

"...*I call your heart, ib, which contains all you love...*"

"...*I call your spirit, akh, which causes you to breathe...*"

Every so often, the chant faltered and there was a muttered curse.

"...*I call your shadow, khabit, which hides behind you...*"

His skin prickled. "Who's in there, Red?"

"Moon's human, of course."

Senu breathed again. "Reonet?" he called softly. "That you?"

The chant broke off and the blue glow died. There was a pause as if the air were holding its breath. Then a fierce cold tore through him and *something* streaked out of the tomb, thumped into his ankles and disappeared along the tunnel with a spine-chilling hiss. He stumbled and caught himself against the wall. The lamp slipped between his sweaty fingers and shattered in a flare of burning oil. Red gave a little shriek and vanished.

For an instant, every detail of the tomb was edged in fire. Reonet, kneeling, her hair tangled across her eyes, her wide eyes turned towards him, a scrap of papyrus in her hand... the rocky shelf with her mother's unbandaged sahu just as he remembered, hands crossed on its shrivelled chest... dried lotus petals on the floor... a temple incense burner, shaped like a human arm, lying on its side near the girl's knees...

The flames gave one last flicker and darkness plunged around them both. Senu froze, the sweat breaking out all over his body.

"Mother?" Reonet's voice, small and scared. "Mother? Is that you?"

Senu opened his mouth but no words would come. He could feel the darkness in his head shifting. His breath came faster. Just like last time—

There was a rattle ahead. A spark, and the sudden flare of another lamp. Reonet thrust the light into his face, destroying the memory before it could form. Her eyes widened. "Senu! I thought you were too scared to come down here any more."

Hardly knowing whether to be relieved or angry, Senu edged round the rock and sat as far from the sahu as possible. Red was still invisible, though he could feel his ka beside him, hovering like smoke. "I've been looking for you all week!" he said. "Was that Miu who tripped me just then? Scared me stupid... hey, what's wrong?"

Only now did he notice how ill she looked. She had dark circles under her eyes. Her hair was greasy, her dress stained and filthy.

She said bitterly, "Haven't you heard? I got thrown out of the temple."

Senu blinked at her. "Thrown out? Your neighbour said a priest came to your house, but I didn't think..."

She tightened her lips. "That was Ankhsheshonq, the *sem*-priest who keeps an eye on us all. He said someone had reported me stealing spells and I couldn't go there any more. I tried to tell him your father was helping me prepare for scribe school and I needed the spells to learn them properly, but he just smiled in that superior way of his and said I could forget working with Craftsman Tefen because he wouldn't be helping anyone for a very long time. When I told him he was a liar and I'd go to his superiors, he said I was very lucky they hadn't summoned Moon and taught me what happens to thieves. So I kicked him. Father told me off for being disrespectful, and I suppose things got a bit out of hand." She shook her head. "Father was *hopeless*. He kept saying I'd grown up wild because I didn't have a mother to look after me, and what could he do? He was working all day and couldn't be looking out for me all the time.

Making excuses, like it was my fault I was born! When I found out they'd arrested your poor father, I didn't know what to do. I went down to the lagoon, but some motherless dung-snake had stolen my canoe. I couldn't face going back home just to see Ankhsheshonq smirk at me, so I came down here to be with Mother. I'm sorry, Senu. You must be feeling awful. But I couldn't face talking to anyone, and you were up on site all day, and – oh, it's all gone wrong! The stupid spell doesn't work, anyway." She flung the papyrus at the wall.

Senu stared at her. "How long have you been down here?"

She gave him a distracted look. "Oh, I don't know, a few days I think. Miu can feed herself now, and I brought lots of dates and stuff."

"You're crazy, Reonet! A few days? More like a week! Weren't you afraid?"

"What of?"

"The dark... the kas of the dead..."

She gave him a withering look. "I've got a lamp. I was just conserving oil when you tried to start that fire just now. And I'm not a baby. There isn't anybody here, I know that now. The kas are all gone."

"No they're not."

She stared at him.

"Red can talk to them. I've got heka."

For a moment she looked as if she were going to cry. Then she started giggling. "Oh Senu! You're so funny. Like that story you made up about the robbery! At least you made me laugh. Don't think I've laughed so much in days."

Senu got to his feet, forgetting the low roof. He hit his head and the pain banished what remained of his fear. "Stop it! Stop it, Reonet! This is *real*, can't you see? Father's been taken to Khnum's Cataract. He might die. I'm trapped up on site, and you're down here making yourself ill. So you stole a spell. Why don't you just give it back and say you're sorry? It's not as bad as what's happening to me. Someone found out about the robbery. That's why they arrested Tefen. It's not a joke. It never was. And if you... if you said anything..." He couldn't go on. His eyes filled.

They stared at each other.

The giggles died in Reonet's throat. "Oh, Senu, oh no... I'd never... I didn't say a word, I swear! On Moon's life!"

He sat down again. "I knew you wouldn't betray us on purpose. I just thought that if you didn't believe me..."

"I didn't tell anyone."

He nodded, trying to think who else it could have been.

"You're going to rob Lord Khufu's Horizon? Really?"

"Yes. Except it'll all go wrong because Red won't help. He keeps saying Lord Khufu's ka won't attack the intruders, but Captain Nemheb thinks he will, and he ought to know. He's done Temple service—"

Reonet paled. "You don't think your Captain had anything to do with me being thrown out of the temple, do you? He knows we're friends."

"I never thought of that."

"Ankhsheshonq's probably in on it, too." She clenched her fists. "I hate those *sem*-priests! They go round with their noses in the air and their leopard skins swinging from their shoulders as if they're some sort of human-headed gods! I don't think I want to be a scribe if that's how they get treated." She drew a deep, shuddering breath. "Oh, that's not true. Yes I do, I want to be a scribe more than anything else in the world, and now I'll never be one. I shouldn't have said all those things to Ankhsheshonq, but he made me so *angry*!" She sat back, shaking her head. "It's a mess, isn't it? What are we going to do?"

Senu reached for a date to gain time while he thought. "I suppose I should tell someone about Red, but I don't know who to trust. Captain Nemheb's got spies everywhere, and if I don't do what he says he'll send Mother and Tamuwy to beg at the White Wall."

Reonet's head snapped up. "He can't do that."

"He can. I'm the only working member of our family now."

She frowned at the wall for so long, he suffered a brief, cold terror that she was working for Captain Nemheb too. "I still can't work out why a Captain needs to steal anything," she said. "They're all stinking rich already. When's the robbery taking place?"

"Nemheb wouldn't tell me. He said I'll be contacted."

"Lord Khafre's visit is next week. They probably won't do anything until after that, so we've got a few days at least. What about that old dwarf down at the lagoon? He seemed to be on your side."

Senu shook his head. "Too risky. Pehsukher's worked for Nemheb for years. Nemheb saved his life or something, and he used to have heka. I don't trust him."

"Batahotep, then?"

"Who?"

"Old Batahotep – you must remember him! He whacked you often enough." She giggled again, though it sounded strained. "He's still in the village. They don't pack teachers up with the awning and slates when school finishes, you know."

Senu scowled. "What can *he* do?"

"He's a scribe, isn't he? And he works for the Education Department, which is nothing to do with Buildings, so he isn't one of Nemheb's men. He might be able to help."

Senu breathed deeply. Reonet was so clever, even when she was so upset and ill.

"Maybe we could run away to the Marshes until the robbery's over and everything's back to normal," he said without thinking. "The imakhu all go hunting there. Miu'll love it!"

She sighed. Touched his hand. "Senu, you're so sweet. But we can't just run away. My father might not notice, but what about your poor mother? Besides," she added,

"I haven't got a canoe any more."

She was right, of course. Nemheb would only find some way to punish his mother and sister.

"It was me who took your canoe," he admitted. "I was stupid, thought I saw Father... It got smashed in the flood. I'm sorry."

Another frown. "You smashed my canoe?"

"I'm really sorry."

"Oh Senu! You're such an idiot! All that work!"

"I'll help you make another one."

She sighed again. "Thanks. But it'll take time, and you've still got your ka. If someone saw us, they'd make me bring you back."

Senu's ears burned. "I'll cut off my ka-tail!"

Reonet's eyebrows raised. "Without releasing Red?"

"Yes... I mean... oh, I don't know!" He threw his date stone at the wall. "I don't know what to do."

The dark eyes flickered. Reonet bit her lip and glanced at her mother's sahu. "Go and talk to Batahotep first. Then we'll decide."

Chapter 10

DEATH

*Save me from aggressors in this land of the just, give me
my mouth that I may speak with it, let my arms be
extended in your presence, because I know you... (spell 72)*

BATAHOTEP'S HOUSE OCCUPIED a little rise in the least
crowded corner of the village. It was of the same design
as the other houses, having square mudbrick walls and a
flat roof accessed by steps up the outside of the building.
But Batahotep's status allowed him a private courtyard
which he had filled with pots containing miniature palm
trees. His servants clipped the plants so they formed neat
rows arranged by height, the way he liked to arrange his
pupils in the school. An ornamental wall sheltered the
yard from sand storms and shaded it from the sun.

Senu's steps slowed as he approached the gate. The
old scribe was sitting on a mat patterned by leaf
shadows, frowning over a sheet of papyrus. He couldn't
see Batahotep's rod, but that didn't mean it wasn't within

easy reach. He shifted his slate under his arm (Reonet's idea, to make the visit seem less suspicious in case anyone was watching) and wiped his sweaty palms on his loincloth. Not too late to walk on past and pretend he'd never come.

"It is too late," Red pointed out. "You should've been at the Passage of Purification a lighthour ago. The chief human will be wondering where you are."

"Shh!" Senu hissed back. "I've got to do this right. Don't distract me."

Batahotep heard and looked up from his work. His weak eyes peered at Senu from their folds of fat. "Get off with you!" he growled. "School's finished. If I catch you boys hanging around here again, I'llÑ" The eyes focused on Senu's ka-tail. He frowned. "What do *you* want?"

Senu licked his lips. He'd rehearsed his story with Reonet, but as usual when faced by his old teacher it all came out jumble. "You... the test... finished the glyphs... sir!" He offered the rather smudged slate.

Reonet had completed the glyphs for him last night. Now he wished she hadn't bothered. Batahotep looked down his nose at the smeared slate and pressed his lips together. "What do you call that?"

"I... er... my test, sir! You remember, don't you? You said if I completed twelve glyphs by sunset, you'd recommend me to help in the temple next year, and I thought that since my father's... uh... away, maybe I could help this year?"

The scribe shook his head, as if he didn't believe what

he was hearing. "That was sunset on the first day of Akhet, not sunset on the day we complete Lord Khafre's pyramid!"

Senu flushed and stared at his feet. "That's what I wanted to talk to you about, sir," he rushed on. "I meant to get it to you by sunset, really I did. But something happened, and—"

Batahotep clambered to his feet with an alarmed look. "I don't want to hear your excuses! You boys must think I'm stupid. I've heard them all before, you know."

"But it's not an excuse this time—"

"I *said* I don't want to hear it! If Captain Nemheb's willing to pay good gold to make sure a boy fails a test, I don't need to know why. And if you've any sense in that head of yours, you'll do as you're told and keep your mouth shut. Isn't what happened to your father warning enough?" Batahotep cast a nervous glance at the gates and gathered up his papyrus and ink pot. Without stopping to roll the mat properly, he hurried into his house. "I'm sorry for you and your poor mother," he called over his shoulder as he went. "But don't think it's going to make me recommend you to help in the temple before you're ready. I can see that tail of red hair hanging down your cheek, if no one else can. You'd best get back on site where you belong before Nemheb sends the sapers round your house."

Senu turned cold then hot with anger. Captain Nemheb had paid Batahotep to fail him! He'd never have passed that test, no matter how hard he tried, and his teacher didn't even want to know why.

"Stupid fat old hippopotamus!" Red rippled into view between the scribe and his house and stuck out his ghostly tongue. Batahotep, unable to see the ka, walked straight through him. Red gave an exaggerated shudder and made being-sick motions with his fingers down his throat.

For once, his ka's antics didn't cheer Senu up. Everything he'd been about to say, all the carefully rehearsed words, relied on Batahotep staying to listen. "Wait!" he called.

The scribe ducked through the doorway, catching his wig on the lintel. The wig slipped over his eyes but he didn't stop.

"No, wait!" Senu ran after him. "You have to help me, sir! Please! You see, Captain Nemheb's trying to make me and Red help him rob the pyramid and—"

The door slammed in Senu's face.

Red rippled out of the wood and made a rude sign at the house. "Forget him," the ka said. "He wouldn't have done anything, anyway. He's too fat. If he tried to sail to the Palace to warn Lord Khafre, his boat would sink."

Senu clenched his fingers on the slate and stared at the closed door. "He heard me," he whispered. "I know he did."

"I expect that's why he's leaning against the wall inside looking so ill."

Senu gave his ka a sharp look. Red didn't normally report on other people's physical actions. Suddenly, the courtyard seemed like a trap. Not a breath of wind stirred the leaves of Batahotep's miniature palms. Senu thought he heard the scrape of a sandal in the alley outside the gate but when he turned to look, no one was there. Sweat broke out all over his body. "Do you think he'll betray us to Captain Nemheb?" he breathed.

Red shook his head. "Not if he's got any sense. You heard what he said. He doesn't want to know what Nemheb's up to. He's probably afraid he'll get sent to Khnum's Cataract with your father."

This time Senu did laugh. The image of their flabby teacher breaking granite in the mines with a gang of mertu conscripts was just too funny. Then he remembered Tefen would soon be doing exactly that, and the laugh died in his throat. He looked at his slate, Reonet's careful lines smudged by his sweaty fingers, and suddenly it seemed responsible for all that had gone wrong in his life. He raised the slate above his head and flung it as hard as he could at Batahotep's door. The limestone broke with a loud, satisfying *crack*.

"That's what I think of your stupid test!" Senu shouted, stamping on the pieces to break them into smaller ones. "And *that's* what you can do with your stupid school! See if I care! We're going away, and we're never coming back. Never!"

Some women on their way to the lagoon with armfuls of dirty loincloths stopped outside the gate and stared at him as if he'd gone mad. A bunch of small, ka-tailed children ran off screaming and giggling. Senu scowled at Batahotep's house, wondering why none of his servants had come out to see what all the noise was about. He shook his head and brushed fragments of slate off his feet. The door was still firmly closed. Batahotep hadn't even threatened to beat him.

"Come on, Red," he said. "We're wasting our time here. Let's go find Reonet."

They'd agreed to meet by the lagoon to discuss what Batahotep had said. Senu saw the papyrus heads waving and heard the crashing and muttered curses from halfway up the hill. He found Reonet knee deep in black mud, hacking at the reeds with an old sickle. Lumps of mud hung in her hair. More mud splattered her face and arms. Her dress was wet and filthy. He couldn't catch everything she was saying, though 'stupid' seemed to come into it quite a lot.

"...stupid sickle... stupid spells... stupid priests... stupid boys!"

"I think she means you," Red whispered.

Senu bit his lip, embarrassed when he remembered his own outburst.

"Well?" Reonet demanded, hands on hips. "Are you just going to stand there gawping all day, or are you going to help?" She threw him the sickle, which slowly sank in the mud at his feet. "Stupid thing's blunt, my arms are killing me. What did old Batahotep say?"

Senu extracted the curved blade and wiped his hands on his loincloth. The flood was on the retreat, but the mud was still like thick black gruel, not yet dried by the sun. Reonet gave him a push. "Go on! Can't cut reeds without getting your feet wet!"

"Can't make a canoe out of wet reeds, either," Senu mumbled.

"You should have thought of that before you smashed my other one. So? Is he going to sort it out?"

"He wouldn't listen."

She looked at him in disbelief. "Didn't you tell him about the robbery?"

"Yes, but—"

"Well? What did he say?"

"Nothing. He shut the door in my face."

She stared at him again. "What did you do then?"

"I threw my slate at the door." He smiled in memory.

"Oh, Senu, you're hopeless! I knew I should have come with you. He probably thought you were just joking around, as usual."

Senu frowned. "It'd have made more sense if he had. But I'm pretty sure he believed me. He seemed scared. Apparently, that snake Nemheb paid him to make sure I failed the apprenticeship exam, only he didn't tell him why."

Reonet blinked. "Well, he knows now," she said. "Maybe he'll go to the authorities when he's had a chance to think about it. He doesn't have to mention the bribe. There's still time before Lord Khafre's visit..." She broke off and stared towards the site. "Oh, I wonder if that's why!"

"What?"

"I've been thinking about why the priests threw me out of the temple. You're right, they wouldn't have done it just because I stole a spell – everyone working in there has a chance to copy spells and I don't suppose they write the really secret ones on the walls. But sometimes Ankhsheshonq would bring younger priests with him, and they'd talk about all sorts of interesting things. Gods, goddesses, funerals, spells... I kept my ears open, and the day before they arrested your father I heard them talking about a temple scarab and a royal ka. They seemed worried. And I think that was when Ankhsheshonq caught me listening."

Senu stiffened. "A temple scarab? That's some sort of amulet, isn't it? Gef once threatened me with one. What's it do?"

He received a distracted look. "I was forgetting, you've not had your tail cut. Don't worry, you'll get it in full when you release Red. I thought it was just to scare us. They can't order us about any more, so they invent something else to control us with." She took a deep breath. "The priests are supposed to be able to summon adult kas and trap them inside temple scarabs to punish people. I didn't think there could really be a horrible thing like that but now I'm not so sure. And they spoke of a royal ka..." She looked round and lowered her voice. "Oh, Senu, what if they're planning to trap *Lord Khafre's* ka in a temple scarab?"

Senu's breath tightened as he imagined Red imprisoned in a tiny amulet. "But why should they want to trap Lord Khafre's ka? And why wait till he comes here?" He shook his head. "Forget it, Reonet. We've more important things to worry about, like what we're going to do if Batahotep doesn't help us. And I need to find out more about my heka."

Something passed behind Reonet's eyes. "Don't ask the priests, Senu, whatever you do."

"After they threw you out? No way!" He grinned. But he kept thinking of what Nemheb had said about the temple, of how children with heka were taken there to be properly trained. The priests would be able to answer his questions.

They spent the rest of the afternoon cutting reeds for a new canoe, though it was obvious they wouldn't get a platform made for it before Lord Khafre's visit. With the royal party due on site in a few days, the sapers were too watchful for them to risk taking any wood.

Reonet grew quieter and quieter as they worked. She kept glancing at him, especially when Red fooled about and made him giggle. Finally, she said in a little voice, "You're so lucky, Senu. I miss Moon. I really, really miss her."

"Reonet..?" Senu lowered the sickle and took a step towards her, but stopped, feeling awkward.

"It was all right at first," she said without looking at him. "There was Miu, and school, and canoeing with all my friends. Even when I was in the temple, it was all right. There was so much going on, so many new things to learn. Then your father got arrested and everything started to go wrong... " She sniffed. "I can't get Mother's ka to talk to me. And Moon's so hard to reach now, even when I dream."

"You can't reach her in dreams?" His stomach did peculiar things. "But I thought—"

"So did I! That's what they tell you when they cut your ka-tail. 'Don't worry, your ka will always be there when you need her.' But it's not true! We grow up, and the kas go off on their own. They don't care about us, not really."

Red rippled uncomfortably in the shadows under the huge, feathery papyrus heads. Senu frowned at him. Reonet's shoulders were shaking. He had a sudden, chilling thought.

"Red?" he whispered. "Are there really such things as temple scarabs?"

Red began to fade until his ka-tail was a mere smudge against the water. "Come back!" Senu snapped. "This is important!"

To his surprise, the ka reappeared. "The priest-charm exists," he whispered. "But humans don't have the power to make them any more. There are very few left."

Senu turned cold. "Could... could Moon be in one?"

"Maybe." His ka's tone was strange. "But the spells stop kas from looking inside."

Reonet was staring at him with wide eyes. "What?" she demanded. "What's Red saying?"

He passed on his ka's words and Reonet gave a little moan. "Then it's true. They really can imprison kas. I wouldn't put it past Ankhsheshonq! If he's done that to Moon, I'll... I'll *kill* him."

"I'm sure he hasn't—"

They were interrupted by a high pitched scream from the river bank.

Reonet's head snapped round. Premonition breathed across Senu's neck. Red whirled from the reeds like a bird startled from its nest and momentarily lost all shape before winking out like a star at dawn. They raced towards the sound, jumping irrigation ditches and splashing through channels, black mud sucking at their ankles. They were among the last to arrive. Nearly everyone from the village, including some mertu boys who'd splashed round the end of the Wall to see what all the excitement was about, were crowded on the bank staring at something stuck in the reeds. Senu saw torn, muddy linen, bloated flesh... One of the mertu boys prodded the body with a stick, triggering more screams.

"Dead," he pronounced in a satisfied tone.

The women pulled their little ones away and told the older children to stop staring. They sent one of the boys to fetch the sapers. The men who'd been working in Lord Khafre's river temple, alerted by all the screaming, came running along the bank.

Reonet elbowed her way through the crowd. Reluctantly, Senu followed. As he stared at the body he turned colder than ever. The wig and sandals were gone, the fine clothes ruined by the mud. But there was no mistaking the identity of the drowned man.

"Batahotep," he breathed.

Reonet paled. They stared at each other. Without speaking, they pushed out of the crowd and took cover under the palms.

"I'm scared, Senu," she whispered.

It didn't take a genius to work out why.

"So am I."

Chapter 11

BLIND ROOM
...your vision is clear in the House of Darkness...
(spell 169)

BATAHOTEP'S DEATH CHANGED things. Whether the scribe had tried to warn Lord Khafre about the robbery and been caught, or one of Nemheb's medjay had followed Senu and heard him pleading for his teacher's help, they had no choice. The moment Nemheb discovered Senu had also told Reonet, her life too would be in danger.

Senu was all for stealing a canoe that very night and fleeing while the sapers were still busy investigating Batahotep's death. But Reonet said no, they would be watching for unregistered vessels leaving the site and probably searching them for Batahotep's murderer. Also, she refused to leave Miu behind and said she had some things to take care of before she left. In the end, it was agreed that Senu should go back to work and act as normally as possible until the eve of Lord Khafre's visit, when hopefully everyone would be too excited and busy to notice two hemutiu youngsters on the river.

Those two days were the longest of Senu's life. He wasn't sure Sobek believed his excuse for his day off, that his cheek had got infected again, but the big Gang-Chief didn't press the matter. The gangs were kept working an extra hour after sunset in an effort to finish the ninth layer of the new pyramid before Lord Khafre arrived, and everyone was tense and snappier than usual. Even the boys' traditional amulet game seemed subdued, though how much of this was due to Gef's absence and how much to the imminent Royal Visit, Senu didn't know. He and Red were instructed to distract Lord Khufu's ka several times, which Red handled in his usual manner of insisting they didn't need to worry. If only.

On the final evening, Senu scrambled down the pyramid and raced for the Passage of Purification as soon as the Overseer gave the order to down tools. Sobek called something after him which he pretended not to hear. He headed straight for the lagoon, terrified Reonet would think he wasn't coming. But when he reached their meeting place, she wasn't there.

He hung about in the shadows of the palms for what seemed like hours, long enough for guilt to set in. His mother would be worried when he didn't come home from work. He wondered if he should leave a message with someone in the village. Then he spotted a saper working his way slowly along the bank, prodding the reeds with his spear, and shook his head. His mother and sister would only send someone after him. If they didn't know where he'd gone, Nemheb couldn't make them tell.

Above the plateau, a dazzle of stars came out. The new pyramid was beginning to show above Amun's Wall, flat topped and solid. Beyond its scaffolding, Khufu's Horizon reflected the starlight, pale and majestic. Sapers on patrol behind the Wall called to one another, their voices loud in the night. He shivered, finally realizing what a stupid, crazy thing the Scorpions were intending to do. Even if they broke in at night, someone was bound to see them.

"Red," he whispered. "Red, you can come out now. It's all right, we're not going up there again. Ever."

He didn't expect his ka to appear so promptly. For once Red had no clever comment. He simply stood there, rippling gently, a dark palm trunk visible through his ghostly body. "Please don't make me talk to Batahotep's ka," he said in a subdued voice.

Senu blinked, realizing he hadn't even thought of it. "Don't be silly, he wouldn't listen to us when he was alive, let alone now he's dead!"

"Or Moon's human's mother?"

"I won't make you talk to any of the kas of the dead, ever again. I promise. We're getting away tonight. We're going to rescue Father, then everything will be all right." He peered up the path to the village. Still no sign of Reonet.

"You really promise?" Red said.

"Yes. I know how scared you are. So am I. It's just Nemheb was so— oh, never mind, come here. Please?"

His ka's face brightened. He wrapped his ghostly arms around Senu. Love and relief surged through him. He closed his eyes, drew a deep breath and burst into tears.

That was how Reonet found him, still hugging his ka with the tears streaming down his cheeks. He hastily wiped his eyes, cheeks burning. Reonet didn't say anything. In one hand she carried Miu in the same basket they'd taken hunting. In her other, a second basket bulged with bread and smoked fish. She'd tied a rope around her waist. A long cooking knife glittered in its coils. "Sorry I'm so late," she panted. "Took me ages to catch Miu. Little devil had gone off hunting rats. Are you going like that?"

Senu tore his gaze from the knife and looked down at himself. He was still wearing the old, stained loincloth he wore on site. "Like what?"

"Aren't you going to take any spare clothes, or anything?"

Senu shrugged. He experienced another flicker of guilt about his mother and Tamuwy. "I've got Red. He's all I need."

Reonet's serious expression melted into a grin. "Good job I'm coming with you, then, because you'd never make it on your own, Senu son of Tefen! It'll be cold at nights with no shelter, you know." When he flushed, she giggled. "Don't worry, you'll keep warm enough tonight paddling. We'll grab you a tunic off someone's drying stones tomorrow."

Getting the canoe wasn't as difficult as they'd feared. With Lord Khafre's visit due the next day, most of the hemutiu children had been pressed into helping with the preparations and they had several decent vessels to choose from. But Reonet suddenly decided to be fussy, tugging at the reed bindings and jumping up and down on the wooden platforms, rejecting one perfectly good canoe after another, as Senu hopped from foot to foot and cast nervous glances along the bank. The moon rose, reflecting silver in the water and bathing the site as bright as day. "Just take the first one," he hissed. "Quick, or the sapers on the Wall will see us."

But Reonet refused to be hurried. "None of these are as good as mine was," she grumbled. "They'll be leaking before we're halfway out of the lagoon."

"At this rate, we'll both be caught before we're halfway out of the lagoon!" Senu snapped back, tension making him short-tempered.

They had another argument about which way to flee. Reonet said they should go downriver to the Marshes, of course. Quite apart from the fact that paddling with the current was much easier and faster than paddling against it, there would be plenty of cover, lots of wildlife to hunt and a kinder climate. They'd have to get past the site and, later, the Temple of the Sun without being seen. But that was nothing to getting past the Palace of the White Wall at a time when Lord Khafre was preparing to set out on his Royal Tour. "Besides," she added. "It was your idea, wasn't it? Plenty of hunting for Miu, you said."

Senu set his jaw. "They took Tefen the other way."

"It makes no sense! How are we supposed to rescue someone from a conscripts' barge, even if we do somehow catch up with it? Do you *want* to join your father in the mines?"

Tears filled Senu's eyes at the thought of never seeing any of his family again. "Perhaps we shouldn't go, after all?" he said in a small voice. Red stayed very quiet, sitting cross-legged on the front of the canoe, barely visible.

Reonet threw down her paddle with an angry glint in her eye. "You're impossible! No wonder old Batahotep gave up on you!"

"That's not fair. It's not *your* father they've taken to the mines!"

"At least *your* father doesn't hate you because your mother died giving birth to you!"

They'd been shouting. Realizing how stupid this was, they glared at each other, panting hard.

Senu blinked, flooded with strange emotions. "I didn't know..."

"How could you know? Why do you think I want to contact mother's ka so badly? I've never had a chance to get to know her. Never."

"I'm sorry."

Reonet sighed. "No point being sorry. Father's right. It won't bring her back — Shh!"

A rustle in the reeds made them both freeze.

"Someone's there," Senu whispered, the hairs on his neck crawling.

Reonet listened a moment. "No, it's just a duck." But she quietly picked up her paddle. "Come on, then, we'll go upriver. But you can help. There's two paddles. I'm not fighting Hapi's whole flood on my own."

As they pushed through the reeds, cleared the mud banks and joined the main river, Senu started to sweat. The stars reflected in the black water exactly as they had on the night he'd almost drowned. But despite Reonet's grumbles, the flood was nothing like as strong as that night and they made steady, if slow, progress along the safe channels near the bank. His arms were soon screaming but he didn't dare ask Reonet for a rest. She knelt in front of him, her paddle rising and falling in perfect rhythm, her turquoise clip glinting in the moonlight. He watched the far bank anxiously as Nemheb's fields slid into view, but all seemed quiet. Then Nemheb's house came into view, white under the moon. He missed with his next stroke and water landed in Miu's basket, making the cat flatten her ears and hiss.

Reonet turned her head. "Careful! Are you trying to drown us or something? We'll be nearing the Palace soon. We ought to cross over, try to sneak up the far bank."

The sweat came again. "No! Not yet."

"This bank will be heavily guarded further up. If we cross now, we've a chance of getting over without being spotted."

"But the currents—"

She gave him a hard look. "This was your idea, remember. If you're scared, we can go back right now."

Senu glanced over his shoulder. Nemheb's house was growing smaller behind them. He began to relax then stiffened again, neck prickling. "I think there's a boat following us."

Reonet peered at the wide expanse of water. "I don't see anything."

"It went into the reeds back there."

They stared a bit longer, but nothing moved in the shadows. Senu began to think he'd imagined the boat.

Reonet gave him a hard look. "This is no time for one of your silly jokes, Senu!" She narrowed her eyes at him and angled the canoe's bows into the current.

Senu was so busy staring at the reeds behind, he didn't see the danger ahead until Reonet gasped, "Quick! Paddle for your life!"

He caught a glimpse of two sleek black vessels arrowing towards them out of the night. There was a sudden rush of speed as the current caught them. Then they were racing downstream with the black and silver water, desperately angling their paddles to keep the canoe from turning broadside. As they drew level with the reeds where he'd seen the first boat, it came out of hiding. Two dark-skinned men crouched over the bows, shouting. Reonet waved her fist at them as the canoe slid under their noses. Senu crouched low, back prickling, hoping they didn't have spears.

For a moment he thought they'd escaped. Then there was a deadly hiss as something flew past his ear. The canoe gave a sudden, unexpected jerk as a hooked spear with a rope attached thudded into the bunched reeds at the stern. He lost his balance. The paddle flew out of his hand. Miu's basket, with the cat still imprisoned inside, slid across the platform and splashed overboard. Reonet gave an anguished cry and made a grab for it. Her paddle went spinning away in the flood. She stared round wildly, not understanding what had happened. "Hippopotamus harpoon!" Senu yelled, lying on his stomach and desperately trying to untangle the rope. Before he could work the hook free, a net descended over the canoe entangling them both in a mass of thick cords.

"No!" Reonet screamed, fighting the net like a crazed crocodile. "Miu's drowning! *Do something, Senu!*"

In those first few breaths, the panic was too great to think. Senu saw the cat struggling to keep its head above water as its basket was swept away by the current. He kicked in terror as the net dragged him and Reonet into the river too. Then he realized he could still breathe. The black water wasn't closing over his head. They weren't even in the river any more, but were being bumped across channels and through the reeds.

Red's anxious face appeared on the other side of the knotted ropes. "Senu! Senu! It's all right, I'm here. Grab my hands!"

The ka's ghostly fingers reached through the net, glowing faintly blue as they had when he'd rescued Senu from the falling stone. Senu's heart lifted. He reached for his ka, but a dark foot descended on his arm, pinning it to the mud.

"Your knife!" he shouted to Reonet through the tugging, tangling ropes. "Use your knife!"

Her struggles lost their panic. She twisted in the net beside him, trying to pull the knife free of its folds. A dark hand got there before her and extracted the weapon. There was a chuckle. "No you don't, my little wildcat," said a voice with a thick Kush accent. And a black wing blotted out the stars.

Senu cried out as its weight pressed him to the mud. It reeked of blood and death. Under the skin's smothering folds he could barely breathe, let alone see. The cords of the net cut into his chest and one of his legs was bent at an awkward angle. He heard Reonet screaming and cursing nearby, interspersed with sobs as she cried again for Miu. An image of the cat trapped in its sinking basket flashed before Senu's eyes. He closed them in sympathy. There were more voices, speaking in the language of Kush. Someone snapped an order and Reonet's screams cut off.

"Reonet!" he called, his words muffled by the skin. "Red! What's happening?"

"Senu!" shrieked his ka. "Senu, he's making me, it's the summoning spell... no... I don't want to go..." Red's words whirled away like sand before the wind.

"Red!" Senu screamed. "Red!"

Nothing.

Senu's struggles ceased. His limbs were trembling like a baby's. They've killed Reonet, was all he could think. They've killed her like they killed Batahotep. And they've got Red. And now they'll kill me too and throw my sahu in the river. I'll float back down to the Place of Truth, where Mother will find me, and —

The hippopotamus skin was wrapped tightly around him, stealing his remaining breath. He felt more ropes being wound around outside, imprisoning his arms and legs, tight about his neck. His muscles spasmed in terror.

"Re..e..ed!"

At his strangled cry, something punctured the smothering skin near his mouth. He sucked air gratefully through the tiny hole as strong hands picked him up and carried him a short distance. They dropped him on to something hard that wallowed from side to side. There were splashing sounds beneath. He fought unconsciousness as long as he could, trying to work out if Reonet had been taken captive with him and whether they were headed up or down river. But the skin muffled his hearing and destroyed his sense of direction. Not enough air came through the tiny slit. Worst of all, he couldn't feel his ka.

Not long after the start of that nightmarish journey, he lost the uneven battle and fainted.

When he woke, his bonds were gone but he still couldn't see. It was black with the absolute nothingness of a tomb. He clawed at his eyes, only this time they were not blindfolded. He pressed his hands against cold stone and swallowed a whimper of fear.

There'll be a door, he told himself. Somewhere. There has to be.

Very slowly, dizzy with the blackness, he sat up and tentatively felt around. More stone, its surface marred by unexpected little bumps and grooves.

"Red?" he whispered. "Reonet?"

His whisper bounced off the walls, giving him the size of his prison. Frighteningly small.

He stretched an arm upwards. His fingers brushed yet more stone, encountered more of the strange lumps and grooves. He shuddered and forced himself to crawl, feeling in front of him with one hand. Another wall. Crawled back. Wall.

Crawled to his right.

Wall.

Crawled left.

Wall.

All the surfaces were covered in the little carvings. He traced one of them with his finger, recognized a glyph, and suddenly realized what they were.

Spells.

He huddled as small as he could and wrapped his arms around himself.

It was so dark, so small. There was no air. For the first time in his life, his ka was not with him.

His fingers clawed uselessly at the stone spells.

"Please," he sobbed. "Please, let me out. There's been a mistake. Let me out. Please. I'll do anything, just let me out, please let me out."

But no one came. And, as he knew it would, the old nightmare returned to haunt him.

He was eight years old again, back in the hemutiu tombs with the kas of the dead. There were human bodies with the heads of lions, and cat's bodies with human heads. There was a strange creature with a serpent's body, scaled wings, and the face of a woman who reminded him of his father's pictures of the old queen. They were glowing blue and they were trying to tell him something. He couldn't quite hear the words.

"Where's Red?" he whispered. "What have you done to him?"

The kas clamoured louder. For the first time, he understood what they were saying.

"TRAPPED! TRAPPED! THE GREAT ONE IS TRAPPED!"

He was trapped, all right. Senu put his hands over his ears. "Go away," he sobbed. "I can't help you. Go away..."

A long time later, there was a scrape on the other side of the wall. He sat up, stiff with terror, and stared at the crack of light slowly widening in front of him. After so long in the dark, it dazzled. He flung up a hand, thinking for a moment that he was back in his nightmare and the kas of the dead were coming for him again. But the thin silhouette against the light was human. And the ghostly shape that rushed past the silhouette was—

"Red!" he gasped, wrapping his arms around the ka and squeezing until they met in the middle of Red's body. Tears of relief and love ran down his cheeks.

His captor stood outside and watched. After a pause, the familiar, clipped voice said, "You should realize, Senu, that I know exactly what scares you. You're in what is called a Blind Room. The spells stop your ka from finding you. If you try to run from your duties again, I can make things a lot worse for you than that small demonstration. Now come on out. I want to make quite sure we understand each other before you go back to the Place of Truth."

Senu raised his tear-streaked face. "It was you, wasn't it?" he whispered. "*You* sent my father to Khnum's Cataract!"

A little smile played at the corners of Nemheb's mouth. "So. You're not quite as stupid as everyone says you are."

A terrible rage banished the echoes of Senu's fear. He launched himself across the Blind Room and flung himself at the scribe, beating the golden collar with his fists. "I hate you! *I hate you!*"

Nemheb backed into a windowless passage lit by flaming brands set in the walls. He neatly side stepped, allowing the medjay who accompanied him to seize Senu's ka-tail and pull him away. Senu struggled, but the medjay's thick arm went around his neck. Nemheb jabbed his scribe's staff under Senu's chin. "Want to go back in there? In the dark without your ka?"

His struggles ceased. The sweat came again. "You can't keep him from me!"

One of Nemheb's perfectly groomed eyebrows rose. "Can't I? Ask him."

"He summoned me," Red said. "But he hasn't got a priest-charm, so he can't hold me."

"See these spells?" Nemheb took a brand from the wall and ducked into the cell. He swept the flame around, making the tightly carved glyphs writhe like spiders. With the medjay's dark arm still clamped across his throat, Senu shuddered. "I carved them myself." The scribe seemed proud of his achievement. "Kas can't see through them."

"Don't worry," Red whispered. "If he puts you in here again, I'll know where to come. Those silly spells can't keep me out. Look—" To demonstrate, his ka floated calmly across the cell and vanished through the far wall.

"Red..!" Senu cried, struggling afresh.

Red reappeared from the wall, grinning. "See?"

Nemheb, who had been following Senu's gaze, must have guessed the gist of this conversation. "Granted your ka knows about this room now. But I've other rooms where he'll never find you. Your little friend is in one right now."

"Reonet!" Senu gasped, flooded with guilt. In his

own terror, he'd forgotten that cut-off cry. "Where is she? She's got nothing to do with this! Let her go."

Nemheb smiled. "That's where you're wrong. I think you'll be more motivated if you know she's going to be inside the pyramid with us when we go in."

Senu stared at the scribe in horror. "No!"

"Yes." The smile broadened. He patted Senu on the cheek. "I'm sorry it had to come to this. I'd hoped we could be friends. But from now on, you and Red will do exactly what I tell you or I'll make sure you never see your father or your friend again. Understand?"

Senu swallowed. "Let me see Reonet," he whispered. "How do I know she's still alive?"

"You'll just have to trust me, won't you? Like I'm going to have to trust you."

"Soon as I get back on site, I'm going to the authorities. They'll arrest you and search this place and find her and—"

Nemheb laughed. "Oh yes? Like you did last time, perhaps? Running to your teacher like a little ka-tailed baby?"

"So you did kill him." His heart dropped.

Another twisted smile. "Batahotep fell in the river and drowned. No one's going to believe the sun-ravings of a criminal's son over the word of a Captain of the Royal Works, now are they? Be sensible, Senu. Just do what I want. That way no one else need suffer."

Senu glared at Nemheb, hating him more with every moment. "I thought you were helping us! All that fine stuff about getting gold for the mertu families so they would have plenty to eat and wouldn't riot... it was all lies, wasn't it? You don't care about any of us! You're in it for yourself!"

"Of course."

The tears came again. He fought them. "Why? Why do you need gold? You've got a beautiful house. You've got power. You're a Captain! An imakhu! You can have anything you want. Why do you have to make us all suffer like this? I don't understand—"

"That's enough," Nemheb said in a hard voice. "Take the boy back to the site. Watch him every moment. If he even so much as breathes when he shouldn't, kill the girl."

"I'll rescue her," Senu whispered. "I won't let you take her into the pyramid." But the scribe only laughed.

"You do a good job today, and we'll see about reuniting you with your loved ones. Otherwise..." He left it hanging.

He didn't have to say a word more.

Chapter 12

ROYAL VISIT
You have appeared as Lord of the Two Lands...
(spell 183)

TWO SILENT MEDJAY escorted Senu back to the site in one of Nemheb's work-boats while the Captain himself stayed behind to dress in proper attire for the royal visit. Unlike last time, the medjay watched Senu constantly as if they thought their charge might dive overboard the moment they took their eyes off him. Senu thought about it, but discarded the idea. The image of Reonet, locked in a small dark room without Miu or her ka to comfort her, was too strong. It was all his stupid fault for suggesting that they run away. Without him, she'd still be safe in the hemutiu tombs with her mother's sahu.

He knelt in the bows of the boat, folded his arms on the rail and rested his head on top. He watched the water swirl past with dull eyes as Nemheb's servants worked the big keel-paddles to keep the vessel straight. They barely had to row. The flood might be easing but the current was still strong enough to carry a small boat such as this. They glided effortlessly past the lagoon where he and Reonet had stolen the canoe, past the school site, past the place where the women did their washing and Batahotep's sahu had been found in the reeds. Senu wanted to thrust his hands into the water and hold the boat back. But that would have been as futile as trying to fight Nemheb.

At least he and Red were unlikely to be asked to contact Lord Khufu's ka today. Excitement had stirred up the Place of Truth like a swarm of invisible bees. Women rushed along the bank with strips of linen dyed in bright colours, stringing them from every available palm tree and winding them around the necks of the statues that guarded the entrance to Lord Khafre's river temple. Blue lotus petals had been scattered on the steps, which had been freshly scrubbed until they gleamed in the morning sun. The hemutiu children seemed to have been let off their morning apprenticeships. Dressed in their best clothes, they chased one another around the lagoon, shrieking wildly like ka-tailed babies. Senu spotted Iny among them, wrestling two of the smaller boys in the mud. Their whoops and laughter made him feel very old. Up on site work appeared to be continuing as normal. The cracks of the Gang-Chiefs' whips reached Senu on the wind, together with the familiar whiff of sewage. In spite of everything, he smiled. Lord Khafre was unlikely to stay long.

"We'll tell Sobek everything, Red," he whispered. "He'll know what to do. Don't worry, I understand why you're so scared now. That woman with the snake's body and the wings was pretty fierce."

For once, his ka did not fade. "I only made you forget because I thought it would help you."

"I know. I'm not angry with you."

And he wasn't. After the terror of Nemheb's Blind Room, he felt very calm. "Will you look like that when I'm dead?" he asked, curious.

"Kas take their own shape when their human dies. I don't know what mine will be yet."

Senu shivered.

Red rippled closer. "I love you."

"I know."

"I need to tell you something about Lord Khufu's ka."

Senu stiffened. "What?"

"He's trapped in his pyramid. That's why all the other kas in the tombs were so upset."

Senu's stomach fluttered as he recalled the voices from his nightmare. *TRAPPED, THE GREAT ONE IS TRAPPED!*

He glanced round to check no one was listening. The medjay had been distracted by the preparations on the bank and the helmsman was shouting to someone on the Landing, ordering one of the other barges out of the way. "But that's terrible! He's bound to see the men when they go inside! Why didn't you tell me before?"

"He won't. He's trapped inside the sarcophagus. That's why we didn't need to distract him when the humans were digging. Don't worry, he won't be able to see the robbery happening and he can't attack anyone. So we can just pretend, like we did before."

Senu frowned. "But isn't Khufu's sarcophagus made of granite? I thought kas could walk through stone."

Red rippled uncomfortably. "They can usually. I don't understand it either, but it's true. The kas said so, and I've checked."

There was no time to think about it. The boat bumped against the Landing and the big medjay who had taken Senu to the tombs on the first night gripped his arm. "Come on, you," he said. "I'm to escort you to your Gang-Chief."

Senu climbed out of the boat on numb legs. He did not resist as the medjay hustled him up the path to the site. A few curious eyes followed them. But one of Nemheb's medjay escorting someone across the Place of Truth was a common sight. The gangs probably assumed Senu had been caught throwing sticks in the wrong place.

Senu longed to ask Red more about Lord Khufu's trapped ka, but the medjay's presence made this impossible. As he was marched through the dust and the cracking whips to the ramps at the base of Lord Khafre's pyramid, his thoughts churned furiously. The most important thing was to get Reonet out of Nemheb's clutches before he had a chance to take her into the pyramid. Then they could go to the authorities. They'd have to go higher than Captain Nemheb, he realized that now. The Chief of Works? Maybe he'd be on site today since his Lord was visiting.

Up on site, the mertu were singing gustily. Sobek's voice carried above the others, louder and more enthusiastic than everyone else.

"Scor–pi–ons! Scor–pions FOR EV–ER!"

Senu smiled.

The medjay gave him a suspicious look. "No tricks," he muttered, giving his arm a warning squeeze. "Captain Nemheb's a powerful man. He can do all he threatened, and more."

Senu bit his lip. "He's a snake! Why do you work for him?"

The medjay's black eyes hardened. "He pays well. Quick now, and remember. Keep your mouth shut, or the girl dies."

The hand-over was done efficiently and quickly. Sobek stared hard at Senu, then nodded to the medjay. "Thanks for bringing him back. I'll be responsible for him from now on."

"You're to tie blocks to his ankles," instructed the medjay. "So he can't run off again. Captain's orders."

Senu's heart beat faster. But Sobek growled deep in his throat and said firmly, "You tell your Captain I run my gang with safety first. Tyin' blocks to a boy's ankles and havin' him fall over the edge ain't going to make a good impression when the Lord Khafre comes to see his pyramid, now is it? You can tell Captain Nemheb I've my own methods of keepin' my boys in line." He fingered his whip and glowered. But under the fierce scowl, Senu caught the big man's wink.

He hung his head to hide his smile. The medjay looked at him uncertainly, before giving a curt nod. "I expect you know best, but watch the boy. Captain doesn't want any trouble today."

When the medjay had gone, Sobek gathered Senu against his sweaty chest in an unexpected hug. "I thought you were a goner," he muttered.

Senu buried his face in the big mertu's shoulder with a rush of relief. "Nemheb's up to something," he whispered back. "You have to tell the others! He—"

The thick arms crushed him tighter. "Don't worry, we're not as stupid up here as you hemutiu seem to think! Nemheb wants somethin' special out of that pyramid. He's not goin' to breathe till he gets it. By then, we'll be well clear. You'll see."

"But—"

"Just do your stuff. I'll make sure you're all right, don't worry. I expect Nemheb's given you your instructions, so I'll not waste time repeatin' them. Stay alert."

"But—"

As he tried to tell Sobek that Nemheb hadn't given him any specific instructions, the other gangs eyed them curiously. This attracted the attention of the Overseer and his scribe, who peered down to see what all the fuss was about. Sobek released him and gave him a light cuff on the ear. "Got me water-boy back, sir!" he called. "Medjay found 'im dossing down the lagoon. Get up there, boy!" he added in a loud voice. "An' give t'other lads some help!"

A second playful cuff sent Senu scrambling up the pyramid to the accompaniment of whistles and jeers from the other boys. Red shinned up beside him, for once not fooling around on the scaffolding. The Overseer yelled at the men to get back to work. He wanted ten more stones lifted up each side before Lord Khafre's visit interrupted things. "How we're expected to finish this pyramid with His High and Mightiness breathing down our necks, I don't know!" he grumbled to his scribe. "We're nearly a week behind, as it is, and that Captain's been messing with the schedules again..."

Senu slipped out of sight before they remembered he'd been brought back in the company of "that Captain" last week. In spite of everything, it was a relief to be back on site in the fierce sunlight under the open sky with his ka, surrounded by men whose speech was direct and whose threats were made with their fists, not their tongues. He looked hopefully for Gef, but there was still no sign of the mertu boy. Hemutiu stone dressers crawled across the raised central area, frantically smoothing and chiselling the final rough edges. Boys crawled behind them with water jars, washing off the dust. The ninth layer was almost complete. Ladders had been arranged up the eastern side in case Lord Khafre wanted to climb up and inspect the work. Boys from the other gangs were betting amulets on how far the great Lord would climb, which crown he'd be wearing, how many amulets, how many rings, and just about anything else it was possible to make a wager on.

A lighthour crawled by. The tension in the air was almost thick enough to eat. Senu collected a water jar and half heartedly helped Patep and Teti, who seemed to have forgotten in the excitement that they weren't supposed to be talking to him. As they knelt shoulder to shoulder, washing the last specks of dirt from the stones, the two Scorpion boys chattered non-stop about the royal visit, trying to impress Senu with their knowledge. He didn't hear a word they said.

Then someone shouted, "He's coming! Look! It's his barge!" and everyone – labourers, Gang-Chiefs, Overseer, scribes, water-boys, hemutiu stone dressers – rushed to the east side of the pyramid, jostling one another dangerously for the best view. Senu lost sight of Patep and Teti and found himself squeezed on the northeast corner surrounded by boys he didn't know. They dug him in the ribs with their elbows, pointing and shouting excitedly. "Look at all them sapers! Must be hundreds of 'em down there!"

Senu shivered. Armed sapers in full uniform surrounded Lord Khafre's river temple and guarded the path from the Landing to the steps. More sapers lined the route Lord Khafre would take to his pyramid. Extra spearheads glinted in the sun along the top of Amun's Wall, one guard for every four cubits. Yet more guards had been posted along the west bank of the river to make certain no unauthorized vessels landed during the royal visit.

From the edge of the water, a cheer rose into the dusty air. Senu shaded his eyes. An enormous gilded barge that shone like a second sun was tying up at the Landing. It had a striped blue and gold awning which hid the passengers from view, but it was obvious who was on board by the way people scurried along the bank, making the barge fast and organizing planks and cloths so their Lord would not have to step in the mud. The sheer size of the vessel had caused it to overshoot slightly and shouts and curses mingled with the cheers. One of the boys next to Senu gave a mocking laugh. "He should've come in a canoe! It'd have bin a lot easier."

Hemutiu women threw lotus petals to cover the cloths as servants disembarked with fringed sunshades. There was a long pause. An expectant hush spread from the river up the hill and across the plateau. The excitement was infectious. In spite of everything, Senu discovered he was holding his breath.

At last, Lord Khafre was carried ashore on a golden throne supported by two long poles that rested on the shoulders of four shaven-headed men. The Double Crown of the Two Lands balanced on his head, a false beard protruded from his chin, his crook and flail were crossed precisely on his chest, and his kilt had been pleated in strict royal style about his knees. He sat stiffly, staring straight ahead like a living statue.

A great shout carried up the hill.

"HIDE YOUR EYES BEFORE KHAFRE THE GREAT! MIGHTY BULL! LORD OF THE TWO LANDS! SON OF RE!"

No one obeyed. They were too busy ogling the royal party. After their Lord had disembarked, five important looking imakhu in wide collars of gold, red and blue stepped off the barge, each carrying a staff with a different symbol glinting on top. Senu squinted curiously at the symbols, but they were too far away to see details. After the imakhu came twenty young women dressed alike in shining white linen pleated in the latest fashion, wearing gold in their ears and around their arms and ankles. Some shook sistrum-rattles, some clapped their hands, some sang, some danced. Standard bearers took up position before the throne. Finally, there came a pure white ox with a garland of rare creamy lotus around its neck, led by a girl with blue flax in her hair.

The boy next to Senu peered closely at the throne. "There he is!" he said, pointing in excitement. "He *has* still got it! I said he had!" He grabbed the arm of another boy and hissed, "You owe me two amulets! Prince Menkaure's still got his ka-tail!"

Senu's heart gave a little jolt. He squinted at the procession, which had reached the entrance to Khafre's river temple. The throne was lowered to the ground and the living statue stepped stiffly from it on to the gleaming white steps. In the shadow behind the throne, a smaller, chubbier replica of Lord Khafre stood just as stiffly and clad in just as much gold, except the Prince's head was bare of crowns having instead a single tail of braided hair twisted with blue cloth. It was difficult to see from such a distance, but Senu thought the small figure ran a finger under his tight collar.

He experienced a flash of sympathy followed by a daring idea.

"Red?" he whispered, glancing round.

The boys next to him were busy exchanging amulets. Everyone else was still ogling the royal party. Senu eased backwards through the crush. "Red!" he hissed more urgently.

His ka became visible at once. "I told you we don't have to worry. Lord Khufu's ka is still trapped..."

"Never mind that now! Can you see Prince Menkaure's ka? He must be down there somewhere if the Prince has still got his tail."

Red's eyes went wide. "I can't talk to the ka of the *Crown Prince*!"

Senu sighed. They'd be in a lot of trouble, true. But they were in so much trouble already, it no longer seemed to matter. "Red! Just do it. Tell Prince Menkaure's ka to tell him to tell his father that Captain Nemheb's planning to rob Lord Khufu's pyramid and that he murdered Scribe Batahotep and has kidnapped a hemutiu girl called Reonet. That ought to do it."

Red stared in horror. "I can't tell him that!"

"Yes you can. Prince Menkaure's not dead, is he?

What's the problem? You do this, and you won't have to worry about Lord Khufu's ka."

Red glanced at the pyramid behind them and returned his gaze to the royal party. He grinned. "Look at him posing down there, the podgy little snob! This'll be fun!"

"Be polite, Red!" Senu called, suddenly worried. But his ka had already gone.

The royal party, including Prince Menkaure and the ox, had by this time disappeared into the river temple. The sapers guarding the temple, who had been very alert and correct as their Lord was carried passed, relaxed and leant on their spears. During the wait, the mertu who'd scrambled up the new pyramid for a better view sprawled on the stepped layers, chattering and laughing and sharing out gruel and bread. Judging by the smell and the flushed faces, some of the gruel had been fermented, but the Overseers turned a blind eye to this flaunting of site rules. The party mood spread to the sapers, who surreptitiously passed a jar of the fermented gruel down the lines. Meanwhile, the pyramid Overseer decided it would be a nice idea to have a "show team" lift a slab from the bottom of the ramps to the ninth layer, so that Lord Khafre could see how efficiently his pyramid was being built. Anxious it should all go smoothly with no hitches, he rushed about organizing a gang for each layer. For the crucial final lift to the top, he called for the Scorpions and was furious when it turned out that half their gang, including Gang-Chief Sobek himself, had mysteriously vanished.

Senu assumed they had gone to find some more fermented gruel and thought no more of it. He was too busy trying to see if Red had gone into the river temple after the Prince and worrying about Menkaure's reaction. When the royal party eventually emerged from the temple and began the slow climb to the site, he had eyes only for the chubby, ka-tailed figure puffing up the hill in the dust behind the throne, his golden collar and sandals glinting in the sun. Did that wary look in the Prince's eyes mean Red had already spoken to his ka? Was the Lord Khafre, with his fierce stare, even now on his way to arrest Senu and the Scorpions?

His heart thudded faster with every step the royal party took. But before the Lord of the Two Lands reached the pyramid, the throne was lowered on to a convenient rock. Servants erected a fringed canopy to shade Lord Khafre's head, while more servants waved fans of peacock feathers to keep their Lord cool. A detachment of sapers immediately surrounded the royal canopy, very stiff and alert. The women gave up singing and rattling their sistrums in favour of giggling behind their hands and casting sly glances at the sweaty mertu. The standard bearers stood proudly before the throne, flags snapping in the breeze.

Four of the five imakhu detached themselves from the royal party and strode to the base of the nearest ramp. Prince Menkaure followed, the wary look still in his eyes. Senu stiffened. But the Prince paid no attention to the audience on the pyramid as he poked the demonstration stone to see if it would move. The Overseer gave the Prince a furious look and rested a possessive hand on the stone as he explained the process to one of the imakhu.

Now they were closer, Senu saw the imakhu's staffs were topped by parts of the human head. The man the Overseer was talking to carried a golden ear. The "Ear" listened with a bored expression, staring off across the site.

The imakhu whose staff bore a pair of golden lips interrupted the Overseer with an imperious wave. "The Royal Mouth requests you get this nonsense over with as soon as possible," he declared in a voice almost as impressive as Sobek's. "Lord Khafre is hot and dusty and anxious to continue his tour."

"And the Royal Nose is not accustomed to such bad smells," sniffed the imakhu whose staff bore a golden nose.

The fourth imakhu, whose staff bore a huge golden eye, pushed the Prince out of the way and peered closely at the stone, testing the arrangement of ropes with one delicate finger. He climbed the ramp and peered dubiously up the layers, where the chosen gangs waited with their machines and levers.

"I wouldn't stand there if I were you, Royal Eye, sir!" said the nervous Overseer. "There have been accidents—"

"Accidents?" snapped the Royal Mouth. "You mean these clumsy mertu have dared drop one of Lord Khafre's stones?"

"N–not these particular men, sir!" the Overseer stammered, flustered now. He rushed across from the Royal Eye and bowed to the Royal Mouth, then evidently remembered he should be talking to the Royal Ear and turned in confusion to the first imakhu, who was still gazing across the site. "Just a precaution, you understand... er, Royal Ear sir?"

The Royal Mouth glanced from the Royal Ear to the motionless figure on the throne. With no change of expression, Lord Khafre flicked his flail. The Royal Mouth sighed and pulled Prince Menkaure to a safe distance. He waited until the Royal Eye was clear, banged his staff on the rock and announced, "The Royal Eye will observe this demonstration. Proceed!"

With much unnecessary whip cracking from their Gang Chief, the mertu on the ramp threw themselves against the ropes. The stone grated, creaked, and began to move. Senu looked again at the Prince. He was standing between the imakhu, watching the stone intently. He noted sweat on Menkaure's brow and experienced another flare of sympathy. Still no sign of his ka.

"*Red*," Senu hissed. "You've got to tell him before that stone gets to the top or he'll go back behind the White Wall and then it'll be too late!"

He wasn't as cautious as he usually was when talking to his ka. Everyone on the pyramid was craning over the edge, watching either the demonstration or the royal canopy where Lord Khafre still sat like a copper statue, fanned by his servants and fed wine-soaked dates from a golden plate by the Royal Tongue, who ate half of each date before placing the other half very carefully between his Lord's lips.

When an amused voice whispered in his ear, "Still talkin' to your ka, Red-Tail?" his heart missed a beat.

He whirled. "Gef!"

The boy looked as handsome as ever in his dusty, mertu way. His eye, trophy of their last meeting, had faded to a green tinge. He returned Senu's wary stare with a grin. "So what you been up to, then? Spyin' on the Lord Khafre today, huh?"

"Shh!" Senu looked round anxiously. But with the Lord of the Two Lands sitting on his throne barely ten paces away and the demonstration in progress, no one was interested in the conversation of two grubby water-boys.

"I can keep a secret, you know." Gef pulled Senu round the north side of the pyramid where it was quieter. "Despite what Sobek might think."

This reminded Senu that the Hawk gang had replaced Scorpions on the final layer. A vague sense of unease penetrated his worry over Red and the Prince. He gave Gef a suspicious look. "What are you doing back here? How come you knew about my heka?"

Gef sighed. "You hemutiu aren't the only ones who get it, you know. Used to have it myself – oh, not as strong as you!" he said, catching Senu's incredulous expression. "I cut my tail just as soon as I could. Father said I'd only get caught up in Temple politics otherwise, and us mertu have to work for a livin'. But that don't mean I can't remember what it was like. Reckon you're in some sort of trouble, Red-Tail. Thought you might appreciate some help."

Senu considered the boy, wondering if it were another trick. "Do you know where Sobek and your father have gone?" he asked.

"They're not here?" The boy looked round with a frown as Patep and Teti came racing round the pyramid, their eyes bright with joy.

"Hey, Gef!" They thumped him on the shoulder. "What you doin' back here? You back for good?"

Gef shook his head, still looking for the rest of the gang. "I ain't supposed to be here. But nobody's doin' a stroke of work with his High and Mightiness down there, so I thought I'd come over and check on you lot. Fifty lashes for talkin' to you if I'm caught." He grinned. "Chiefs must want to keep us separate fairly bad."

The other two looked uncertainly at Senu. "It's all right," Gef said. "He won't blab. We understand each other, don't we Red-Tail?"

Senu's shoulders relaxed a bit. Gef was probably one of the few people who *weren't* working for Nemheb. He peered over the edge, twisting his head to see the royal party. Prince Menkaure had gone back under the canopy, the blue ribbon in his ka-tail just visible in the shadows behind the throne.

Gef chuckled. "Red-Tail's spyin' on Lord Khafre."

"No I'm not! I—"

"You're lookin' in the wrong place, you know." Gef went on. "Somethin's goin' on over at old Khufu's Horizon. I just came from over that way. Lots of them black-skinned medjay creepin' around like they're goin' to ambush someone. Forget Lord po-face down there."

A chill shot through Senu. His head jerked up. He stared at the dazzling Horizon and back at Gef, remembering what Nemheb had said before he sent him back to the site and the way Sobek and the others had disappeared.

All at once, everything slotted into place as neatly and fatally as a trap in a pyramid. The sapers normally on guard duty at the Horizon had been called across to swell the ranks protecting Lord Khafre's party. The priests normally on duty in Lord Khufu's ka-temple had gone down the river temple to perform the sacrifice of the ox. Every eye was on the royal visitors. No one was paying any attention whatsoever to the finished pyramid behind them.

"Re's breath! I've been so *stupid*!" He drove his knuckles into the stone and leapt to his feet. "Of course they didn't go for more gruel! They're doing it now. *Right now!*"

Chapter 13

BETRAYAL

I am a crocodile immersed in dread, I am a crocodile who takes by robbery... (spell 88)

THE MERTU BOYS stared at Senu in confusion. On the other side of the pyramid, heads at the back of the crowd began to turn.

Gef moved first. He grabbed Senu's elbow with one hand and scooped up a discarded loaf with the other. He tore off a piece of bread and stuffed it into Senu's mouth, guiding him away from the curious looks they were getting. "Steady on, Red-Tail. Not so loud. *What* are they doin'?"

Senu choked and spat out the bread. "No time! Got to rescue Reonet!" But it had given his brain a chance to catch up. He couldn't hope to rescue her alone. He considered the three Scorpion boys, wondering how much to tell them.

"You know what my father and the other men are up to, don't you?" Gef demanded. "So tell!"

Senu decided to trust them. Casting anguished glances at Khufu's pyramid, he told the boys in breathless whispers. About Captain Nemheb. The robbery. Tefen. Reonet. Everything. Gef sat on his heels, quietly chewing a dirty nail as he listened, his handsome features still and his eyes fixed on Senu's face. The other two giggled nervously.

"Chief Sobek?" Patep spluttered when Senu had finished. "Robbing Khufu's 'orizon? Pull the other one!"

"It's true!" Senu said. "It's why I'm on the gang. I have heka. I'm supposed to lure Lord Khufu's ka out of his pyramid while the robbery takes place, only I can't because he's trapped somehow. I don't think Sobek and the other men know about that, and now Reonet's in there too. Nemheb's up to something bad, I know it! We've got to warn Sobek. Will you help me?"

The others snorted. But Gef frowned and took his nail out of his mouth. "I believe him."

The laughter stopped. The other two stared from Gef to Senu, re-evaluating, trying to work out if it was a joke.

Gef shook his head and whistled softly. "I *knew* something was up! Father's bin actin' real strange lately. He's hardly spoke a word to me since Red-Tail was off sick an' I got transferred. I just never guessed how serious it was!" He turned to Senu. "He's inside now, ain't he? With Sobek and the others?"

"I think so."

Gef's narrow eyes considered the pyramid. He said, "I think we should go over there."

"Why?" Teti said, looking alarmed.

"To make sure the men come out again, of course."

The reply was so matter of fact, it made Senu blink. "And Reonet," he reminded them.

Gef flashed him a grin. "Don't you worry about your girlfriend, Red-Tail. I seen her down at the temple. Lord Khufu's ka won't hurt a pretty thing like that."

Senu flushed and scrambled to his feet, fists clenched. Gef seized his arm and pulled him back. "You got to learn not to be so touchy, Red-Tail! We'll get her out, don't worry. I know a route over there where we won't be spotted, but see them sapers?" He pointed with his lump of bread at the line of royal guards who blocked the route to Lord Khufu's complex. "We got to be careful. Act natural, don't make any sudden moves. I'll go fetch the others. You get hold of some empty water jars. We'll bluff our way through."

As Patep and Teti rushed off to collect the jars, Senu shaded his eyes and considered the line of sapers. They stood as motionless as copper statues, sunlight glittering from their spearheads, their backs turned to Khufu's Parade. Heat shimmered over the pyramid complex. The imakhu graveyard and the area around the ka-temple looked deserted, but Senu couldn't stop thinking of the medjay Gef had seen. Were they across there even now, creeping in the shadows around the base of the Horizon with Reonet a prisoner in their midst? Of course, Nemheb could have sent them to help get the treasure out. But the cold feeling in his gut said otherwise.

"Red?" he whispered. "Red, come back! I need you."

Still no sign of his ka. He looked down at Lord Khafre's party. The canopy fluttered in the breeze. Dust blew across from the lifting machines. He saw the Royal Nose waft it away from his Lord. The ka-tailed Prince was sitting in the shade, eating his father's dates.

Gef returned with eight strong looking mertu lads in tow, all whispering excitedly. Patep and Teti handed out yokes and empty jars. The boys sat on the edge and quietly lowered themselves down the stepped layers. "C'mon, then!" Gef hissed, seeing Senu hesitate. "While everyone's still watchin' that stone."

It was all happening too fast. "Wait," Senu hissed back. "Red's not here yet."

"He'll have to catch up. We need you, Red-Tail!" Gef reached up and grabbed his ankle. It was either jump or fall. Senu elected to jump. In moments, he found himself at the bottom, running after the others towards the line of impassive guards. His heart thumped. But Gef pushed fearlessly between two of the sapers, swinging his yoke to bump their hastily lowered spears out of the way.

"Got to get more water for the demo!" he called. "Chief's orders. Can't hang about, bin told to run!" He set off at an angle that would take him close to the imakhu graveyard, jars clattering.

The sapers saw the group of dusty boys running after Gef as if they had whips at their heels and let them through, chuckling. "Run fast!" they called. "Or Lord Khafre will have your heads on spikes!"

Senu ran as fast as he could, his own jars bruising his knees and dust rasping in his throat. He was certain someone would raise the alarm. But the Overseer was too concerned with the most dangerous part of his demonstration to worry about disobedient water-boys and the sapers, content the boys posed no threat to their Lord, stayed in their ranks. No one noticed the boys duck off the path and slip between the obelisks that sprouted from the graveyard like tall stone fingers.

They pulled up in the shadow of Khufu's Parade, panting and chuckling. Gef flung his jars aside and felt his way along the larger than life carvings. "There's a way up by this hippo," he whispered. "When you're up top, make your way towards the pyramid. Keep your heads down, make no noise."

Senu had never been this close to Khufu's Parade before. The sheer size of the carvings along its walls and the brightness of the colours made him dizzy. But there was no time to stare. Someone boosted him up, and he found himself balanced on the back of a gigantic stone hippopotamus that bulged out of the side wall of the Parade. He followed Gef up and used the ear as a final step. At the top, a low wall ran along each side of the Parade to stop people from falling over the edge. One by one, the mertu boys pulled themselves over this parapet and dropped on to the smooth limestone road that joined Lord Khufu's river temple, far down in the valley, to his ka-temple in the shadow of the pyramid itself. Gef motioned for them to duck so their heads wouldn't show above the parapet. The back of Senu's neck prickled, half in excitement at being in a forbidden place, half terror that they'd be caught.

"What about the medjay?" he whispered. "What'll we do if they try to stop us?"

"Don't know till we get there, do we?" Gef's eyes were glittering. "You might 'ave to do some heka, Red-Tail."

"But I need my ka for that, and Red's—"

"*Shh!*" Patep hissed. "Just shut up an' follow."

Before he had a chance to think, Senu was bent double in a file of grinning mertu boys, running after Gef along the top of the Parade towards the gleaming eastern slope of the Horizon of Khufu. The other boys' eyes sparkled as if this were the greatest adventure they'd had in their lives. Senu's one hope was that Red had made contact, and Prince Menkaure had managed to talk to his father. What Lord Khafre would actually *do* about it was another matter and one he didn't like to dwell upon. But surely the greatest Lord the Two Lands had ever known would recognize the truth when he heard it?

They'd passed the imakhu graveyard and the small queen's pyramids were rising on their left, when the air in front of Senu suddenly shimmered. Already dizzy from the sunlight reflected off all the white stone, he missed his stride and Patep trod on his heels.

"Don't stop," hissed the boy. "If someone catches us up here, we're done for."

But Gef had stopped too. He peered cautiously over

both sides of the parapet. "Can't see anyone," he reported. "They must be round the back. Those steps lead down into the ka-temple, but the doors'll be locked so there's no point goin' down that way. Now, here's what we do..."

But Senu didn't hear Gef's plan. Even as he imagined Lord Khufu's ka raging up the flight of shadowy steps ahead of them, Red materialized and threw himself against Senu's chest with the strength of a storm wind.

"Go back! Get away from here! Oh Senu, this is bad, very bad. Lord Khafre *already knows*! The human with the snake's tongue told him!"

Before Senu could warn the others, there came a wild warbling cry from beyond the northern parapet and the desert on that side erupted with sand-devils.

What happened next was a confusion of swirling sand, shouts, and half-seen shadows running through the copper mist brandishing spears and clubs. From their vantage on the Parade, the boys saw everything. It seemed hundreds of sapers had been lying in wait on the apparently deserted north side of Khufu's pyramid. They'd dug shallow trenches in the sand, covered themselves with their cloaks and piled more sand on top, remaining absolutely still so they looked like part of the dune. Nemheb's medjay must have been sent to give the signal when the men came out. They had the pyramid surrounded in moments. At first it wasn't obvious where the Scorpions had made their entrance tunnel. But cries of alarm and horrible, fleshy thuds from the north side made it all too obvious. Senu thought he recognized Sobek's roar. Then a mertu, covered in dirt, came zigzagging round the corner of the pyramid, head down, arms pumping, pursued by two of Nemheb's medjay. Sapers closed in and levelled their spears. The fugitive slithered to a dismayed halt. The medjay caught up and beat him to the ground with their clubs.

Gef paled. "Father!" Before anyone could stop him, he'd leapt the parapet, landed in a spray of sand, righted himself and was running towards Adjedd's captors with stones in his fists. "Stop it!" he yelled, flinging the stones at the medjay. "Leave him *alone!*"

The sapers whirled in surprise and Gef's next stone hit one of them in the face. He raised a hand to his cheek and brought it away covered in blood. He stared at the blood, pointed his spear at Gef and snapped an order. Two sapers closed in on the boy and seized his arms. They flung him face down beside his father and bound his elbows tightly behind him.

"We got to help him!" Patep hissed, one leg already over the parapet. "C'mon!"

The other boys groaned. But they jumped down after Patep, stooping for stones which they threw with wild yells at the nearest sapers. Senu stayed crouched on the Parade, staring at the scene in horror. He saw Patep felled with a single blow and Teti's legs knocked from under him by a spear. The other boys fared little better. Fury and desperation were no match for an entire regiment of highly trained royal sapers.

"Run, stupid!" Red yelled, pushing at him so hard he almost sent him over the parapet. "Don't let them catch you, too!"

Senu gripped the stone, still expecting to see Reonet's turquoise clip amidst all the struggling, sandy flesh and falling clubs. It was too late to run, anyway. A pair of sapers, alerted by the other boys jumping down, had scrambled up the wall of the Parade and were advancing on him with amused grins. Two more raced up the steps from the ka-temple, trapping him in the middle.

"Too high for you, son?" said the leader, with an amused glance at his ka-tail. "What're you doing up here? Don't you know it's forbidden to set foot on the Lord Khufu's Parade – may his ka roam wherever it pleases – once his sahu has passed along it?"

Senu felt sick. He looked over the edge the way the others had gone. It was a high jump but the landing was soft.

He faced the sapers, heart banging. "I... er... I was only trying to get a better view of Lord Khafre..."

"Watch that boy!" one of the medjay shouted from below. "He's the one Captain Nemheb warned us about, the one who has heka."

The leading saper's amusement vanished. He pointed his spear at Senu. The other three did the same. Senu's stomach churned. He forced a little laugh and spread his hands. "Heka? *Me?*"

The sapers glanced at one another. Senu looked up at

the pyramid, sloping dizzily into the sun. He was close enough to see the glyphs chiselled at eye-height into the pink granite base and repeated around all four sides. He couldn't read all of them, but Batahotep had beaten the curse into his pupils year after year until they knew it off by heart.

I, Khufu, Lord of the Two Lands, made this tomb in a pure place where no one had a tomb, in order to protect the belongings of one who has gone to his ka. As for anyone who might enter the tomb unclean and intending to do evil, the Great One will judge against him.

"Red," he whispered. "If you can do anything, do it now. Open the world, or something, like you did in the tombs —"

"Quiet!" ordered the leading saper. "None of your spells!" He propped his spear against the wall and unwound a rope from his waist. He stepped towards Senu with a look of regret. "Sorry about this, son, but we don't want any trouble. Turn around."

Senu leapt for the top of the parapet, shut his eyes and jumped. He hit the sand in a whoosh of breath and a whirl of blue sky and white stone. He bounced to his feet, already running. Tattooed medjay dodged out of his path, wary of his heka. A line of sapers blocked his retreat to the river. Senu ran the other way, round the northeast corner of the pyramid where they'd dragged Gef and Adjedd and the other captives.

The Scorpions had dug their tunnel in the side of one of the unused boat pits. The pit was surrounded by bristling spears. It was a well laid trap. Caught red-handed, the men who'd been into the pyramid and crawled out again with their sacks of treasure had no way to run except back inside. Most of them had already surrendered their sacks to Nemheb's medjay, hopeless looks in their eyes.

The medjay clubbed them anyway, beating them to the ground so the sapers could tie their elbows behind them. The sapers seemed wary of Sobek, who was bigger than most of them and had a knife in his hand and a furious glint in his eye. But by sheer force of numbers, they disarmed him and tied his elbows too. Then two medjay set about beating him, swinging their clubs at his unprotected body with a cold, methodical efficiency that made Senu's stomach churn. Gef yelled and kicked and spat in his captors' faces, but they lifted him between them and flung him into the pit, too. Most of the mertu boys had now been caught and were thrown down also. The treasure was being piled at the edge, a huge mound of gold that made the rough sides of the pit glow, reflected up the northern slope of the Horizon and lit the faces of the men.

Senu's gaze flew from captive to captive, his heart in his throat. But Reonet wasn't among them.

He dodged another saper, ran to the edge and slithered down. His ka rippled into the pit with him and tried to push him back up. "What are you *doing*?" he hissed. "Get out, or your head'll be on a spike with the rest of them when Lord Khafre gets here!"

Senu set his jaw. "I've got to find Reonet."

The pit was filled with golden shadows and groaning men. The pyramid soared overhead, piercing the sky. Senu had never felt so small and helpless. Gef stared up at him, one eye swollen shut, the other very dark. The way they'd tied his elbows pinched the skin. "Reonet's inside," Senu gasped as he ran past. "Got to get her out." The eye flickered – was it approval? In the shadows at the far side of the pit, Sobek was a motionless heap of blood and bruises. He hoped the big Gang-Chief was still alive. The medjay, who were busy retrieving the last of the treasure from the prisoners, didn't notice Senu at first. But as he dodged towards the pyramid, a black hand closed on his arm.

"Don't touch that boy!" someone yelled. "He's got heka!" The medjay's grip loosened and Senu twisted free.

The mouth of the tunnel lay ahead. It was small and rough and led down steeply under the pyramid. Senu plunged into darkness that smelt of men's sweat and something burnt. He took ten stumbling steps into the unknown, his shoulders brushing the low roof, before he stopped. Sweat broke out all over his body. It was no good, he couldn't do it. A medjay's shadow already blocked the entrance. Any moment now, he'd come in after him and drag him out.

"I'm sorry, Reonet," he whispered.

Then a familiar, clipped voice called from the edge of the pit. "Don't bother chasing the boy! He can't do any damage in there. I'll get him out later."

Senu stiffened.

"Have you retrieved all the gold the traitors stole from Lord Khufu?" the voice continued. "Good! Get a ladder over here. I want to inspect it before Lord Khafre arrives, make sure nothing's missing. You can't trust these mertu. One of them might have swallowed something. They'll need to be properly searched. The priests have a method. Painful, I believe, but scum who dare violate their Lord's pyramid deserve to suffer before they die."

Senu clenched his fists, tears in his eyes. "*Nemheb!*" he hissed. "I bet he meant to betray us right from the start!"

"Humans are unpredictable," Red agreed, hovering like a flame against the light at the end of the tunnel.

Senu took a deep breath and faced the dark. "Red?" he whispered. "Can you ask Moon where Reonet is?"

His ka shook his head.

Senu bit his lip. "Then we'll just have to search the whole pyramid."

He didn't think things could get much worse. But as he put his fingertips against the rough walls and took a hesitant step into the dark, there was an ominous rumble behind and the last of the light vanished in a choking mass of dust and falling rubble.

"No!" he screamed, whirling in the confined space.

Red pulled him back, his hands almost solid. "No, Senu! Not that way! You'll be crushed!"

In terror, Senu folded his arms over his head. He

didn't move until the echoes had died away, leaving a thick, black silence that wrapped itself around him as tightly as the medjay's hippopotamus skin. A terrible coldness entered his heart.

"I'm still here," Red said, pressing against him in the dark like a real person. "You're not alone. They'll dig you out again, you'll see."

But Senu, surrounded by the absolute blackness of Lord Khufu's tomb, could not think of a single reason why anyone should.

Chapter 14

KA-DOOR
...I have come forth from the horizon against my foe.
(spell 11)

SENU WASN'T SURE how long he crouched, sweating, in the dark. Plenty of time to have nightmares about Lord Khufu's ka breaking out of his sarcophagus and roaring up the tunnel to avenge the violation of his tomb. He was aware of every single stone resting above him, a massive weight that made his ears hum. Then another trickle of dirt fell from the tunnel roof, reminding him of more immediate dangers. He shook the hum from his head and forced himself to crawl deeper into the pyramid.

Red stayed close. "I could go and talk to Prince Menkaure's ka again," he offered.

Senu's stomach clenched. "No! Don't leave me!"

"He might be able to help. Get his father to open the official entrance."

"Nemheb'll stop it somehow."

Red sighed. "Yes, I expect so."

Eventually the tunnel levelled out. At the same time, Senu realized he could see lumps of rock ahead, glimmering faintly blue. Air moved somewhere, bringing another whiff of the burnt odour. His heart leapt. Without stopping to consider how there could possibly be a way out beneath the centre of the pyramid, he crawled faster. The blue light brightened and something feathery brushed the back of his skull. He let out a little scream, then laughed in relief. It was only the frayed end of a dangling rope, hanging down a vertical shaft surrounded by that eerie blue mist. Sobek must have been in too much of a hurry to retrieve it.

Refusing to let himself think about what might be making the blue light, Senu used the rope to haul himself up. The shaft was narrow enough to brace his feet against the walls, so it wasn't as hard to climb as he'd feared. The rope ended in a high, sloping passage down which the blue light poured like water. A second, level passage led straight ahead into darkness. All the hairs on Senu's neck rose. He crouched at the junction, listening. The hum was louder here, drowning the thump of his heart.

"Reonet?" he whispered.

"*Reee...onnn...ettt...*" came the echo, repeated strangely as if the chamber beyond were full of ghosts mocking him.

He shuddered and hurried past the dark entrance. The

light was coming from behind a massive granite slab at the top of the slope that blocked the end of the passage but didn't quite reach the floor. The gap looked large enough for a child to squeeze through. Senu crouched and put his mouth to the gap. "Reonet?"

Muffled echoes bounced off unseen walls and came back jumbled. *"Reee...onnn... Reee...onnn...ettt."* Followed by a sound that made Senu's skin prickle. A chink of metal on stone.

"It's Lord Khufu's ka!" He scrambled away from the slab, looking for some way to close it, even if it meant cutting off the light. Then he broke into a cold sweat. He'd forgotten. Granite was no barrier to kas.

"It's all right," whispered Red. "He's not in there any more."

Senu frowned. "I thought you said he was trapped?"

"He is... but not in the sarcophagus any more." Red's tone was puzzled.

Senu's heart pounded. He stared at the slab. "Then who's in there, Red? What's that burnt smell? *And what's making that light?*"

"Human?" His ka shivered, still sounding confused. "Hurt?"

Senu hadn't thought of that. The chink of metal... "That snake Nemheb's chained her in here to die!" Not stopping to consider what might happen if the stone settled when he was halfway through, he wriggled under the granite. It was thicker than he'd thought. Beyond the first slab was a second, and beyond that a third, slightly lower than the other two. His shoulders got stuck. Skin scraped painfully as he dragged his way through. Still sweating, he rose into a defensive crouch.

And stared.

He was inside a rectangular chamber with polished walls gleaming purple in the strange light. Piled against the walls, as if he'd worked his way into the stomach of some enormous metal-eating beast, was gold. So much gold! Chests had been forced open and their contents spilled across the floor. Delicate necklaces, heavy formal collars, armbands, anklets, hair pieces, jars, plates, statues... fiery rubies and rare emeralds larger than Senu's fist... all glimmering eerily in the light which spilled out of the granite sarcophagus in the centre.

"Careful!" Red warned, appearing beside him.

With an extra thump of his heart, Senu saw the lid of the sarcophagus had been slid askew. Soot blackened the opening. Inside, someone was moaning.

He rushed over without thinking. "Reonet!"

But of course it wasn't her. Even before he saw the stunted legs and wrinkled body squeezed in beside the sahu, he knew.

"P–Pehsukher?"

The dwarf's mutilated hand snaked out and seized Senu's wrist. There were peculiar burn marks on his arm – four curved, smoking indentations licked by blue fire. "Where is it?" Pehsukher rasped, ending in a cough.

Senu's stomach heaved as he realized what the burnt smell was. He averted his eyes from the dwarf's roasting flesh. "Where's Reonet?" he whispered. "What have you done to her?"

"Who took it?"

"*Where's Reonet?*" Senu insisted, still trying to prize the dwarf's fingers off his arm. Inside the sarcophagus, he caught a glimpse of Lord Khufu's sahu. The bandages about its neck had been ripped loose.

"Got to get it back..." Pehsukher mumbled. "...didn't know..."

"WHERE'S REONET?" Senu shouted, tearing free at last. His own arm had begun to burn where the fire had touched it. He clasped it to his chest and stared at the dwarf, panting with fear and anger.

At last, Pehsukher seemed to hear. He dragged himself out of the sarcophagus and slid to the floor. He leant his head against the granite and frowned at Senu in his creepy, blind way. "What are *you* doing in here, boy? Didn't I warn you to stay away? Get out while you can!"

"I can't get out! I wish I could! The tunnel collapsed. The sapers arrested everyone. Nemheb betrayed us. And Reonet's still in here somewhere—" He choked on a frustrated sob.

The chamber dimmed as the fire licking the dwarf's arm faded. He sighed. "Your friend's not here. I'm afraid Nemheb lied to you."

"Maybe she's still in the Blind Room at Nemheb's house?" Red said in a small voice. "That might explain why Moon can't find her."

Fury at his own stupidity banished some of Senu's fear. He kicked a golden jug, sending it bouncing off the far wall. Plates and goblets rattled down.

Pehsukher's head turned at the noise. "Sounds like the others left in a hurry," he said, clutching his burning arm. "Must have given them quite a scare when I got knocked out like that. Did you see the treasure they took out of the pyramid?"

"Yes, but—"

The dwarf leant forward. "Was there a little beetle on a chain? About so big? Carved with spells underneath? Glowing blue eyes?"

Senu started to shake his head, thinking the dwarf had gone crazy. Then he turned cold. "A beetle... you mean a scarab, don't you?"

A grim nod. "Did Nemheb take anything from the prisoners?"

"I didn't see... but he was checking the treasure. He said he wanted to check it was all there before Lord Khafre arrived."

Pehsukher sighed again. "Then I think we have to assume Nemheb's got it. If only I'd been more careful, checked before I unwrapped it... Nemheb's wanted one ever since he realized the power it would give him. When he discovered a temple scarab had been buried with Lord Khufu, the temptation was just too great. Neither of us suspected it might still be in use. It's my fault, I should have checked." He closed his eyes with a little moan.

A lot of things suddenly fell into place. Senu stared

across the burial chamber, where Red was rippling curiously through all the gold. "So *that's* what Nemheb wanted all along. This whole thing, just for a stupid amulet!"

At this, the dwarf roused himself. He had another bout of coughing. When he spoke, blood flecked his chin. "Not just an amulet, unfortunately. The trapped ka managed to hit me even through the spells." He touched the marks on his arm and winced. "It's very, very angry. I suspect its power is spent for now, but if that amulet's ever opened..." He shook his head. "I wonder whose ka it is, the poor thing. To be buried in a pyramid, never to be released!"

"The royal ka," Senu whispered.

Pehsukher stiffened. "*What did you say?*"

"It's Lord Khufu's ka. The kas of the dead tried to warn me six years ago that the Great One was trapped, only Red kept making me forget what they said. I didn't remember until last night in Nemheb's Blind Room when Red wasn't there to stop the nightmare, and then I was too upset to realize what they meant... But when she was in the river temple, Reonet overheard the priests talking about a royal ka trapped inside a temple scarab. She thought they meant Lord Khafre's, only they didn't mean anyone living after all! It's got to be Lord Khufu's. Red's known all along that his ka was trapped in the sarcophagus, only he didn't understand how. At least he can't attack us if he's not here any more." He tried a smile, then looked at the marks on Pehsukher's arm and felt ill again.

The old dwarf whistled through his teeth. "Re's breath! If that ka ever gets out, it'll rip the Two Lands apart trying to find the human who dared trap it! But that's not the worst of it. Once Nemheb finds out the scarab is occupied, he'll probably try to force it open. There's a rumour spread by those who oppose the temples that the spells can be broken by offering a free ka as a sacrifice. It's nonsense, of course, but that won't stop Nemheb trying and you said he still had your friend..."

Senu stared at the dwarf in horror. "Sacrifice?" he whispered. "You mean he's going to sacrifice *Moon*? But that'll kill Reonet! We have to stop him!"

Pehsukher grunted. "Yes, you do, and quickly." More coughs drained the blood from his face as he dragged himself to his feet and lurched across the burial chamber. He felt his way to the gap under the slabs and cursed. "Sobek jammed the mechanism, but the stones are sinking. You've got to find Nemheb and get that scarab off him before he manages to open it. Take it to *sem*-priest Ankhsheshonq at the Temple of the Sun. He'll know what to do. Quickly, this way, before the gap closes."

Senu scrambled after him, his heart starting up again at the thought of being trapped inside the burial chamber. Not that it mattered which part of the pyramid they were trapped in since they couldn't get out, anyway. "Are we going to dig our way out with one of Lord Khufu's golden bracelets?" he said. "Or should we just walk out through the wall like Red does?" He managed a little laugh. It emerged high-pitched and made his head spin.

The dwarf was already squeezing under the slabs, so his voice was muffled. "The wall's quickest. You're going to need some help, though."

"Don't listen to him," Red said in a strange voice. "It's not safe."

Senu squeezed after Pehsukher, wondering if he'd heard right. "What did you say?"

"I said the wall's quickest." As they stumbled down the sloping passage, the dwarf went on calmly, "I almost got through it once, but I lost my ka because my mind had grown old and inflexible. Nemheb thought if I could get in here using the ka-tunnel, it'd be a lot easier than organizing a robbery. I was stupid to agree and we failed. But I could have done it when I was your age, no trouble. The spells on the ka-door in the temple are good ones, and I'll help you all I can. The first door's in here—

They'd come to the small level passage. With Pehsukher's burning arm acting as a lamp, it was no longer dark. Blue light licked the stones. The hum, that had eased off while he was in the burial chamber, increased.

Senu hung back. "What's in there?" he whispered.

"I told you, the first ka-door. This is the heart of the pyramid. You hear it, don't you? That's the heka working. People like us awaken it in places of power like this, whether we want to or not."

At least he didn't try telling Senu he was lucky.

The chamber was empty except for a large niche in the eastern wall, surrounded by an archway of gold engraved with spells that glinted blue as Pehsukher pulled Senu nearer. Beyond the arch lay shadow, but there was enough light to see that the back of the niche was solid stone.

"The tunnel slopes downwards and brings you out in the ka-temple," Pehsukher said. "You shouldn't have too much of a problem. The heka's strong in you and your ka is young."

Senu stared at the spells, skin prickling. The dwarf, he realized, was deadly serious.

"No!" Red rippled in front of him and pushed at his chest with remarkably solid hands. "It's dangerous!"

Senu frowned. *A way out.* "Red... if you knew this was possible, why didn't you tell me before?" His words emerged sharper than he had intended, full of his desperate need to find Reonet before Nemheb hurt her.

To his surprise, his ka didn't vanish or sulk. He hung his head like a boy being told off by old Batahotep. "Please, Senu. Don't make me do it. I'm scared I'll lose you."

"I'm scared too. But we have to try."

He straightened his shoulders and faced the golden arch. "What do I do?"

Pehsukher smiled. Even as he'd done outside the

hemutiu tombs on the first night of Akhet, he reached up and placed his knobbly finger to Senu's forehead. A shock rippled from Senu's scalp to his toes. He flinched, expecting to faint as he had before. But this time it was the dwarf who slumped to the floor. "Go!" he gasped. "Go now!"

Senu reached for the dwarf's hand, but Pehsukher shook his head. "The next time I cross the boundary between worlds, I won't be coming back. I've given you the last of my power. Go!"

Senu looked helplessly at the shadows beyond the arch. "But I don't know how to use the spells..."

Pehsukher convulsed, let out a final moan and lay still. The burns on his arm dimmed and cooled. The chamber darkened.

"No!" Senu fell to his knees beside the dwarf. "You're supposed to teach me! Don't die, please don't die! I don't know what to do!"

"All you have to do is believe," said a gentle voice inside his head. "Go with your ka, boy. Hold on tight... don't let go of each other... you'll be all right."

"The small human's ka has come back," Red whispered. "Listen to him."

Senu stood very still as Red gripped his hands in his ghostly ones. He began to glow. The blue fire spread like cool water up his arms, into his heart, down his legs, until he could no longer feel the floor. Very slowly, Red began to walk backwards into the niche, pulling him towards the wall at the back. His ka's grip tightened as they drew closer. Then Red rippled into the stone and Senu tugged back in sudden panic.

"Close your eyes," Pehsukher's ka advised. "Hold on to your ka's wrists. Pretend he's human. Pretend you're walking through air, not stone. *Believe*, Senu. It's what this place was built for. You can do it... can do it... do it..."

Senu closed his eyes. The fear vanished. His ka's wrists were as solid as a human's. The stone under his feet softened and shifted like sand. There was light, blue-green and very bright, shining on the other side of his eyelids. He walked forwards, further than the back of the niche. There was a moment of silence. Then an enormous, thick door whispered open before him. Red gently drew him through, and the door swung shut behind them. The strangest thing was that although Senu still had his eyes shut, he seemed to be walking along an avenue of palm trees swaying in a warm breeze with the river flowing beside him and green fields stretching as far as the eye could see. People working in the fields waved. Small children ran alongside him, pointing at his ka-tail and giggling in delight. Under the trees, strange half-human creatures lay in the shade. A winged shadow much bigger than any bird flew across the sun.

Senu hesitated, curious to see what it was. But Red tugged him onwards to a second huge door that whispered open like the first one had, the spells on its other side shining blue. Before he was ready, it closed with a soft thud. The air turned chill, there was a whiff of incense, and his ka's wrists became insubstantial again. He grabbed for them, lost his balance and sat down in a bowl of dates.

He opened his eyes, blinked round the deserted ka-temple with its rows of silent columns, and turned to stare at the wall behind him. The ka-door was there, just as his father had described, painted in spells on the solid wall. He realized he was sitting on one of the offerings left by the priests for Lord Khufu's ka. He picked up a date, put in back in the bowl, then began to tremble uncontrollably.

"We just... I... you..."

"We did it." His ka sounded tired, but triumphant. "We're still together."

Senu looked at the doors and heard a saper call outside. He shook himself. "We've got to get out of here, Red!"

His ka grinned. "Don't panic. The humans with spears are guarding the tunnel, not the temple. I'll help you get to the house of the human with the snake's tongue. But if he's opened the priest-charm, you're on your own. I'm not going near any dead Lord's furious escaped ka, no matter what you say."

Chapter 15

TEMPLE SCARAB
The clouded eyes of the Great One have fallen on you... (spell 35)

AFTER THE TERROR and wonder of his journey through the ka-tunnel, getting to Nemheb's house seemed a small thing, though if Senu had stopped to think about it he could have been caught a hundred times. Night had fallen while he'd been inside the pyramid, and the site was crawling with sapers. But Red went ahead to spy on the guards and the doors of the ka-temple opened easily from the inside. In moments, Senu was racing down the starlit Parade to the river temple. He stole one of the canoes moored between the feet of Lord Khufu's statues, crossed the flood with none of the difficulties he'd experienced before, and kept to the reeds under the far bank as he paddled upstream. Some of the guards shouted after him as he struck across the open water but nobody gave chase.

He'd abandoned the canoe, raced past three of Nemheb's medjay, dodged through an open door, and stopped to catch his breath in a corridor with blue tiles underfoot, before he started to wonder at the ease of his escape.

"Why doesn't anyone try to stop me, Red?" he panted.

His ka, still glowing blue, mumbled about heka, contamination from the Land of Dreams and something complicated about the spells on the ka-doors.

Senu shook his head. "Never mind – we've got to find Reonet. Where's Nemheb?"

His ka pointed silently. Nemheb's servants stared as Senu ran through the corridors. A few shouted for him to stop but they seemed afraid to touch him, shrinking against the walls as he raced past. One silly woman dropped her tray. Jugs and goblets rattled across the corridor, tripping Senu so he couldn't avoid staggering into her. He righted himself and hurried after Red. Behind him, the servant clawed at her skin and screamed.

There was no time to wonder what she was so scared of. They descended some steps to an underground corridor lit by flaming brands. Two black-skinned medjay with folded arms stood in front of a closed door.

Red rippled unseen between them, vanished through the door and came out again shuddering. "He's got the priest-charm in there," the ka whispered. "Be careful, Senu!"

Senu slithered to a halt. The medjay started and grabbed their spears.

"Let me through!" His voice startled him, emerging deeper than it ever had before. His heart banged. But he'd been so scared in the pyramid, the two Kush warriors with their tattooed cheeks seemed no more frightening than kittens trying to be fierce.

The two medjay stared at him in disbelief.

"It's *important*," Senu said. "Captain Nemheb's expecting me."

The tallest guard recovered first. "Master said we're not to open this door for anyone."

"Oh, I know all about the temple scarab." Senu folded his arms and raised his chin so he could look the medjay in the eye. "He'll be furious if you don't tell him I'm here."

They glanced at each other uncertainly. "He's got the priest-fire," whispered the other.

"Master didn't say anything about a boy."

"Want to risk it? You watch him while I go in."

The tall medjay still looked doubtful, but pointed his spear at Senu and nodded. The other guard opened the door. Bitter red smoke curled into the passage, making Senu's eyes sting. The light beyond was thick crimson, the colour of blood. An ominous chanting broke off when the door opened. Nemheb's clipped voice called, "I thought I told you I didn't want to be disturbed! This had better be important."

The spear in front of Senu wavered as the smoke made the tall medjay sneeze. Senu ducked under the shaft and was through the door before anyone could stop him, Red close on his heels. His ka was still glowing blue. So were the backs of Senu's hands. Beginning to suspect why everyone was so wary of him, he covered his nose and stared in trepidation round the underground chamber.

Nemheb stood before a granite altar, every scrap of the red stone carved with spells. Incense burners in the shape of hands hung on chains from the ceiling, pouring out that choking red smoke. Lamps had been placed in a circle on the floor where they glowed like orange stars in a sand storm. Nemheb's bare chest gleamed with sweat. Around his neck, on a thick golden chain, hung the scarab amulet the dwarf had described. Its wings were red but its eyes shone bright blue. Nemheb had been in the process of trying to open it with a pin. There was no sign of Reonet.

Senu hesitated.

Nemheb's kohl-lined eyes widened. "How did you get out?" he whispered.

"Tell him you used the ka-tunnel," Red said.

"I used the ka-tunnel, of course," Senu said.

Nemheb's face drained of blood. "It's not possible... even Pehsukher couldn't..." Something flickered behind his eyes and he put the pin down. He smiled at the medjay, who'd rushed in behind Senu but stopped at the sight of their Master working spells. "Leave us," he told them. "Bar the door on the outside. No one goes in or out of this room until I call you."

When the guards had gone, Nemheb smiled again and came around the altar. He dropped an arm across Senu's shoulders. "So. You've got stronger heka than that useless old dwarf of mine? Perfect. I assume he was the one who told you how to use the tunnel? Seems Sobek was hasty in thinking him so easily killed, but we don't need old Pehsukher any more. You'll be well rewarded if you help me, Senu. You can start by opening this little amulet. It's a real nuisance, but I just can't seem to get the trick of it..."

Senu twisted out of his embrace and dodged round the granite slab. "Where's Reonet?" he demanded. "What have you done to her? Do you really think I'm going to help you after the way you betrayed everyone and left me sealed in the pyramid like that?"

Nemheb frowned. "Now, now, don't let's get over excited. You're fresh from using your heka, and that always put old Pehsukher in a terrible mood, too. Couldn't let the sapers arrest you could I? I was going to dig you out of the Horizon just as soon as I got a chance."

"The same way you were going to bring my father back from Khnum's Cataract?" Senu glared at him. "And help the mertu families by giving them their share of the gold?"

Nemheb's lips tightened. "You really ought to be more grateful after all I've done for you, hiding your power from the priests and awakening your heka so successfully. If it hadn't been for me, you wouldn't have been able to use that ka-tunnel, remember."

"If it hadn't been for you, I wouldn't have been in the pyramid in the first place!"

Nemheb sighed. "All right, if you want to play this the hard way, I'll tell you why you should help me." His tone hardened. "Because if you don't open this scarab right now, I'll have your precious girlfriend killed. It'll take but a single order to those medjay waiting outside."

"Don't open it!" Red whispered urgently.

A shiver ran down Senu's spine. But at least he knew Reonet was still alive. "I don't know how," he said to gain time while he decided what to do next.

Nemheb scowled. "Don't give me that! With heka as strong as yours, you can do anything. Just don't try spreading any more evil rumours about me." He shook his head. "You're so stupid, Senu! Did you really think the *Crown Prince* would listen to an insignificant hemutiu ka-baby like you? Now let's be sensible, shall we? Open this for me, and I'll let your friend live. In fact, she and her ka can help us test it." His lips curved into a cruel smile.

Senu clenched his fists. The scarab's glowing eyes drew his gaze. Blue. Burning. Angry. And Nemheb wanted it *opened*? Then he realized. Nemheb not only had no idea what it contained, he still thought it was empty. He obviously believed it had jammed shut during the robbery and could be opened without danger.

Senu's heart beat faster as he saw the opportunity to play the trick to beat all tricks.

He hung his head to hide his expression. "Please sir," he said in a trembling little voice. "Don't do that to Reonet."

Nemheb's eyes narrowed. "So you do care about her? I was beginning to wonder, after that trick you played with the mertu boys. How sweet. All right, if you open this for me, I'll consider keeping her here. She can serve you while you serve me. You'd like that, maybe?"

Senu could just imagine Reonet's reaction to *that*. But he hid his disgust and managed a small grin. Nemheb chuckled and raised a hand to the chain around his neck.

"No, keep it on, sir... I, er, don't need to touch it. Red'll open it. Won't you, Red?" He turned to his ka, who was rippling wildly and shaking his head in horror.

"Have you gone crazy? You heard the small human! We've got to take it to the *sem*-priest so it can be opened safely."

"Can you open it or not?"

His ka shivered again. "I... maybe."

"Then do it. Otherwise Nemheb will hurt Reonet, and then we'll have to do it anyway."

Nemheb's cruel smile widened. He was only hearing Senu's half of the conversation, and he liked what he heard. Senu searched for something that would let Red know what he had in mind. "Red?" he whispered. "Remember the curse? The Great One should know the whole truth."

Red stared at him. "You want me to tell Lord Khufu's ka whose idea it was to rob the pyramid, don't you?"

Senu nodded, trying to look defeated. "We haven't any choice."

His ka looked at the scarab about Nemheb's neck and gave a weak grin. "All right. It might work. But get ready to run."

Red floated across the room. Whispering under his breath, he reached his ghostly fingers towards the scarab. Senu met Nemheb's gaze across the blood-red granite, letting all his hatred show.

The Captain smiled. "I know you hate me, Senu," he said. "Pehsukher did in the end, too. But I need someone with heka working for me, and you don't have to like me to enjoy the proceeds of our work. I can help your family and friends. I'm sure when you've had time to think about it, you'll realize your co-operation is the best thing for everyone—"

He never found out what lies Nemheb would have told next. There was a sigh as if the air had settled. In perfect silence, glittering redly in the smoke, the wings of the scarab unfolded.

"Duck!" Red cried, diving into the floor.

Senu crouched behind the altar and covered his head with his arms. There was a loud roar that made his ears ring and the whole room filled with blinding blue light. Nemheb began to scream.

A great wind roared around the walls, tugging at Senu's ka-tail and extinguishing the lamps. He caught glimpses of claws the size of canoes... vast blue wings like pieces of the sky... a long scaled tail... The light brightened until he could see it even with his face pressed to the stone and his eyes squeezed shut. Nemheb's scream went on and on, as the wind whirled faster and the terrible light blazed. Dust and chunks of plaster fell from the ceiling. Then, abruptly, the scream stopped.

Warily, Senu opened one eye. Blue feathers spiralled down and settled softly on the smoking altar. More plaster fell on top of them. Nemheb was nowhere in sight.

The door crashed open and the medjay rushed in. They took one look at the carnage and fled, yelling. Screams spread throughout the house. Still trembling, Senu dragged himself to his knees and peered over the altar. A smoking patch on the floor, licked by blue flames, showed where Nemheb had stood. The scarab amulet lay in the fire, its chain still fastened but its wings broken.

For a moment he couldn't move. Then another chunk of the ceiling collapsed and Red rippled out of the floor, pushing at him with his ghostly hands. "Run!"

Senu didn't need telling twice. Wrapping a strip of his loincloth around his hand to protect it from the flames, he snatched up the broken amulet and darted out the door to join the medjay and servants fleeing through the falling masonry. Elbows caught him in the eye, bodies shoved at him, walls and columns collapsed all around. He was halfway up the steps to the ground floor before he remembered.

"Reonet!" He looked at the falling bricks in despair.

"This way!" his ka said, surprising him.

"But how..?"

"Moon says she's down here. Quick!"

Senu didn't waste time asking for an explanation. He fought his way out of the panicking crowd and followed Red down some more steps into another underground corridor where he experienced a sickening jolt of recognition. "This is where he kept me! She was right next to me all the time, and I never knew."

"Hurry!"

Part of the roof had collapsed. Dust showered into his ka-tail as he clambered over the pile of rubble, coughing and choking. Moonlight streamed through the hole, lighting the way. He raced to the door Red indicated. His ka went straight through and came out again. "She's in there! But she's asleep! Oh, quick Senu!"

Asleep? Through all this? Senu's stomach churned uncomfortably. In the confusion, might his ka have mistaken death for sleep? He unbarred the door and wrenched it open.

Reonet was curled in one corner with her cheek pressed to the spells. Her hair fell in greasy tangles across her eyes and she had blood on her fingers. She blinked sleepily at the light. "Moon..?" Then she recognized him and gave a shaky smile. "Senu! I knew you'd come."

He put his arms around her. He didn't care what she thought or how much Red teased him afterwards. He squeezed her tightly, tears running down his cheeks. "I thought you were dead! Nemheb tried to seal me in the pyramid, but Pehsukher told me how to use the ka-doors and Red got me out... Lord Khufu's ka killed

Nemheb... you should have heard him scream... blue feathers everywhere... but Gef and Sobek and the others got arrested! They'll be taken behind the White Wall and put on spikes... all my fault... we've got to help them..."

"...so hungry..." Reonet was crying too. "So hungry, Senu... I thought Moon would never come. I broke my clip... my turquoise fish-clip... it used to be Mother's, you know. But Moon came back! She came when I needed her, she came..."

As Senu peered at the walls, wondering how Moon had seen through the spells, another chunk of the corridor collapsed.

"No time!" Red interrupted them, tugging Senu's ka-tail. "You've both got to get out of here. Right now!"

Outside, they found more chaos. The servants who had fled the house were shivering in Nemheb's garden, staring dazedly at a great coil of blue wind that was sucking up into the sky rubble, bricks, painted plaster, pots, plates, goblets, expensive linen kilts, and everything else Nemheb's house had contained. The wind whirled the debris round and round, higher and higher, then started to spit the objects out again. The dazed looks on the blue-lit faces changed to fear. People screamed and ran for the river with their arms over their heads. Some jumped into the water, others into boats and canoes. Because they were too panicky to rig the sails, most fled downstream with the current. But when they reached the bend that marked the boundary of Nemheb's estate, the boats turned round, their occupants struggling to get the sails up, shouting and pointing behind them.

Reonet had managed to snatch a jug of gruel on their way out of the house. She gulped hungrily as they ran, the thick, dark liquid spilling out of her mouth and staining her dress. It must have been fermented, because her eyes burned very bright and she hiccuped as they raced for the last of boats. But as they skidded down the bank, an unnatural wind blasted upriver, bending the palm trees and creating moonlit waves on the dark water. A great rushing and creaking noise was coming out of the night, accompanied by the roars of hippopotamus and cries of woken geese. All the hairs on the back of Senu's neck stood on end. "Reonet! Stop! Something's wrong."

"It's the ka-wind!" Red shouted in his ear. "They know the truth now, and their humans are coming."

At first Senu didn't understand. Then he saw them. Racing upriver, using the entire width of the flood, came the black silhouettes of hundreds of sails. Great lumbering barges that usually ferried stone to the building site, elegant sailing craft owned by the Overseers and scribes, reed canoes fitted with makeshift sails to catch the ka-wind... crammed into these vessels was what looked to be the entire work force of the Place of Truth. Mertu rubbed shoulders with hemutiu, men with their wives, ka-tailed babies with older children, scribes with Gang-Chiefs.

"They've gone on strike!" Reonet said, her eyes still wild. She tossed the empty jug away. "C'mon! We'll catch that wind if we're quick!"

Senu shook his head, still half expecting to wake up on his mat with the lamp burning beside him and Red telling him it was all just a bad dream. The blue coil had died down behind them, but everything still felt unreal.

Reonet seized his hand and dragged him to the nearest landing stage, where she snatched the tether of a small boat from under the nose of a frightened servant. "Important business at the Palace!" she announced, but ruined the effect by giggling hysterically.

The man looked ready to fight her for the boat. Then his eye fell on Senu and he backed away, clutching the amulets he wore and muttering a prayer.

"What's wrong with everyone?" Senu shouted. "Why do they keep looking at me like that?"

"You are an idiot, aren't you?" Reonet scrambled into the boat and hoisted the sail with another hiccup. "Do you think you can use a ka-door and come back the same?"

"But I haven't changed."

She shook her head. "Still stupid, maybe. Hurry up and get in! I can't hold it against this wind much longer."

Senu glanced uncertainly at the speeding armada. "I think I'd better get back home. Mother will be frantic, and—"

Reonet grabbed his wrist and pulled him into the boat. "Do you want to get your father back, or don't you?" she said. "This is your one chance to speak to Lord Khafre himself! Sit down. I can't see to steer with your ka-tail in the way."

Senu sat down. It was either that or fall overboard. Reonet handled the little craft with reckless skill. Before he had time to think, they were racing between a hulking barge still laden with slabs of white limestone destined for the site, and a flotilla of reed canoes. The wind whistled in the ropes. Sails bulged and strained. Startled ducks flapped from their nests and the night filled with whirring wings. Senu looked up uncomfortably, remembering the blue feathers in Nemheb's cellar.

One of the boys in the canoes waved. With a start, Senu recognized Iny. "We're going to petition Lord Khafre so he'll let the mertu robbers go!" he yelled. "Where have you two been? You've missed all the excitement!"

Reonet scooped a handful of mud from the bottom of the boat and threw it at him. "Hey!" Iny steered off at an angle, her missile dripping from his cheek. The others laughed and started a splashing battle with their paddles. They seemed to have no idea how serious it all was. The adults were little better. Mertu called to one another and laughed as the wind carried them faster and faster.

Senu gripped the sides of the boat and stared upriver, little chills going through him. The sky was paling rapidly, the dunes taking shape. Ahead on the west bank, the White Wall could be seen glowing pink with dawn, high and beautiful and terrible. Spear glints along its top showed the positions of the royal guards.

He thought of Lord Khafre, who was too important to speak to his subjects personally, and his own stupid attempt to get Red to contact Prince Menkaure's ka. A waste of time, because Nemheb had already spread his poison as far as the Royal Ear.

"Red," he whispered. "Red, make them turn round. They'll all be killed! Make them go back."

His ka shook his head. "I can't. Their kas are too angry. Lord Khufu's ka has roused them. It's too late to stop it, Senu. Too late."

Chapter 16

TRIAL
I come to you with my hands bearing Truth, and my
heart has no lies in it. (spell 183)

As THE ARMADA sailed into the shelter of the White Wall, the ka-wind dropped. Hundreds of sails, red with sunrise, flapped as the boats turned towards the west bank. Saper eyes watched them silently from the battlements. At first it seemed the guards wouldn't try to stop them landing. Then a side gate opened and a pack of lean, four-legged shadows bounded out.

Reonet sucked in her breath. "They're letting the dogs out! With all those people down there!"

Senu's stomach twisted. On the narrow bank between the retreating flood and the Wall, still in shadow, a whole village of sagging tents had been erected in the drying mud. Dirty, ragged people slept in the open, rolled in mats. With a shiver, he realized they were the beggars Nemheb had mentioned, who lived on the scraps thrown over the Palace wall. Most were still asleep. Into these defenceless, sleeping people bounded the greyhound pack, barking excitedly.

The mats and tents erupted with terrified screams. To add to the confusion, the morning refuse was thrown over the Wall. As the stale bread and rotten fruit showered down, the beggars forgot about running away and rushed to the food, scrabbling on their hands and knees and fighting the greyhounds for every last scrap. Growls, snarls, and cries of pain as people got bitten, filled the air. The guards watched the scene from the safety of their sunlit battlements, impassive.

"Do you think they do that every morning?" Senu said, imagining his mother and Tamuwy and her two little girls scrabbling in the mud with the big, fierce dogs.

Reonet shook her head. "Of course not. They're just trying to scare us."

Senu wasn't so sure. But the demonstration had its desired effect. The armada hesitated, paddles raised as people watched the scene in horror.

"Workers from the Place of Truth!" called a saper from the Wall. "Return to your labours! If you do not, your families will be down there with the other beggars before Re sets tonight!"

"See?" Reonet whispered, her knuckles white on the steering-paddle. "Let's show them we mean business." She adjusted the sail and angled the little boat towards the nearest landing. Heart pounding, Senu grasped an oar, hung over the bows and fended off the other craft.

Red rippled anxiously in front of him, distorting his view. "Make yourself useful!" Senu hissed. "Go and talk to Prince Menkaure's ka again!"

Red shivered. "What do I say?"

"Tell him the truth. Tell him about Lord Khufu's ka and Captain Nemheb."

Red, still in his strangely obedient mood, went. But he was back before they reached the landing, shivering and rippling in agitation. "I can't. There's a *sem*-priest in the Judgement Hall and he's made a spell barrier to stop kas from spying. You'll have to go yourself."

Senu glanced at Reonet, wondering whether to tell her about the priest. Her gaze was fixed on the landing, her jaw set, her eyes still unnaturally bright. He shuddered and felt for the scarab, which for safety he'd knotted into a corner of his loincloth. It made a small hard lump against his thigh. He squeezed it tightly. "We have to get this scarab to Lord Khafre," he said. "It's the only evidence we've got that Tefen and the others are innocent."

Reonet nodded and renewed her efforts to reach the bank. The workers were muttering angrily in response to the saper's threat. A few boats had followed Reonet's lead and were almost at the royal jetties when a door opened in the enormous main gate of the Palace and a regiment of sapers ran out, armed with spears. The greyhounds bounded up to them, wagged their tails, and raced to the bank where they snarled at the approaching boats. The leading canoe hastily back paddled, but the barge behind, unable to stop in time, crashed into it. There was a dreadful splintering. The occupants of the canoe jumped into the river and swam desperately for the bank, only to scream in dismay as two greyhounds splashed into the water and arrowed towards them.

Senu winced as he saw a dog catch one of the swimmers' arms in its jaws. "We'll never get past those dogs!" he said. "We'll have to find somewhere else to land."

Reonet's eyes glittered black fire. "They can't stop us all." She balanced dangerously on the stern rail and shouted at the boats hesitating in the middle of the river. "They've got the Scorpions behind that wall! Lord Khafre's going to execute them! Come *on!*"

The sapers on the bank looked at Reonet with narrow eyes. One raised his spear and took aim, making Senu's stomach churn. But their leader put a hand on his arm and shook his head.

"Workers from the Place of Truth!" he called, holding a snarling greyhound back by its collar. "This is your last chance! Return to your labours, otherwise we'll consider this an attack on Lord Khafre's Royal Person and be forced to take appropriate action."

"Don't listen to him!" Reonet shouted. "Stay together! We outnumber them. We can get over the Wall if we stay together!"

But the workers had been scared by the dogs and the fate of those in the smashed canoe. One of the women called to Reonet to come away from the bank before she got herself killed. The men muttered uneasily. The Overseers tried to encourage them to hold firm by promising to take their petition before Lord Khafre through the official channels. But scarcely had they begun shouted negotiations with the sapers on the bank, than a furious yell went up from the barge that had smashed the canoe.

"SOBEK!" a mertu Gang-Chief called in his booming voice, pointing at the top of the Wall.

The negotiations broke off as people shaded their eyes. Senu squinted at the sunlit battlements, heart thudding afresh. On the top of the White Wall, between two of the execution spikes, Sobek stood with his elbows bound behind him and blood running down one side of his face. He was bigger and stronger than the two sapers who flanked him, but it was obvious all the fight had been beaten out of him. He swayed groggily, staring in confusion at the armada.

"Workers from the Place of Truth—!" began the saper.

"They're goin' to put 'im on a spike!" yelled the Gang-Chief.

A great cry of rage rose from the river. As one, hundreds of red sails turned for the bank. The sapers waved their arms and shouted further warnings but it was no good. Seizing oars, throwing sticks, crusty lumps of sun-dried mud, stones, whatever came to hand, furious mertu and hemutiu threw themselves into the shallows and splashed up the bank.

"Sob–ek! So–bek!" they chanted, making it into a gang-song. "SO–BEK! SCORPIONS FOR–EVER!"

"C'mon!" Reonet yelled, caught up in the frenzy. "Before they shut that gate!"

Senu's breath came faster. Blood pounded in his ears. Somehow, he was out of the boat and on the bank, breaking through the mud, trying to keep up with Reonet. On all sides, struggling knots of men and women yelled and screamed and whacked each other with their primitive weapons. Iny led the hemutiu children in an attack on the royal barge, moored upstream. The dogs growled and snarled. The sapers were disciplined and used the shafts of their spears to knock people down, but they were outnumbered and soon lost control. The Overseers and scribes shouted in vain, clutching their scrolls to their chests, saying the petition must be taken to Lord Khafre by official routes. The beggars, seeing a chance to get at some real food, joined in. The sapers gave up trying to make arrests and started spearing people in the feet to stop them trying to climb the Wall.

They've killed Sobek, was all Senu could think. They've put him on a spike and Father will have to stay in the mine for ever. We're too late.

"The chief human's not dead," Red said in his ear. "They took him back inside— Look out!"

A spear plunged into the ground near Senu's toes, sending a shiver through him. He plunged after Reonet, breath rasping in his throat. It hadn't looked like much of a slope from the river but the short dash to the Palace was all uphill. When they stopped to catch their breath, he braced himself for another look at the battlements and realized Red was right. There was nobody on the spikes.

His relief was short lived. The sapers had retreated to the gates. They slipped through the little door and barred it firmly in the rioters' faces. A muffled gong sounded inside and a line of dark heads appeared on the battlements with bows. The rioters beat at the gates, not realizing at first what was happening. Then arrows began to fall from the sky like black rain.

Along the length of the White Wall people dropped with surprised expressions, clutching at shafts buried deep in their flesh. The arrows did not discriminate. They brought down mertu, hemutiu, scribes, women, children, anyone who got in their way.

Reonet tugged Senu against the wall. They pressed their backs against the warm stone, gasping for breath. "The arrows can't reach us if we keep really close," she shouted above the screams. "We have to get inside somehow. Can you climb?"

They looked up. The limestone was smooth, perfectly finished and vertical. Some of the mertu were trying to build a human pyramid to reach the top, but the wall was much too high and the pyramid collapsed, spilling men into the mud. He shook his head helplessly. Reonet frowned. "We'll try round the back. They might have left one of the other gates open." She grasped his hand in a determined manner.

They worked their way to the corner and up a slope where the mud gave way to drifts of sand blown out of the desert. It was quieter round here, but the entire western section of the Wall was smooth and high, no gates at all. Reonet thumped the stone in frustration. "Any ideas?"

Senu kept quiet. The sight of people dying had reminded him what would happen to his father and the others if they didn't get inside before the prisoners were sentenced. He shivered in the shade beneath the Wall and wished he could start Akhet all over again. He'd do it right this time.

"Then we've no choice," Reonet tugged him back into the sunlight towards the main gate.

Senu followed, too weary to think. The strange energy that had filled him since his escape from the pyramid was fading. Red hardly glimmered blue at all as he danced away from the wall and back again, giving advice such as "Stay where you are!" "Look out!" and "Duck!". An arrow went right through his ka and shivered in the mud. Senu simply stared at it.

Now Reonet was thumping on the gate. It gave back dull thunks. She found a sliding hatch and forced her fingers into it. "Guard!" she shouted. "This is the boy who helped the robbers. The one with heka! He's come to give himself up!"

Senu came to with a start, grabbed her wrist and dragged her along the wall until a crowd of angry mertu hid them from the spy slot. "Are you crazy?"

"It's the only way!" she hissed. "If you let them arrest you, they'll take you to the others."

"Bound and beaten senseless, maybe! You saw what they did to Sobek. A lot of good that would do. Besides, it's not the only way—"

A delighted yell cut him off. "Red-Tail! I *said* it was you!" A bruised and filthy mertu boy came pounding up, followed by a gang of others in the same state. With a start, Senu recognized Patep and Teti and the boys who'd tried to help the Scorpions. They stared curiously at Reonet. She glared back, hands on her hips.

"Er... these are the Scorpion boys and the others from the site," Senu said, looking closely at the dirt-smeared faces.

Patep anticipated his look. "Gef's inside with the men. Sapers were goin' to let us boys go, but Gef punched one of 'em in the eye so they decided he must be guilty. We're tryin' to get in."

"So are we," Reonet said. "Senu's got an idea. Shut up and listen."

Senu flushed, wishing he hadn't said anything. He licked his lips. "You know I've got heka. Red and I might be able to... Red and I can walk through walls. If we have a ka-door."

The mertu boys looked at one another. Teti giggled. Reonet scowled at him. "Shh! How do you think he got out of the pyramid?"

They all stared at Senu.

"Of course it's impossible," he said, not knowing if he

was relieved or frustrated. "We'd need a priest to make the door."

"No we wouldn't." Reonet chewed her lip. "I know the spells."

The mertu transferred their incredulous looks to her. "Re's breath!" Teti swore. "I think they're serious!"

Patep looked at Senu with new respect. "You can really do it? Walk through the White Wall?"

"I can't get you through, too."

The boy grunted. "If you can walk through walls, you don't need us!" He turned to Reonet. "Well, go on then! Do the spells."

Reonet gave him a scathing look. "I can't just magic a door out of the air, you know! I need ink. Soot from one of the fires will probably do. And some brushes. It'll be quicker of there's several of us drawing the glyphs..."

She organized the boys, sending some to raid the beggars' camp for burnt wood, Teti to the river for reeds, and Patep to fetch Iny and the others from the barge. While they were gone, she picked up an arrow that had missed its mark and scratched the outline of a small door on the wall. She gave Senu an apologetic grin. "You'll have to duck. It'll take too long to do a full-sized door."

The scratch of the arrowhead in the stone set Senu's teeth on edge. The riot was working itself into a frenzy, people running everywhere trying to scale the Wall, arrows raining down, stones and mud flying up. Through the confusion, Patep and Teti returned with Iny and the others puffing behind them. Iny listened in silence to the plan, gave Senu a long hard look and grinned. "Always knew you were keeping that ka of yours for something special!" he said. Under Reonet's instruction, the hemutiu children set to work, while the mertu boys created a diversion with a very realistic fist fight. Senu watched the door take shape, shivering with fear that it wouldn't work, then with fear that it would.

Before he was half ready, Reonet pushed the others back. "Good luck!" she said, kissing him on the cheek.

Senu was still worrying about what the others would say if he walked straight into the wall and bloodied his nose, when Red drew him gently into the stone. The ka-door whispered open. He shut his eyes hastily. There wasn't nearly enough time to think about Reonet's kiss before the ka-door closed and he was on the other side of the White Wall.

The Palace was much bigger and busier than Senu had imagined it would be. At every junction, he had to hide while servants rushed past carrying jugs or baskets of bread and fruit, or platters of roasted fowl. He followed a group of important looking imakhu wearing scented wigs and golden sandals for a while, until they turned off into a room with a pool where naked girls were splashing each other and giggling about the "dirty mertu" outside. They obviously didn't believe the rioters would get over the wall. Senu ducked out again, cheeks hot. He thought about asking someone where the prisoners were being judged, but Red was glowing blue again and he didn't want a repeat of what had happened in Nemheb's house.

As he worked his way deeper into the Palace, using the statues and gilded pillars for cover, the noise of the riot faded and he had to keep reminding himself why he'd come. In every shadowed corner enormous vases of blue lotus perfumed the air, making him want to curl up and go to sleep. Royal ladies in fine linen reclined on couches, fanning themselves and watching the servants hurry past with bored, kohl-lined eyes. One of the women stared straight through Senu without seeming to see him. He shuddered. But as he opened his mouth to ask his ka about it, Red hissed, "Sapers!" and the slap of sandals marching in step sent him scurrying behind a jar of lotus blooms. He parted the petals and saw a detachment of four men turn down a corridor, dragging in their midst a bloody and bruised mertu with his elbows tied tightly behind him.

"Sobek!" he whispered.

The sight of the Gang-Chief penetrated his lotus-daze. He trailed the sapers until they turned into a hall so big the entire hemutiu village would have fit inside. Gilded, lotus-shaped pillars marched down both sides to a raised dais where Lord Khafre sat on a black granite throne wearing the Double Crown of the Two Lands, his crook and flail clasped across his chest. As he had on the site, Khafre stared fiercely straight ahead. The hall was lined with imakhu men and women, standing silently in the shadows of the columns. A square of sapers formed a solid wall of flesh between the audience and whatever was happening in the centre of the floor. More sapers stood to attention before the throne, arms folded and faces impassive. On the lowest step, the Royal Ear, Eye, Nose, Tongue and Mouth sat in a row with their staffs of office balanced across their knees, watching the proceedings with bored expressions.

For those first few heartbeats as the sapers dragged Sobek to the centre of the Hall and thrust him roughly into the guarded square, it was all Senu could do to absorb the scene. Then he caught glimpses of dark-spotted golden fur rippling inside the wall of spears where the prisoners knelt and his stomach tightened.

"A leopard!" he whispered in horror.

"Shh!" an imakhu lady hissed from the side of the hall, craning her neck to see what had happened to Sobek. "It's just the priest, silly. Get back to your place—" She turned to frown at him and her eyes widened. "Who are you? What are you doing here? You're not—"

Senu dodged under her arm before she could stop him. He squirmed between the tightly packed bodies and worked his way closer to the prisoners. The guards had closed up again so he could no longer see the leopard fur. But Red, rippling reluctantly after him, whispered in a strange little voice, "It's the *sem*-priest. Careful! If you cross those spells he's drawn on the floor, I won't be able to hide you any more."

So *that* was why no one had noticed him creeping through the Palace. They'd see him soon, though. With a shiver, Senu realized that the decorative tiles around the edges of the Hall had been hastily painted with glyphs. But what he'd thought was a beast was only a man with a leopard skin draped over one shoulder. Then his confusion returned. The priest was an old man. Yet a thin, tightly braided ka-tail sprouted from the side of his shaved skull. He wanted to ask Red about it, but someone was bound to notice him if he spoke. He pressed himself against a column, hoping the invisibility effect would last until he'd decided what to do.

Sobek's arrival had interrupted an argument between the priest and the Royal Mouth. This took forever, since when the *sem*-priest spoke he had to address the Royal Ear, who then turned and whispered to the Royal Mouth, who then spoke to the priest. Sometimes the Royal Nose or the Royal Eye would add something to the whispered discussion, and there was an even longer pause before the Royal Mouth spoke. Meanwhile, the Royal Tongue took the occasional bite out of a date or sip from a goblet, before passing these to Lord Khafre for consumption. The great Lord himself seemed to take as little interest in what was being said as he had in the building of his pyramid. But when Sobek had been thrust to his knees with the other prisoners and a saper reported that the riot was getting worse, Khafre leant forward and whispered something to the Royal Ear.

The Royal Ear whispered to the Royal Mouth, who climbed stiffly to his feet. He banged his staff on the step to get everyone's attention and announced, "The Lord

Khafre requests that this trial be concluded. The prisoners' guilt is not in question. Half the robbers should be executed at once. Since there are spiritual matters to clear up, the other half may be interrogated out of his presence and executed at sunset. He gives *sem*-priest Ankhsheshonq of the Temple of the Sun full authority in this matter. The rioters should be escorted back to the Place of Truth. Anyone disobeying this order is to be arrested and sent to Khnum's Cataract. Insurrection will not be tolerated. Khafre the Great, Mighty Bull, Son of Re, has spoken." He banged his staff again, the sound echoing in the high roof.

A sigh rippled down the Hall. The kneeling prisoners moaned and their guards stiffened. Senu's heart thudded. He felt short of breath. Red rippled around the column in dizzy circles. "Oh this is bad, very bad..."

Senu pushed himself from the column and staggered across the line of spells into the clear space between the square of sapers and the royal dais. "Sir!" he shouted, addressing the throned figure directly. "Lord Khafre, you have to listen to me! These men are innocent. Captain Nemheb—"

He got no further. A gasp of horror went up from the watching imakhu. A heavy saper fist knocked him on his face and at least twenty spears pricked him flat against the floor.

"Impudent hemutiu wretch!" someone shouted. "How *dare* he speak to the Lord Khafre directly?" ... "How did he get in here?" ... "Still got his ka-tail." ...

"Glowing." ... "Priest-fire." ... "It's a trick." ... "Thief!" ... "Desecrator of tombs!" ... "Only a child."

Amidst all the frightening shouts, it was this last one that made Senu's blood run hot. He raised his head as far as he could with the spears pricking the back of his neck and searched the shadows. "Red," he whispered. "Where's Prince Menkaure?"

"Behind the throne."

"Tell his ka—"

"Silence, boy!" a saper thumped him on the back of his head, slamming his nose against the floor. He tasted blood. A rope went round his elbows, drawn so tight he gasped. Tears of pain flooded his eyes. "Don't you try any of your magic in here, boy," hissed the man tying his arms. "Or we'll kill you, minor or not."

"I have to tell—"

"Silence!" The spears poked harder. "The prisoner will be silent!"

"I won't be silent!" Senu said as loudly as he could with his cheek pressed to the floor. "Captain Nemheb is a traitor! He used these men. I can prove it! Red," he added in an undertone as more shouts of protest rang around the hall, "tell Prince Menkaure to come over here. Tell him to look in my loincloth."

Red seemed reluctant to leave him, but after a final nervous ripple he disappeared into the shadows behind the throne.

Senu kept very still, terrified one of the sapers would get carried away and push a little too hard on his spear.

Then a pair of papyrus sandals came into view and a soft voice said, "Let him up."

The spears retreated. Senu raised his head thankfully. A leopard claw dangled into his line of vision as the *sem*-priest gazed down at him with eyes so deep and dark, Senu's head started to spin.

"Such strong heka," breathed the priest, crouching to see him better. "Where have you been hiding all these years?"

Red hastily rippled back. "Say nothing," his ka advised.

Ankhsheshonq's gaze flickered to Red, almost as if he could see him. He gave Senu another long stare, then pushed at the nervous saper spears and helped him to his feet. The rope bit the soft skin of his elbows but Senu grit his teeth, determined not to cry.

"I'll take care of the boy now," Ankhsheshonq said. "Don't worry, I can control him." He addressed the Royal Ear again. "If the Great Lord Khafre will give his permission, and considering the boy was not caught with any of the royal treasure upon his person, I request this prisoner's life for service in the Temple of the Sun."

Senu opened his mouth. "No—"

Ankhsheshonq's hand went across it. "Shh! I'm trying to help you."

Lord Khafre sat up a bit straighter. There was more whispered discussion on the lower step. Then the Royal Mouth said in a bored tone, "The *sem*-priest's request is granted. The other prisoners will be executed at the appointed time. Take them away."

"No, Father!" said a high, shrill voice.

A hush fell over the hall.

Senu's heart stirred in hope as Prince Menkaure, wearing a simple kilt that made him look much more comfortable than he had on site, pushed through the sapers. He met the Prince's gaze and his heart sank again. It was dark with hatred, as Gef's had been the first time they met.

"Look in his loincloth," ordered Menkaure. "He *has* got some of the treasure on him."

Senu tried to explain as the sapers searched him, but when they found the knot containing the broken scarab they stopped listening. They tore the amulet free and held it up triumphantly. The scarab's broken wings glinted red in the torchlight. Another sigh rippled through the Hall.

The Royal Mouth banged his staff. "Since the boy has been caught in possession of an item of royal treasure—"

"That's not Lord Khufu's treasure, you imakhu idiot!" a rough voice yelled with site-trained lungs. Senu twisted his head and saw Gef struggling to get through the line of guards. "That's a temple scarab! Nemheb's spyin' dwarf got it out of the sarcophagus, but it killed 'im and—"

His words ended in a grunt as a saper knocked him to the floor. Ankhsheshonq sucked in his breath and snatched the scarab from the saper's hand. He examined it carefully, closed his fist and stared hard at Senu.

He spoke to the Royal Ear in stiff tones. "The boy

cannot be considered a thief, since this amulet is indeed Temple property that Lord Khufu – may his ka roam wherever it pleases – was wearing when he died. There is no longer any need for me to interrogate the prisoners. They are judged free of spiritual crimes."

Prince Menkaure frowned at Senu. "What were you doing with Grandfather's amulet?"

But all eyes were on the dais, where Lord Khafre had risen to his feet. He descended two steps, stared straight at the *sem*-priest and demanded in a raspy voice, "How did that thing get inside my father's pyramid? I was told the priests who prepared his sahu took steps to free his ka before the sarcophagus was sealed."

Senu, who was closest, was the only one who noticed Ankhsheshonq's flinch. "It must have been a mistake, Lord," the priest said smoothly. "But I can confirm your father's ka is now free, so you have nothing to worry about—"

Khafre cut him off with a flick of his flail. His gaze flickered across the prisoners and lingered briefly on Senu before returning to the Royal Ear.

"Where's Captain Nemheb? Is he behind this riot?"

The Royal Ear prostrated himself and stuttered that he didn't know, but there had been reports of strange events at the Captain's house last night. A blue light in the sky and an unnatural wind. The Captain himself had not been seen since.

Lord Khafre seemed to consider this then returned his attention to Senu. The weight of the royal gaze was like a yoke with ten full jars attached. Again, the flail flicked.

"I will speak to the hemutiu boy." The gasps and whispers had barely died away when Khafre the Great uttered two words that would set every tongue in the Two Lands wagging for the rest of the year. "*In private.*"

Chapter 17

ROYAL PARDON
I am a Great One, the son of a Great One... (spell 43)

SENU'S INTERVIEW WITH Khafre the Great took place in a
small inner chamber off the main Hall. It passed in a haze
of blue lotus mingled with the perfume of the royal wig
and the sweetness of the honeyed wine a servant brought
to revive Senu. His bonds had been removed at Lord
Khafre's order, but they'd been applied so tightly by the
frightened guards in the Judgement Hall that his arms
tingled and his fingers wouldn't work properly. He spent
much of the interview staring at his hands clasped about
the precious royal goblet, willing himself not to drop it.
Prince Menkaure sat at his father's feet and frowned at
every word. Two sapers stayed in the chamber with them,
but remained so motionless in the shadows by the door
that Senu soon forgot they were there.

The servant positioned a stool for Senu before the
plain wooden throne before bowing out of the room.

The Lord of the Two Lands removed his false beard and leant forward. He rested his elbows on his knees, propped his chin in his hands and stared straight into Senu's eyes as he asked his quiet questions. He never once raised his voice above the raspy whisper he'd used in the Judgement Hall. He didn't need to. The whole story came out, every detail of it, in a wild flood interrupted only by the occasional reminder from Red, who stayed very close to Senu throughout.

When Senu ran out of words, Lord Khafre sat back, closed his eyes and let out a weary sigh. "The truth," he said quietly, "comes by unexpected means. Thank you, young hemutiu. It's refreshing to listen to someone who hasn't forgotten how to speak directly. I now see there is much more to this robbery than meets the eye. I must talk to the *sem*-priest and reconsider my verdict." He raised a finger. The guards jumped to attention.

"Er... Lord?" Senu stammered, leaning forward to touch the smooth knee. "There's one more thing. My father—"

The royal forehead creased. He sat back, heart hammering. He'd *touched* the Royal Person! But Lord Khafre smiled and, so briefly Senu couldn't be sure it happened, rested his beautifully manicured hand on Senu's head. "A messenger will be sent. Now, perhaps you'll allow me to attend to this matter before your friends outside rip my palace apart stone by stone?"

Senu blushed as the guards opened the door. The servant reappeared and carefully reapplied his Lord's beard and touched up his kohl. The crook and flail were placed back in his beautiful hands. Without another word, the Lord of the Two Lands rose to his feet and left the chamber, shadowed by the two sapers.

Senu thankfully put down the goblet. He'd taken only a few sips of the wine, yet his head was spinning and his hands trembled. He looked uncertainly at the Prince, who remained on the floor. Menkaure was still frowning at him, though the hatred had gone from his eyes to be replaced by a thoughtful look.

"Er... shouldn't we go back too?" Senu eyed the open door.

The Prince shook his head. "Not unless you want to sit through another lighthour of listening to the Royal Mouth bore everyone to death," he said.

"But—" Senu bit his lip. Suddenly it seemed wrong to be sitting on the stool when the Crown Prince was on the floor. He stood up, only to sit down again in embarrassment when Menkaure made no move.

The Prince laughed in his high voice and patted the tiles beside the throne. "Come and sit on the floor with me, hemutiu, if it bothers you so much. You look like you're going to fall off that stool, anyway."

More embarrassed than ever, Senu slithered down beside the Prince. Red rippled down beside him, eyeing the air where Menkaure's ka must be. They sat in stiff silence for a few moments. Eventually Menkaure said, "I'm sorry I called you a thief out there. I misunderstood."

Senu mumbled something stupid about forgiving him.

Menkaure went on, "When your ka tried to talk to mine on the site, I was too stupid to listen properly. I thought it was some silly hemutiu joke. People get jealous just because I get to wear golden sandals in public. It's so stupid. They make my feet blister. It's really much more comfortable to go barefoot, only I'm not allowed." He glanced sideways at Senu. "Then when I saw you in the Judgement Hall, glowing blue like that, and your ka came over to mine... well, I was frightened. And you had the scarab Grandfather used to wear all the time. His favourite amulet, or so I thought. I'd no idea his ka was trapped inside it! No one ever tells me *anything* interesting like that. But I should have listened to your ka. I learnt a valuable lesson today."

He stared at the open door, then grinned, suddenly mischievous. "Do you know how many private audiences my father grants?"

Senu tried to make his brain work. There were all the important imakhu. And the foreign ambassadors, he supposed. Then there were the priests of all the temples, and the Chiefs of all the government departments... "Uh, I dunno. Maybe a hundred a week?"

Prince Menkaure's eyes sparkled. "Try again, hemutiu."

"Er... a hundred a day?" Senu amended.

This time the Prince laughed, his amusement ringing high and clear around the chamber. "My father speaks through the Royal Mouth and listens through the Royal

Ear. He eats from the Royal Tongue and sees through the Royal Eye and smells through the Royal Nose. The only people he speaks to personally are members of his immediate family. Even the Chief Priest of the Sun has to speak in the presence of the Royal Ear and Royal Mouth, though sometimes he's graced with a direct question, as you witnessed out there. As far as I know, you're the only living hemutiu ever to speak to Lord Khafre directly. Certainly the only living hemutiu to *touch* him."

Senu stared at the Prince in despair. "Then I'm dead, aren't I?" he whispered. "He can't let me live now."

Menkaure giggled. "Oh, he won't have you executed, if that's what you mean. He'd be too worried about your ka coming back for revenge."

"*Red?*" It was Senu's turn to laugh. "Don't be silly! Walking through walls is one thing, but—" He broke off. What did he really know of Red's power?

The Prince slithered closer, curiosity burning in his eyes. "What's it like? Walking through a wall? I wish my ka could do that! All he ever does is hang around moaning at me to hurry up and grow into a man so he can be free."

Senu eyed Red. His ka perched on one arm of the throne, swinging a ghostly leg, holding a whispered conversation with an invisible presence on the opposite arm. "It's... different."

"Oh come *on*!" Menkaure wasn't satisfied. "You went to the Land of Dreams, didn't you? What did it look like?"

255

Senu shrugged. "Like here, sort of. Only nicer. Brighter. More water."

"More water?"

"A bigger river, more green, stranger creatures... oh, I don't know." He shook his head helplessly. "We were in a hurry. Red wouldn't let me stop for a proper look. Why don't you ask your ka?"

Menkaure scowled. "He never tells me anything! And when he does, it's all boring stuff about protocol and acting like a prince. He's as bad as the Royal Mouth."

Senu peered curiously at the throne arm opposite Red. "What does your ka look like?"

Menkaure gave him a startled glance. He was afraid the Prince would tell him it was none of his business and summon the sapers to drag him off to some dark dungeon. But Menkaure smiled. "Like me, of course."

"Red always looks like me, too! Bruises, dirt and frizzy ka-tail included!"

The Prince made a face. "Chubby—" He gave an embarrassed cough. "Chubby always looks really solemn and serious. And he's always perfectly dressed and clean. He's so boring."

"Red pulls faces at people."

Menkaure gave him a wistful look. "I wish Chubby'd do that."

"Red's frightened of the kas of the dead."

Silence. The Prince chewed a fingernail, then admitted, "So am I. One day I'll have to build a pyramid too. It's horrible, knowing your sahu will lie under all that stone. I wish I could walk through walls like you."

"No you don't. It makes you feel ill."

"I feel ill just thinking about it. What if Chubby can't get out after I'm dead? What if he gets trapped inside, like Grandfather's ka?"

"That won't happen to him if he's not in a temple scarab."

"But what if he can't find the way out? Father's pyramid is going to be so *big...*"

"Maybe you could have a smaller one? The walls wouldn't be so thick then."

The Prince gave him a long, thoughtful look. "I've never talked to a hemutiu before. You've got such funny ideas. Do you go to school? All they ever teach us in here is boring court stuff and stupid stories about gods and goddesses that no one believes. Tell me what it's like in the hemutiu village."

"It's smelly."

"You have those blue lotuses too? Yeah, they stink — "

"Not the lotuses! Sewers..."

And so it went on. Their kas joined in, and the two boys became so engrossed in comparing their lives that they missed the revised judgement in the main Hall. Senu supposed everyone else must have forgotten about them in return, because when a passing saper looked in to find them sitting on the floor beside the throne with their heads together giggling like lifelong friends, he gave a little disapproving cough.

"Er, the Royal Mouth is asking that the hemutiu boy

be taken to the baths, my Prince. And then the *sem*-priest wants a word with him."

Both boys jumped to their feet, equally embarrassed to be caught sitting with the other. The Prince brushed himself off and resumed the regal expression he'd accused his ka of wearing. Senu's heart banged with fresh fear. Ankhsheshonq had seen him glowing with the light of the other world. There was no hiding Red's skills now. He looked at his ka.

"He can't make us do anything we don't want to," Red said, rippling close. "Not now."

The prisoners were granted a royal pardon for their part in freeing Lord Khufu's ka. They were released from the main gate of the Palace, bathed and fed and wearing new loincloths made of good linen. Senu, his skin still tingling from the bath and his shoulders smarting from the Scorpions' grateful slaps, brought up the rear with Ankhsheshonq. As the gates creaked open, the priest's hand tightened about his elbow. Everyone assumed the grip was to steady Senu after all the excitement. But Senu suspected, with a coldness that took the edge off his triumph, that Ankhsheshonq wasn't going to release him in a hurry. He looked for Reonet, hoping she'd have enough sense to stay away.

The riot had quietened while Senu had been inside the Palace, but groups of stubborn mertu were still flinging themselves at the Wall in periodic attempts to climb under the defenders' arrows. Although the sapers had shouted news about the pardon from the battlements, it seemed no one really believed it. When the gate was unbarred, the frustrated men and women surged to their feet with angry shouts and ran in a yelling, stick-waving mass for the opening. The sapers were forced to lower their spears in an attempt to hold them back, which only made the rioters more furious.

At first no one recognized the freed men, and they were all in danger of being trampled in the confusion. Ankhsheshonq hissed through his teeth and held Senu back in the shadow of the gates. It might have turned nasty, had not Sobek jumped on an overturned cart and bellowed in his trained Gang-Chief's voice, "What are you all doing, sittin' on your backsides out here in the middle of the day? Get back to the site, you lazy scum! We've a pyramid to build!"

There were a few confused shouts. Then a great cry went up.

"SOBEK! SOBEK! SCORPIONS! SCORPIONS FOREVER!"

The next moment, everyone was leaping to their feet and rushing towards the cart. All the pardoned men, including the huge, highly embarrassed Sobek, were hoisted into the air and carried down the slope to the waiting boats. Patep and Teti arrived, out of breath, and the mertu boys crowded around Gef demanding to know everything that had happened. As he was lifted on to their shoulders, Gef reached down and briefly clasped

Senu's arm. "Thanks, Red-Tail!" he said. "Don't forget to come an' see us when you're a high and mighty priest, will you?"

Senu mumbled something about hoping Gef won a lot of amulets next time the Scorpions were lifting, and promised to bring him the ankh he owed him one day.

Ankhsheshonq frowned after the mertu boys and beckoned to the sapers. "We'd better hurry," he said. "We've wasted enough time already. My barge is at the north landing." Without waiting to check they were following, he led the way at a smart pace along the White Wall, leopard claws swinging round his knees.

Senu hung back, still searching the crowd for Reonet. He was starting to regret his promise to accompany Ankhsheshonq to the Captain's house and show the priest exactly where the scarab had been opened. Once Ankhsheshonq had him alone, who knew what awful spells he would use on Red to persuade him to serve in the temple?

"He won't do that," Red whispered, rippling alongside. "He knows what it's like."

Before Senu could work out what his ka meant by this cryptic comment, there was a shout behind and a wild-eyed, tangle-haired apparition came racing down the slope after them. The sapers whirled in alarm, spears lowered, but put them up again with a chuckle when they saw it was only a girl, alone.

Reonet flung herself at the *sem*-priest and clung to his staff. "Where are you taking him? Let him go! He doesn't want to go to your stupid temple – do you, Senu?" Her eyes searched his, desperate.

Ankhsheshonq's expression clouded. He snatched his staff free and tightened his lips. "I might have known. The girl who was too curious for her own good. This has nothing to do with you, Reonet. Go home with the others."

Reonet set her jaw. "Senu's my friend and I won't let you hurt him."

The priest shook his head sadly. "I'm not going to hurt him."

Reonet's flashing eyes said she didn't believe a word of it. She put her hands on her hips and planted herself in Ankhsheshonq's path.

"It's all right, I agreed to go with him," Senu whispered quickly. "We're going to Nemheb's house." Reonet's eyes flickered, and he knew it would be hard for her to go back there. "You don't have to come," he said, forcing a smile. "I'll be fine. I've got Red. I'll see you back at the village. Tell my mother and sister I'm fine and I'll be home as soon as I can."

Reonet frowned at Ankhsheshonq's hand, which rested once more on Senu's arm. She gave the priest a sly smile. "Of course I have to come! You might need another ka-door." Still smiling at the priest, she waved casually at the White Wall.

His gaze snapped up. He stared at the Wall, where the door she'd sketched on the limestone still showed in the morning sun, despite Iny and the others dutifully rubbing out the spells with the corners of their loincloths. Iny waved cheekily at the priest and winked at Senu.

Ankhsheshonq sucked in his breath. "You... you *dared* to... *you* drew a ka-door on the *White Wall*?" He didn't seem to know whether to summon her ka on the spot or rush back up the slope to check the spells.

Reonet kept smiling. "How do you think Senu got into the Palace?" she said sweetly. "He might be able to walk through walls, but he's useless at glyphs."

The sapers frowned at her. Red had a big grin all over his face. Despite his fear of what the priest might do to Reonet, Senu had a sudden urge to giggle.

Ankhsheshonq sighed. "You, my girl, have been trouble from the start." He motioned to the sapers. "All right, let her come."

The journey downriver to Nemheb's estate was made in silence. Ankhsheshonq stood alone in the bows of the Temple barge, his leopard skin glowing in the sun and his ka-tail straggling in the wind. Senu sat with Reonet against the mast under the burnished disk of Re, while Red pulled faces at the crew of solemn young imakhu doing their temple service. News of Senu's part in the trial had obviously spread. The celebrations taking place on the boats returning to the Place of Truth quietened as the Temple barge passed them. People stared curiously at Senu and clutched their amulets.

Senu clenched his fists. "If I'd known what it was like to have real heka, I'd never have played all those tricks on everyone," he said.

Reonet squeezed his hand. "Yes you would. You'd just have played better ones." But her gaze was thoughtful.

In the same tense silence, the barge docked at Nemheb's flood-landing. Ankhsheshonq and the sapers jumped ashore. One of them tried to help Reonet, but she shrugged off his hand and marched towards the house alone, her back very straight.

She stopped at the steps leading to the courtyard, staring in confusion. Senu stared too.

Where Nemheb's fancy house had been, there was only a crater in the ground, slowly filling with water. Not a brick, not a painted column, not a plate, not a goblet, not a scrap of linen, remained. The edges of the crater smoked, but the blue fire had gone. A few servants, who had been picking around distractedly in the remains of the garden when the barge tied up, straightened and stared at the *sem*-priest. Two of Nemheb's medjay started towards them, but stopped and shook their heads, as if unsure what they were supposed to be guarding.

Ankhsheshonq strode to the rim of the crater, pulled out the broken scarab and closed his eyes. He began to chant softly. Blue flames flickered around his hands and licked his ka-tail. Red hissed through his teeth. Senu took a rapid step away from the priest as the air began to hum like it had inside the pyramid. The sapers backed off nervously. Reonet stared wide-eyed, but stood her ground.

"What's he doing?" she whispered. "I thought Lord Khufu's ka was free now? He's not summoning it again, is he?"

Senu searched the sky in alarm, but it was empty of blue-feathered wings. Finally, Ankhsheshonq sighed and opened his eyes. The blue fire died.

He turned to the sapers. "You can tell Lord Khafre that Captain Nemheb's sahu has gone from this world. I'll need to return to the temple in order to deal with his ka, but his name can be erased from the official lists. He will die the second death."

The sapers shuddered and clasped their amulets. They took a final look at the smoking crater, turned and broke into a disciplined run, heading south along the bank, back to the safety of the Palace of the White Wall.

When they'd gone, Ankhsheshonq passed a hand across his eyes and sat heavily on the remains of a broken wall. He looked very tired. "Perhaps you see now how dangerous heka can be in the wrong hands?" he said. "The imakhu do temple service to learn how the world of the kas connects to the world of the flesh, so they might better serve their Lord and the Two Lands. But Captain Nemheb tried to use heka to help himself, and this is the result."

Reonet set her jaw. "All I can see is a big hole. What happened to his sahu? Why do you have to deal with his ka? Do you mean Nemheb's ka can *come back*?"

Senu tried to catch her eye, but she was too scared and angry to heed his warning. Besides, he had questions of his own. "Why did the priests trap Lord Khufu's ka in that scarab?" he blurted out. "How come it was buried with him? Was it really a mistake like you told Lord Khafre, or...?"

Ankhsheshonq sighed and held up a hand. "I really shouldn't give away Temple secrets to hemutiu, but these are unusual times and you're unusual youngsters. Sit down."

Reonet looked as if she might refuse, then realized she'd trapped herself and sat with a stubborn expression. Senu settled himself beside her. Red stuck out a half-hearted tongue at the air beside the priest, before sitting on Senu's other side.

"You no doubt already know from your history lessons that Lord Khufu closed the temples when he was building his pyramid," Ankhsheshonq began. "He needed every grain of the harvest to feed his work force, nothing could be wasted on offerings to the gods. Most of the priests accepted this, but not all. There was some bad feeling. A few of my predecessors got together, summoned Lord Khufu's royal ka and imprisoned it in a temple scarab. They just meant to teach him a lesson, persuade him to reopen the temples and then let his ka go again. But Lord Khufu –" His lips tightened. " – Lord Khufu sent his sapers to arrest them, confiscated the temple scarab and murdered all but the *sem*-priest who'd imprisoned his ka. The captured *sem*-priest panicked and killed himself before he could be forced to open the scarab."

He paused, looking thoughtfully at Senu. "It would have been better for all of us if someone could have set the old tyrant's ka free, but no one else had strong enough heka. Many sem-priests were horribly tortured and killed. Meanwhile, Khufu wore the scarab containing his ka constantly, refusing to take it off even when he bathed or slept. When he died, the priests who prepared his sahu had a dilemma. Should they keep the scarab in the hope that one day they'd find someone with strong enough heka to open it? Or would it be safer for the dead Lord's ka to remain imprisoned where he could do no harm? You see, they were all too aware of the power that would be unleashed when that ka got free. All kas become more powerful when their human dies, and the ka of a powerful man is a fearsome thing. What happened to Nemheb would have happened to whoever opened the scarab. So we told Lord Khafre it was taken care of and buried his father with some relief, giving thanks to Re that Khufu had spent so much effort making his sahu's resting place the most secure in the history of the Two Lands. We never reckoned on someone like Captain Nemheb, so keen to get his hands on part of the royal treasure that he'd dare rob the Horizon of Khufu itself! Of course, he didn't have any idea what was inside the scarab. That was the best kept secret of all."

Reonet said, "But Senu opened it! He's not even a priest—" She bit her lip, looking furious with herself.

Ankhsheshonq smiled. "Nevertheless, he's got powerful heka, the most powerful I've ever seen. Our Temple training obviously isn't as effective as we thought. Maybe we could learn something from Captain Nemheb's methods."

Senu couldn't help a groan.

Ankhsheshonq patted his arm. "No, don't worry, we're not monsters despite what your friend seems to think. I understand it hasn't been easy for you. Awakening your powers in such an uncontrolled way could just as easily have destroyed you. That's the whole problem with heka. It's strongest when we're young and know nothing of the world. When we start to use it wisely, it deserts us. Which is why the Temple needs you, Senu. You and Red have a great gift. Wouldn't you like to grow up knowing you need never say goodbye to your ka? It's not a prison sentence. You can serve in the Temple of the Sun and still visit your family. You can even marry, if you want." A glance at Reonet, who flushed. "All we ask is that you use your heka for the good of the Two Lands and not for selfish purposes."

The air around Senu stilled. "Would Red have to talk to the kas of the dead?" he asked.

Ankhsheshonq was watching him closely. "Yes."

He knew it had sounded too good to be true. "Red?" he whispered.

His ka was silent a long time. "I'm still scared," he

said in a faint little voice. Then added quickly, "But if you want me to stay, I will. I love you, Senu."

"And I love you." Senu closed his eyes, his head spinning. Reonet was breathing heavily.

"There are so few of us left who have the true power, Senu," the priest continued in his persuasive voice. "The power to use spells and work with our kas as the Creator Khnum intended. I'm getting old. It gets harder and harder for me to cross the boundary and walk in the other world. Maybe one day I'll have to cut my ka-tail. Before I do that, I've sworn to find another to take my place. I'd like it to be you."

Senu didn't know what to say. He thought of Pehsukher, who had lost his ka and died in the pyramid. He'd got old, too. Old and tired and made a mistake. But Ankhsheshonq still had his ka, and if he agreed he'd be able to keep Red and no one would tease him for it. No one would dare tease a *sem*-priest who wore leopard skin and had spoken personally to the Lord of the Two Lands. He took a deep breath. "I..."

Reonet jumped to her feet. "No, Senu! Red'll be miserable! Moon told me about the kas who never grow up. They're slaves, Senu! Nothing but slaves. Ask Red! Ask Red to ask his ka. *He'll* tell you the truth!"

Ankhsheshonq frowned at her. "All right, Senu, ask. My ka is here."

Senu eyed the wall next to the priest. Reonet was biting her lip. Ankhsheshonq wore a confident little smile.

"Red?" Senu said.

His ka rippled in confusion. "He says I've nothing to be afraid of because I'm so strong. But I'm afraid of Nemheb's ka! He hates me now."

Senu pushed the *sem*-priest's hand away and got to his feet. He met the deep, dark eyes. "What about Captain Nemheb's ka?" he asked.

Ankhsheshonq pressed his lips together. "I won't deny he's still loose and looking for revenge. But we'll deal with him before you enter the Temple, so you needn't worry."

Senu nodded. "I've another condition. You've got to let Reonet back into the river temple. She's a good scribe. You saw the ka-door she drew for me. Ask her how she got out of Nemheb's Blind Room."

Ankhsheshonq's frustrated expression changed to professional curiosity. "Mmm," he said. "I've been wondering about that. How *did* you get out of that Blind Room, Reonet?"

Reonet scowled. "I changed the spells, of course. Took me ages, and I ruined my hair clip. But I thought if I made the restraining spells into passage spells like the ones you put on ka-doors, then maybe Moon would be able to find me and tell Red where I was—" She broke off.

"And it worked!" Senu finished for her. "See? Reonet will be a lot more use in a temple than me."

Ankhsheshonq frowned. "A *girl*," he said in his stern priestly voice, "cannot be a temple scribe. She can only be a chantress or an official mourner." He frowned at Reonet a moment longer. "But I suppose it'll do no harm to let you complete your Akhet apprenticeship. All right, if you promise not to draw any more ka-doors where you shouldn't, I'll see what I can arrange."

He turned to Senu. "Becoming a *sem*-priest is not a decision to be taken lightly. The next ka-ceremony at the Place of Truth isn't until the end of Akhet, so you've plenty of time to discuss it with your family. I'll not interfere. We can't force you to join us if you decide not to, though of course I hope you will. Meanwhile, I hope I can trust you both to be discreet?"

Senu, relieved, managed a nod. Reonet stared suspiciously at the priest. "Thank you," she mumbled in the end.

Ankhsheshonq acknowledged her thanks with a stiff nod and strode back to the waiting barge. "Must be getting old," he could be heard muttering to his ka as he went. "I come to interrogate tomb robbers, only to see them walk free with a royal pardon. Then I end up divulging Temple secrets to a hemutiu boy with more heka than anyone's possessed in years and a girl who wants to be a temple scribe, of all things. Re's breath! What is the world coming to?" He paused on the jetty to look at something on the river, smiled to himself, and climbed into his barge which immediately cast off.

Senu let out his breath. "He's not as bad as I thought he would be."

Reonet scowled. "He might have offered us a lift home! He has to go right past the Place of Truth. I suppose we'll have to walk now. All Nemheb's boats have gone, in case you hadn't noticed."

"No, we won't. There's another boat coming, look."

Reonet ran to the jetty and started to wave her arms. But after a moment she let them drop and stood, staring, the river breeze blowing her unclipped hair across her eyes. Senu arrived in time to see an unkempt hemutiu climb clumsily out of the boat and fold Reonet to his broad chest. "Thought I'd lost you, girl," he grunted.

At first Senu didn't recognize him. Then he understood why Reonet was laughing and crying at the same time. The man was her father, sober for once.

He pushed Reonet back and looked her carefully up and down, before transferring his gaze to Senu. "Let's go home," he said.

Chapter 18

SPHINX

...he shall come out into the day, he shall walk on earth among the living, and his name shall not perish for ever. (spell 70)

FOLLOWING THE SCORPIONS' royal pardon the gangs and craftsmen at the Place of Truth worked twice as hard as before, as if they were thoroughly ashamed of their attack on their Lord's Palace. By the final week of Akhet, Lord Khafre's pyramid had grown to about a third of its eventual height with the burial chamber completed and the ka-temple foundations marked out in the shadow of the eastern wall. Black granite statues of Khafre stood in a neat row at the edge of the site, awaiting finishing touches and transportation. The Parade that would lead from Khafre's river temple to his ka-temple was in progress, and hemutiu craftsmen had already begun carving the animals into the lower section.

No one mentioned the robbery. Officially, it had

never happened. Unofficially, the Scorpions paid for their crime by working three darkhours each night inside Lord Khufu's Horizon after their full day's work on site. Under close supervision they returned the treasure, tidied the burial chamber, fixed the traps, filled in the tunnel they'd dug and levelled the northern pit – which the Chief of Works decided was no longer a suitable place to bury a star-boat. Gef's little brother, who had replaced Senu on the Scorpion gang, thought all this was highly exciting and rushed about telling everyone that he'd seen Lord Khufu's ka watching them inside the pyramid. The mertu smiled, tweaked his ka-tail and told him not to tell stories. Captain Nemheb was replaced by an Overseer promoted from the site, a man the gangs respected for his willingness to get his hands dirty. Nemheb did not get an obelisk to keep his name alive, either in the imakhu graveyard or anywhere else. The remainder of his estate was levelled and planted with flax. The members of his household were given the option of staying to work the fields with the provision that the flax they grew would go to the Palace, or banishment from the Two Lands for life. All stayed except Nemheb's medjay, who left to seek more lucrative employment elsewhere.

For a week after the robbery, Senu lay awake worrying about Nemheb's ka raging out of the Land of Dreams to take his revenge. But as the days passed and nothing out of the ordinary happened, he started to wonder if what he'd seen in Nemheb's cellar had been real, after all, or just a final echo of his nightmares. On the ninth night, he took a deep breath and blew out the lamp before rolling himself in his mat. "Don't worry, Red," he whispered to his ka. "You'll be free soon, I promise."

He'd thought about it long and hard, as the days when his mother and Tamuwy barely let him out of their sight stretched into weeks. Should he become a priest and force Red to talk to the kas of the dead against his will? Or cut his tail to release Red, which would mean giving up his chance to enter the Temple of the Sun and keep his ka into adult life?

Reonet stuck to her belief that Red would be miserable if he did what Ankhsheshonq wanted. Every time he mentioned the Temple, she distracted him by taking him home to see her new kitten, which was so playful that Senu couldn't help but forget kas and temples and everything else as he rolled balls, dangled rope, and laughed at Red pretending to be the kitten's ka.

His mother refused to take sides. "You must follow your own heart," she told him with tears in her eyes. "Your father will be here soon. Why don't you wait and discuss it with him?"

But it was a long and hazardous a journey from Khnum's Cataract to the Place of Truth, and although the promised message had been sent, extending the pardon to Craftsman Tefen, another message had come back saying that Tefen was too ill too travel. His mother and Tamuwy put on brave faces, yet Senu knew deep down that the chances of his father arriving before the ceremony were slim.

He had to make the decision himself. But there really was no contest. He'd cut his tail, go back to school and work hard at his glyphs until he got into scribe school as Father wanted. Maybe a new teacher would make all the difference. He was a bit worried that when Ankhsheshonq heard he'd decided against being a priest, he might try to trick him and Red into serving the Temple at the last moment. But, true to his word, Senu didn't see Ankhsheshonq again until the morning of the ka-ceremony.

The last day of Akhet dawned fine with a gentle breeze. The flood waters had returned to the river, leaving fertile fields of glistening black mud which were already being worked by the local mertu in preparation for planting. The barges arriving for the ceremony had to use the lower landing. But a new causeway of shining white limestone had been laid by the gangs before they left the site, so the Chief Priest of the Sun didn't have to get his sandals muddy as he led the procession up the hill to the plateau where the ceremony would take place.

There was an unusually large audience this year. Lord Khafre hadn't come in person, but Prince Menkaure made the journey with the Royal Eye to observe the proceedings. The chubby prince and the tall imakhu stood under a fringed canopy a little apart from the crowd, surrounded by their bodyguards. The plateau buzzed with a party atmosphere as those children ready to release their kas gathered outside the village. The River Gate was ceremonially barred behind them, though their families were allowed to watch from the top of the wall. Beyond the Passage of Purification, two pyramids now cut into the sky – one gleaming white and gold, the other still flat-topped and rough-edged in raw yellow stone. The site itself was quiet. On Amun's Wall, a reduced contingent of saper guards leant on their spears and watched with idle curiosity.

Senu stood apart from the others, feeling silly and embarrassed. He hunched his shoulders so he wouldn't tower above the other children. Menkaure flashed him a little grin. Gef and Sobek waved from the front of the crowd. Senu self-consciously touched his ka-tail. Although he'd soaked it in fish oil this morning in an attempt to get it to behave, it still stuck out like a frightened cat's. The younger children kept glancing at him and giggling.

"Ignore them," an invisible Red breathed in his ear. "You've nothing to be ashamed of. None of *them* can walk through walls."

Senu's heart twisted. "Neither will I, after this morning." For the thousandth time, he wondered if he was doing the right thing.

He glanced up at the water tank inside the gate, where Reonet sat on the rim swinging her long, tanned legs. She grinned and made cutting motions with her fingers. Since the attack on the Palace, her father had stopped drinking fermented gruel and they'd come to some understanding about her mother. Although Reonet didn't talk about it much, Senu knew the two of them went to the hemutiu tombs every evening to make offerings and leave letters. He managed a grin back and returned his attention to Ankhsheshonq, who had reached the top of the path. Two priests without ka-tails followed him. One carried the ritual blade. The other carried a little smoking brazier in the shape of an open lotus flower. Behind them came linen-clad chantresses, rattling their sistrums and singing the Spell for the Releasing of Kas.

The children drew together nervously. The wall was hot and high at their backs. There was nowhere to run. Senu saw the others' eyes flicker sideways and knew they were watching their kas for the last time. He wished Red would become visible.

The chantresses fell silent. The crowd held its breath. Ankhsheshonq scanned the line of silent children and his gaze stopped at Senu. Something flickered in the deep, dark eyes. Uncertainty? Fear? Before Senu had time to think about it, Ankhsheshonq looked away.

He raised his arms to the newly-risen sun and made a speech which Senu heard none of. The priest with the knife walked down the line, pushing the children gently to their knees. The second priest placed his brazier in front of the first girl and blew on the coals. Ankhsheshonq held out his hand for the blade, raised it to the sun and chanted under his breath.

The silence and the heat intensified. The ka-ceremonies Senu had watched from the safety of the village wall had never seemed to take this long before. He wondered what Ankhsheshonq was waiting for. Beads of sweat dripped from the priest's chin. At last he finished his chant and stepped forward. Senu was at the end of the line. Ankhsheshonq started at the other end, cutting off the ka-tails one by one and passing them to the priest tending the brazier, who dropped them on to the hot coals where they flared briefly before curling to ash and blowing away as sparks in the wind.

The air above the plateau began to hum. Senu's pores opened. By the time the team of priests reached him, sweat was pouring off him in rivers and he was trembling uncontrollably. He tried taking deep breaths.

Red, he willed. *Red, show yourself. Just once, please, before we do this.*

Ankhsheshonq stepped behind him and pushed his head forward. As the lotus-scented fingers grasped his ka-tail and the blade touched his scalp, a violent shudder ran through him. It was all he could do not to leap up and run.

"Are you sure you want to do this?" Ankhsheshonq's voice breathed in his ear. "It's not too late to change your mind."

Senu grit his teeth. "I won't make Red do anything he doesn't want to," he hissed. "Never again."

The *sem*-priest sighed and his grip on Senu's ka-tail tightened. "I understand," he said very softly. "But I should warn you we were unable to—"

Whatever he'd been about to say was lost in a blast of

stinging sand. Ankhsheshonq lost his grip on his ka-tail and staggered backwards with a cry of warning as a cloud the colour of blood blotted out the sun. Something thumped Senu between his shoulders, knocking him flat. The brazier blew over and rattled across the rock, spilling hot coals. The chantresses leapt out of the way, screaming. The royal canopy went whirling across the plateau. The bodyguards closed about the Crown Prince and the Royal Eye, staring at the sky in alarm. Someone yelled "Sand storm!" And suddenly everyone was running for cover.

Senu found himself alone on the plateau with Ankhsheshonq, surrounded by swirling sand so thick he couldn't see even the village wall. In the amber half-light, Red was a mere smudge. "No!" his ka screamed in terror. "Get it away from me, Senu! Don't let it touch me!"

"What's happening?" Senu shouted, crawling through the sand towards the priest.

"Nemheb's ka!" Ankhsheshonq gasped. "I was afraid of this."

"What do you *mean*?" Senu yelled, too scared to remember he was talking to the Chief Priest of the Sun. "I thought you said you were going to deal with it!"

"We tried... too strong... the ka ceremony opens the hole between worlds... got to close it... with Red's help, maybe..."

Senu stared at the priest in disbelief. "You did this on purpose, didn't you? You knew Nemheb's ka would attack us!"

"No, we—"

"SENU!" screamed Red.

With difficulty, Senu raised his head. His mouth was full of sand, his eyes, his ears, everything. Grains of sand bit his exposed flesh like a swarm of mosquitoes. Ankhsheshonq was chanting, clasping his amulets. He pointed to the dark centre of the storm, where glimpses of red-scaled wings and a long, sinuous tail made Senu's stomach churn. "Tell your ka to help mine!" Ankhsheshonq shouted. "If we're lucky, we might be able to drive him back."

Senu saw one of the monster's wings twist as if something were clinging to the end. Its huge, crocodile-like head swung round and its teeth snapped at the air. Ankhsheshonq clutched his stomach with a grunt of pain as if he'd suffered a blow from a human fist. His chant broke off mid-syllable. The monster's eyes burned red as they sought out Senu. He shrivelled inside. Nemheb was in there, looking out at him, amused, sure of his absolute power over an insignificant hemutiu boy and his ka.

"Run, Senu!"

Red rippled across the plateau, flung himself on the monster's tail and bravely wrapped his gangly, ghostly arms about the glittering scales. Nemheb's ka hissed and spun in a circle, but its teeth snapped harmlessly on Red's ka-tail, coming away with a mouthful of hair. Ankhsheshonq struggled to his knees and resumed his spell. From the way the monster's wings were beating furiously and its head swinging from side to side, Senu guessed the priest's ka had rejoined the fight.

The hopeless feeling faded. "Hang on, Red! I'm coming."

He staggered to his feet and leant into the wind, squinting against the sand. With an almighty roar, Nemheb's ka launched itself into the air and flew straight for Senu, wings spread vast and dark against the storm. Its tail lashed. Red flew off, crashed against an invisible barrier and fell to the rock in a crumpled heap.

"RED!" Senu cried, fighting to reach his ka. "Get up, oh please get up!"

The monster swooped. A wing tip caught Ankhsheshonq and slammed him against the village wall. The priest's spell stopped again. But this time it did not restart.

Now you will die, spoke a terrible voice inside Senu's head. *Slowly and screaming, like my human did. Then I will rip your ka apart and scatter his essence in the Lake of Fire where you will die the second death!*

Senu couldn't take his eyes off Red. Get up, he willed. get *up.*

There was movement by the wall and his heart lifted in hope, only to sink again as a slender figure with wild black hair raced past the moaning priest and fought her way through the storm towards him.

"No!" he yelled. "Get back, Reonet! Stay away!"

She kept coming. Nemheb's ka laughed, reared into the sky and beat its huge wings, tearing up a palm tree by the roots and flinging it far across the river. Reonet did not hesitate. Through all the roaring and the noise of the storm, her voice could be heard, small and determined, chanting a spell.

"I call your heart, ib, which contains all you love.

I call your spirit, akh, which causes you to breathe.

I call your soul, ba, which belongs to the gods.

I call your power, sekhem, which you have made for yourself.

I call your shadow, khabit, which hides behind you.

I call your ka, Khufu, from where it sleeps in the Land of Dreams."

Behind them, Ankhsheshonq groaned. "No," he whispered. "Oh no."

But Reonet continued:

"By the seven segments of being, I call you!

In the name of the Great One, I call you!

Wherever you may be, I command you by your secret name,

Swifter than greyhounds and quicker than light.

Come forth, Khufu, come forth!"

"Tell Red to explain!" she hissed into Senu's ear as they fell flat to the rock and covered their heads.

Senu squinted anxiously at Red as the air began to hum. But the ka was already on his feet, talking rapidly to the sky, just like Senu used to when he was trying to explain things to old Batahotep.

Nemheb's ka stopped laughing and raised its ugly head. It let out a terrible shriek as an enormous, blue-winged creature with furiously lashing tail dropped out of the storm and grasped it with burning claws. For a single, heart stopping instant, the newcomer turned its ferocious stare upon the three humans crouched on the plateau and they had a clear view of the royal ka outlined by blue fire. His lion's body glowed, his tail ended in flame, his great mane was feathers one moment, hair the next, and fire in-between. His wings rippled like the river on a summer's day. And his face was that of Khufu the tyrant, hard and dark, yet with eyes that had seen more than any living man. For a terrifying heartbeat, that otherworldly stare held them. Then, in a wild roar and a shower of blue feathers, both kas were gone.

Senu climbed shakily to his feet and wiped sand out of his eyes. The wind had dropped. The sun glowed dull orange above the river. Amun's Wall became visible again, its guards uncovering their heads and blinking at the sky. Those who had taken cover staggered out on to the plateau arguing about what they'd seen. The Royal Eye stared thoughtfully at the blue speck vanishing over the pyramids.

Ankhsheshonq clambered stiffly to his feet and brushed himself off. He shook his head at Reonet. "That was very dangerous," he said. "But very brave, and by some miracle you seem to have got away with it. I think we can safely assume Nemheb has died the second death, so it seems I owe you both thanks." He frowned at the sand and blue feathers that had been blown in deep drifts across the plateau. "I also seem to have lost the ritual blade. Would you mind waiting until tomorrow to cut your tail, Senu? All things considered, I think it might be best if we didn't open the hole between worlds again today."

Senu glanced at Reonet, who squeezed his hand. Then at Red, who nodded. "You don't have to cut it," he told the priest in a firm voice. "Red's not scared to talk to the kas of the dead any more. I've changed my mind. I want to be a *sem*-priest!"

Ankhsheshonq raised an eyebrow. "You'd join us, even though I tricked you?"

"You didn't trick me. I knew Nemheb's ka hadn't gone. I just didn't want to think about it." He shrugged, embarrassed. "Besides, heka's the only thing Red and I are any good at. We might as well learn how to use it properly."

The River Gate creaked open and the villagers poured on to the plateau. The terror of the duel and Lord Khufu's victory had sharpened their appetite for celebration. Laughing and chattering, they hugged their offspring with pride. The children who'd given up heir kas touched their heads with hesitant fingers, then pushed their mothers' arms away. Still discussing the battle of the kas in excited voices, they raced off to attack the traditional end-of-Akhet feast.

Ankhsheshonq squeezed Senu's arm. "We'll wait for you," he said. "We won't be leaving until the feast's over." He gave Reonet a long, thoughtful look. "And if your friend is still determined to be a scribe, there may be some Temple funds available. It might be a good idea for her to have proper training, too, before she kills someone." Smiling faintly to himself, he picked up the brazier and followed the proud families down to the river bank.

Reonet recovered first. "Well, what are we waiting for?" she said. "There's date bread and honey gruel and fresh fish and fancy fruits sent from the Palace. After all that heka, I'm starving!"

Senu shook his head. "How can you think of food at a time like this? If you hadn't summoned Lord Khufu's ka, I'd be dead and Red—" He choked and looked for his ka, who seemed to have vanished again.

She touched his arm. "It was my fault Nemheb's ka attacked you like that. I wasn't thinking of you and Red when I told you to cut your tail, only getting back at Ankhsheshonq. I was wrong, I see that now. Besides," She gave him a sly grin. "Couldn't let you cut your tail, could I? I still need you to do something for me—"

They were interrupted by high-pitched shrieks from the edge of the plateau. Tamuwy's little girls were scrabbling up the scree beside the path, slipping and grabbing at each other to stop themselves rolling down again. "Uncle Senu!" they gasped between giggles. "Uncle Senu! Come quickly! Grandfather's back!"

Senu's heart gave an extra thump. He stared down the hill, hardly daring to believe. Unnoticed in all the excitement, a small boat had arrived at the landing. A knot of people stood beside it.

"He's really skinny and he's got this horrible twisted

finger," the girls went on. "But he's asking for you. Come and see, Uncle Senu! Come *on*!" They tugged at his arm.

Reonet laughed and relieved him of the smallest girl. "All right, we're coming. But you've got to remember Senu's going to be a priest now. He's got to be awfully dignified and—"

"I'll show you dignified!" Senu picked up the other girl, swung her on to his back and let her cling round his neck as he raced Reonet to the river. Loose stones rolled dangerously under their feet. The little girls shrieked in delight and shouted to their mother and grandmother, who were hugging someone in the golden reflection of Re's sun disk.

"Father...!" Senu called, a choke in his voice. "FATHER!"

The hug broke apart. Tefen took a long look at his son and opened his arms. "Senu," he said quietly. "You've decided, I see."

He nodded. "I get to keep Red this way, at least for a while..." He blushed. It sounded so babyish.

His father smiled. "Your mother and I are very proud of you, son. We've never had a priest in the family before."

Reonet waited nearby, a ka-tailed girl clasped in each hand, a smile on her face. Everyone was so busy laughing and talking at once that Senu didn't see the first ripple in the air above the Temple barge. He blinked over his father's shoulder, thinking the storm must have damaged his eyes. A handsome ka with a beautifully braided ka-tail and admirable muscles clung to the mast with one arm, drumming his ghostly fingers on Re's sacred disk and grinning broadly.

"What are you staring at?" he said. "Kas grow up too, you know. I just wanted to tell you before you start stuffing yourselves that if Moon's human still wants me to talk to her mother's ka, then that's fine." He glanced at Reonet, gave a big wink, did a handstand and disappeared.

Senu laughed. Catching Reonet's suspicious look, he tried to control himself, failed, and spread his arms wide to encompass his whole family, the workers celebrating their end-of-Akhet feast, the startled priests, the river, the pyramids, and both beautiful worlds. "I'm so happy!" he shouted. "Everything's so perfect!"

His mother shook her head. "You wait till next Akhet," she warned. "The Royal Eye is talking about building a likeness of Lord Khufu's ka to commemorate the occasion, and no one can agree what it looks like, except that it's big. More men, more work, more trouble..."

Tefen grabbed her round the waist and silenced her with a kiss. "Senu's right," he said. "Can't you feel it? The air's different. The kas are happy. I'm looking forward to designing this new statue – we'll carve it out of those rocks up there so it faces the river. We'll make this the finest pyramid complex in the Two Lands, and people will marvel at our work long after we've all gone to our horizons. You'll see."

GUIDE TO SENU'S WORLD

SENU AND REONET lived in the Two Lands during Lord Khafre's reign, which lasted twenty-three years from approximately 2555BC to 2532 BC. In this ancient time, few of the words we commonly associate with their homeland existed (being invented by the Ancient Greeks almost 2000 years later), which is why you won't find modern names such as "Egypt", "Pharaoh", and "Mediterranean" in this story! Words like "pyramid", however, are so descriptive that these are used to avoid the need for endless translation. Other words, like "heka", may be more unfamiliar but are used to give the flavour and magic of the time.

The extracts from the spells in the chapter headings are taken from a collection of magical texts called the *Chapters of Coming Forth By Day* (today known as the *Ancient Egyptian Book of the Dead*). These were put in tombs to give the occupant a happy afterlife and to enable their ka to leave the tomb when necessary.

The following guide might help you on your journey through Senu's land:

adze	Sharp copper chisel used to shape stone.
amulet	An object believed to have magical protective powers, usually worn by the person requiring protection.
Amun	A god known as the "Hidden One".
Amun's Wall	The "Wall of Hiddenness", hiding the hemutiu village and the mertu camp from the souls in the Place of Truth.
ankh	A glyph or spell meaning "life".
Bes	Bandy-legged dwarf god with a lion's tail who brings good luck to a house.
darkhour	A twelfth of the night, measured between sunset and sunrise. Its length varies according to the time of the year. In winter, darkhours are longer than lighthours.
Double Crown	The White Crown of the South and the Red Crown of the North, worn together to show mastery over the Two Lands.

faience   Crushed quartz heated with ash and copper ore to produce a blue glaze. Used to make cheap amulets, beads, etc.

glyph   Picture writing.

gruel   Thick soup brewed from barley, sometimes with additives such as dates or honey. Very nourishing and more of a food than a drink, though it can be fermented to produce a potent beer.

Hapy   God of the flood, which occurs annually during Akhet (see Seasons).

heka   Magical powers possessed by children who have an unusually strong bond with their ka. The amount of heka varies from person to person. People with strong heka usually serve as *sem*-priests in temples or become doctors.
Heka powers include:
– Talking with the kas of the dead
– The ability to enter the Land of Dreams and walk through physical barriers in this world.
– Use of spells.

Horizon of Khufu	Lord Khufu's pyramid, which we call "The Great Pyramid". One of the Seven Wonders of the Ancient World.
ka	Person's double, sometimes called a "material soul". Can be seen only by children, who communicate with their kas constantly. When they grow up, their ka moves to the Land of Dreams. Adults can communicate with their kas only when they sleep.
	Some people (like Senu) have an unusually strong bond with their ka which gives them "heka" powers. We do not know what shape the ka took, but in this story they appear as ghostly copies of their human.
ka-tail	Lock of hair left growing from the side of a child's head to indicate that they still maintain the bond with their ka. Upon becoming an adult, this lock of hair is ritually cut off, after which they are free to wear their hair in any style or wear a wig.
	The only adults who retain their ka-tails and keep their kas past puberty are the *sem*-priests, who have "heka" powers.

Khnum   Ram-headed god who lives at the first cataract (rapids) of the river and sends the flood every year. He also creates baby humans and kas on his potter's wheel.

Kush   Land south of Khnum's cataract, populated by fierce black-skinned warriors.

lighthour   A twelfth of the day, measured between sunrise and sunset. Its length varies according to the time of the year. In summer, lighthours are longer than darkhours.

lotus   Flower like a water lily that grows in the river. The most common form is blue and highly scented, though larger white blooms exist. Has mild narcotic properties.

medjay   Fierce mercenary soldiers from Kush. Sometimes employed as bodyguards by high-ranking officials like Captain Nemheb.

obelisk   Tall, finger-like monument with pointed top, often inscribed with glyphs.

papyrus	Tall plants that grow along the river bank and are used to make a form of paper.
Place of Truth	Pyramid site.
Re	Sun god. In Senu's time, Re was the most important god of the Two Lands. Many people were named after him. For example, Khafre means "appearing like Re".
River (The)	Today known as the Nile.
Royal Ear Royal Mouth Royal Nose Royal Tongue Royal Eye	Five imakhu officials who act in public for the Lord of the Two Lands, protecting him from his people. The Eye, Ear and Mouth are empowered to make minor decisions on his behalf without the need for the royal person actually to be present at the proceedings. The Nose and Tongue smell and taste for poison at official banquets.
sahu	A corpse, usually wrapped in linen bandages. Sahus of the rich were...

... mummified by having their organs removed and stored in jars before wrapping the rest of the body, but when poorer people died they were left to dry out naturally in the hot atmosphere.

sapers   Police responsible for guarding the pyramids and ensuring the good conduct of the workmen. They also guard the Palace and patrol the desert with greyhounds.

scarab   A beetle found in dung. A popular amulet, sometimes inscribed with spells.

    Special amulets called "temple scarabs" are made by priests with heka powers to imprison people's kas so they can be controlled. A temple scarab, once sealed, can only be opened magically. If it is broken, the ka inside will be killed.

sem-priest   Priest allowed to wear leopard skin who has kept his ka and ka-tail beyond puberty. Normally has "heka" powers, although these vary in strength from person to person.

    A type of rattle with sliding metal bars attached to a frame which jangle when shaken.

sistrum   A corpse, usually wrapped in linen bandages. Sahus of the rich were mummified by having their organs removed and stored in jars before wrapping the rest of the body, but when poorer people died they were left to dry out naturally in the hot atmosphere.

sphinx   Powerful creature with a lion's body, a human head, and possibly wings. In this story, the form taken by a royal ka when its human dies.

Two Lands   The narrow strip of fertile land bordering the river between Khnum's Cataract and the Temple of the Sun (White Crown), combined with the marshy area between the Temple of the Sun and the Great Green Sea (Red Crown). Their climates were different enough to be considered separate "lands".

Week   Ten days.

SEASONS

1
Akhet

Flood. June–September. Hottest time of the
year. Holiday for everyone except those
drafted to work on the pyramids.

2
Peret

Coming Forth. October–January. Planting
time.

3
Shemu

Drought. February–May. Harvest time.

MAIN CLASSES OF SOCIETY

1. Lord of the Two Lands
The supreme ruler, Khafre.

2. Crown Prince
Khafre's son, Menkaure.

3. imakhu
Members of the royal family and important
civil servants.

4. scribes
People who can write.

5. hemutiu
Craftsmen (artists, sculptors, etc.).

6. mertu
Labourers in the fields and on
building sites.

7. slaves
Foreigners captured in wars.

GLOSSARY

Lotus

Sun Disc

Double Crown

Crook & Flail

Winged Sun Disc

Snake